Blowtorch

By the same author

Thermal Image
Burn Out

Blowtorch

Pat O'Keeffe

Hodder & Stoughton

First published in Great Britain in 2004
by Hodder and Stoughton
A division of Hodder Headline

ISBN 0 340 82019 5

Typeset in Plantin by Hewer Text Ltd, Edinburgh
Printed and bound by Mackays of Chatham Ltd, Chatham, Kent

Hodder and Stoughton
A division of Hodder Headline
338 Euston Road
London NW1 3BH

This book is dedicated Blue Watch Lambeth 1976 to 1979
Funny, outrageous and professional in equal measure

ACKNOWLEDGEMENTS

My sincere thanks to Gary Francis of the Metropolitan Police for his help and advice on technical details.

1

My skin felt like it was crawling.

The sticky late summer heat had turned the fire appliance cab into a sweatbox and reduced my undress uniform to a crumpled rag. I took off my jacket and loosened my tie while Dave Chase, my driver, went back to cursing quietly as he struggled to negotiate the heavy traffic in the Romford Road.

Shifting uncomfortably in the appliance seat, I tried to read the newspaper as Dave leaned across and turned up the air-blower, giving a tight smile as it blew the paper in my face.

'Sorry, guv.'

I nodded and despite the queasiness brought on by the stop-start motion, I shook open the paper again and scanned the front page.

Reading about other people's fires always put the hook in me. Essex Fire Brigade borders London, but is nothing like it in terms of ethos or organisation. Whenever I read of another brigade fighting a large fire I try to decipher the hack journal-ese that often warps the real story, but between the lurid prose and the blind attachment to cliché it was a greasy slope.

The local weekly rarely rose above media-ocrity, so that when it came to the recent triple fatal in a Basildon disco and they went for smart, they missed by a mile.

Their headline read – 'The Great Fire of Laindon'.

Three dead, twenty injured, many more suffering shock and smoke inhalation – it was a tragedy that deserved a little more sensitivity. Whether it was lazy journalism or indifference I didn't know, but the dead had been ill-served.

My own prejudices undoubtedly played a part, for it irritated me intensely that it seemed beyond the abilities of the press to capture what actually happens at a fire. It was first impression writing, skin deep and bone stupid.

They saw only the surface and you can't see fire, you experience it; every sense comes into play.

Firefighters inside a building work blind, reacting by touch, smell and body sensation. And by listening; to the fire, to the building being consumed, to the movements of your crew.

You tune into the fire: only onlookers, outsiders, 'see'.

So I told myself to reverse the logic and try to tune into the report – decipher the language and sieve the crap.

It was obvious even from this distance that the Essex crews had earned their wages for the year. It was a ten-pump fire. Ten pumps! In most metropolitan brigades it would have been twenty and there would still have been work to do.

There were other reasons for reading the article; reasons that cut deep with me.

It was the same process that every day drew me to read and re-read the summaries of fires across the brigade. These consisted of stop messages listing proportions of the building, percentages of the floors destroyed by fire, the extinguishing media and the deaths and injuries to both the public and firefighters.

It wasn't the gore that drew me. It was reassurance.

Reassurance that I wasn't the only one confronted by dangerous and difficult situations and not the only one who'd lost a firefighter. But the feeling was always temporary, for the glaring reality of Sandy Richard's death ambushed me whenever I dropped my guard; the sense of isolation like a cold wind at my back.

And on days like this it had the capacity to crush me.

The phone had gone just after nine and the control room operator had been oddly formal.

'Station Officer Steven Jay you are to cancel outside duties and go straight to Eastern Command Headquarters for an interview.'

It was only on arrival that I was informed of the purpose, to discuss a no-blame inquiry into Sandy's death.

For five months the rumour mill had been grinding out half-truths about what had happened, now the Brigade wanted to pick over his bones.

Part of me wanted to believe that finally the truth would come out and the matter, like Sandy, be laid to rest. But experience argued against that. From the day I returned from the therapy centre in Wales people had seen the uncertainty in my eyes and read it as confirmation that I'd screwed up.

The interview would not help; it would merely prime the speculation, with truth a helpless bystander.

No one regretted Sandy's death more than I, but I couldn't bring him back.

My own watch knew that, but other people, firefighters who had been nowhere near the fire, found it easier to accuse. They, of all people, should have known better, but a man had been lost and someone needed to take the blame.

They were human enough for that and I was human enough to resent it.

The Senior Divisional Officer who had interviewed me was Maurice Charnley; a man whose short career was noticeably lacking in operational command and control experience.

It wasn't accidental.

Being operational meant that you were tested in ways that couldn't be duplicated by other processes. Ways that forced you to be honest about your abilities – or the lack of them. Charnley's career had been shaped by lengthy spells in fire safety, training and Brigade Headquarters. A two-year spell as a Temporary Divisional Officer at the Fire Service College completed the process of under-equipping him to lead men on the fireground – or anywhere else if it came to that.

Not that he would ever admit to it.

So I fought hard each and every day to avoid the ignorant and to circumnavigate the false mirrors of doubt and despair; I wasn't always successful.

I left the interview fully aware of the pit that had opened up before me. A no-blame inquiry meant that I wouldn't face disciplinary charges, but it could damn me forever. My only possible refuge would be to walk straight and tell the truth.

Mike Scott and Rob Brody, the crew in the rear cab, were restless, reading my silence as trouble and betraying their uncertainty by complaining softly about the weather while watching my face for reaction. They wanted something by way of reassurance, but my head felt like it was going to explode and I didn't trust myself to speak.

Dave Chase also sensed the mood and kept glancing over at me; a question building.

'Sandy then, guv?' he said eventually.

'Yes, Dave.'

'And it was Charnley who interviewed you?'

'Who else?'

He sniffed. 'He's a diamond that man – I've never met anyone with so many faces.'

Dave Chase was a sound hand, but a fierce critic of what he perceived as a detached and self-serving senior management.

He wasn't alone in his view. The alienation of operational personnel from those above them was running at frightening levels. It wasn't that firefighters were hostile so much as beyond expecting anything else.

You can't run a fire brigade like a bank – can't run a profit and loss account with people's lives. Yet senior management persisted in treating fires and special service incidents as unwelcome distractions, setting unrealistic admin targets and requiring each and every action to be supported by paperwork. Leadership was non-existent; statistics and image everything.

The firefighters saw through it and despised the clowns who fought shy of the real work of firefighting. The gulf was growing wider every day – and no one had the balls to do anything about it.

Dave Chase may have epitomised the bleak ethos that shrouded the brigade, but he was also sensitive to the watch and its needs. Along with Harry Wildsmith and John Blane, my Sub Officer, Dave formed the hub of the watch, the centre to which they all looked.

The instinctive support of all three had been crucial to me for the last five months. I'd never thanked them – but they knew.

As Dave fell silent again I stared out the windscreen.

The area through which we were driving was Forest Gate, a richly diverse area of Newham which itself boasted over thirty languages spoken within its nurseries and schools. It had its share of problems – not helped by a chaotic local authority that was long on politics and short on joined-up action – but that didn't detract from the community, which was in every sense of the word, vibrant.

Maybe it was naïve, but the sight of mosques and temples in East London still surprised and delighted me. If I saw people dressed in traditional clothes from the subcontinent or West Africa I smiled. Maybe because it took me back to when I was child and the countless hours I spent in Canning Town public library – a place of refuge and dreams – or maybe because in their faces lay perspectives of life I would never know.

Either way Forest Gate was a community of differing ethnic groups that by and large were tolerant of each other yet unapologetic about who they were and what they wanted from life. It wasn't utopia and it wasn't hell – just people getting on with the business of living.

'Is it me or is something going on out there?' asked Dave quietly.

I turned to him. 'Come again?'

He pointed towards the traffic lights at the junction of Upton Lane. 'Over there, guv.'

I glanced up and saw a group of Asian youths gathering on the street corner. Another, smaller group were running towards them. One was waving his arms about and pointing back down the road, towards Manor Park.

I shrugged. 'I've no idea, Dave.'

As we drove on further it became obvious something was happening; groups of Asians, mainly youths but some older people as well, were either standing around talking or walking towards Green Street. From the dress of the elder men it was apparent that they were Muslims.

'Might be something to do with that geezer the Bill arrested yesterday afternoon.'

'What geezer, Dave?'

He braked and swore as a youth ran across the road just in front of us. Mike Scott and Rob Brody, the other crew members in the rear cab, leaned forward, their heads appearing in the gap between Dave Chase and myself.

'Late yesterday afternoon,' continued Dave, 'the Bill nicked a Muslim imam for a driving offence – apparently he refused to take a breathalyser and it all kicked off. They arrested him and in the scuffle the old boy went down and bashed his head on the pavement. He's not too good by all accounts.'

'Nice one, Dave,' said Rob Brody, 'and you drive us right into the blow-back.'

I scanned the road again. More and more Asians were coming on to the street. As we passed Forest Gate police station on the corner of Green Street and the Romford Road I saw a mob in the distance, marching towards us. There were around ten policemen and women directly outside the police station.

Another five were stretched in a thin line across the width of Green Street.

'Lock your doors,' I said to Rob Brody and Mike Scott in the rear cab. 'Dave, take the next left. Let's see if we can avoid all this,' I said.

Dave nodded and turned into Balmoral Road.

With the change of direction we lost the gathering crowd. Balmoral Road was empty with the exception of a solitary old man walking slowly with his head down. Each junction we came to I looked around, but the side streets were just as deserted.

A movement up at a first-floor window caught my eye. I saw a glimpse of a brown face and then the curtain fell back.

Dave Chase glanced at me. 'Seems a bit moody – trouble, guv?'

'Don't know, Dave,' I said slowly. 'It's almost too quiet.'

'I'll keep on till we reach Wanstead Flats then chuck a right into Capel Road and head up Blake Hall Road. It's the quickest way out of here.'

We drove on, coming to a humpback bridge over the railway line and then went under a bridge at the junction of Sebert Road. Almost immediately Dave shouted.

'Guv!'

He pointed off to his right.

A veiled Muslim woman was running down the centre of Sebert Road, screaming. Behind her, by a set of wrought-iron cemetery gates, a black Audi was slewed across the road with its front doors open and the engine running.

I turned to Mike Scott and Rob Brody. 'Stay here.'

I opened the cab door and jumped down just as the woman reached us. She was hysterical and speaking rapidly.

Three times I tried English, but it was obvious she didn't understand me. She started pulling my arm and looked back at the car. I nodded and shouted at Dave to follow in the appliance, but emphasised that everyone should stay on board.

As we reached the Audi the woman pointed at the empty driver's seat and then at the cemetery. I reached in the car, turned off the ignition and followed her through the gates.

She was running now, waving her arms above her head. She kept calling out, the same thing over and over. Then we came to a junction with a tarmac pathway that led off to the right.

'Dave, pass me a radio.' He took the radio off my tunic and threw it down to me, 'Drive straight on and see what you can – stay in contact on the radio. Rob, come with me.'

'What are we looking for, guv?'

'I don't know – the driver? And keep all the doors locked!'

The Muslim woman was rushing down the path thirty yards ahead of us. Rob and I sprinted after her.

That's when we heard the screaming – the high-pitched screaming of a creature in terror and pain.

The Muslim woman had stopped at an unmade sunken track that meandered between the gravestones. Her eyes were wide and she began pulling at my shirt before dropping to her knees with her hands clasped in front of her.

I scanned the area.

'It's coming from over there, guv,' said Rob, pointing towards a line of bushes twenty yards away.

'Right.'

We ran along the sunken track till we reached the bushes, which shielded a chain-link fence. I realised straightaway that it was the edge of the railway line and led the way along the bushes looking for a gap. Rob stuck close to me.

The desperate screams sounded very near now and I tried to climb through the hedge and reach the fence, but the bushes were too thick. Then ten yards on the bushes thinned and the fence was partially broken down.

On the other side of the fence was a five-foot drop down to a series of rail tracks.

'There!' shouted Rob.

On the far side of the tracks and thirty yards off to our left, four men were savagely beating an Asian woman on the ground. She was trying to stand up and one of them was hitting her with a baseball bat.

I jumped down on to the trackside.

They looked up, saw me and I shouted just as the tallest one, a man in a hooded black tracksuit, grabbed her by the hair and wrenched her head back.

He drew a machete from inside his tracksuit and struck two massive blows to her neck. Bright red blood pulsed from the gaping wound and her long wailing moan became an obscene gurgling as the steel sliced through her windpipe; her eyes bulging in disbelief.

I rushed forward.

'No, guv!' screamed Rob.

On the edge of my vision I saw a movement and jumped back a fraction before a train came racing down the track.

Just before it passed the hood of the knifeman slipped and for an instant our eyes met. Then with a long looping cut he hacked off her head and ran off down the track.

2

Rob Brody climbed the fence and jumped down beside me. His face was pale as he shouted above the roaring of the train.

'Jesus, guv, did you see that? Did you see what they did?'

'I'll go after them–you stay with the woman,' I shouted, 'Rob, did you get that?'

He didn't respond at first, but then nodded.

The goods train moved fast and the bright sunlight strobed between the wagons, flashing us in and out of shadow. As soon as the last wagon passed we ran across the tracks and Rob knelt by the body. I threw him the radio.

'Contact Dave and get him to call the police. Tell them there's four armed men on the permanent way between Manor Park and Forest Gate stations.'

He didn't look up, absorbed by the horror of the headless body.

'Now, Rob!'

I left him and ran after the killers.

I covered the first hundred metres fast, but the trackside gravel was hard going and in the midday heat sweat started to pour off me.

At first I couldn't see anyone and ran blindly, trying only to gain distance. Then I thought I saw something up ahead, a figure distorted by heat haze. I kicked harder, fighting my ragged breathing and focused only on catching the faint dancing shape. By the time I'd covered another hundred yards I was fighting for breath and losing co-ordination.

My feet slipped several times as the gravel gave beneath me and I tried digging my heels in to gain purchase. I stumbled once, twice and then fell heavily, the gravel biting deep into the palms of my hands and knees.

Instinctively I tried to get to my feet, but I was breathing so hard and my legs shaking so much that my right leg collapsed under me and I went face down again.

For the minute I lay there soaked in sweat, my whole body shaking as I sucked in air and tried to ignore the pain from my rapidly swelling ankle.

As the sobbing breaths subsided I raised my head and peered through the haze – the figure had vanished.

Fuck! Fuck! Fuck!

I sat back, angrily picking sharp stones from my flesh and wiping at the blood that oozed from my knees. I was covered in white dust from the gravel and reeked of diesel oil, yet I knew I had to concentrate and remember as much as I could about what had happened.

I tried to focus on the killer's face, but the only image that had shape was the head of the woman – the bloody trophy held aloft in obscene victory. In the same instant I felt helpless and close to despair, for a part of me recognised this as one more bone to carry, one more shard of guilt.

I closed my eyes and sighed – needing the minute – the allowance of weakness, albeit brief and inadequate.

Then another mechanism kicked in and angrily I forced the self-pity away. I got to my feet and welcomed the pain from my ankle as an immediate penance. As I limped back towards Rob I glanced at my watch, realising that I had to make a note of the time.

It was ten past twelve.

Soon the place would be alive with police and they would want some answers not a witness obsessed with his own problems.

Focus on what happened – remember what you did, what was done.

I found Rob on his knees moving around the body. He was agitated, unsure of whether to touch it or not and as he hunched over her his hands were opening and closing, as though he wanted to resuscitate her but didn't know how.

'They cut her head off,' he said softly. 'The wicked bastards cut her head off.'

Blood was oozing from the severed neck forming a dark sticky pool that was soaking into the trackside. Heavy spots of blood marked the direction of the killers' escape.

It struck me then that the act of taking the head dehumanised her – reduced her to the level of a carcass. Was that the intention?

The body was dressed in a dark grey two-piece business suit, well-tailored and expensive though now soaked in blood. A broken string of pearls lay alongside, almost invisible amongst the white gravel. I could see no other jewellery.

Then my eye fell on the radio beside the body.

'Did you get hold of Dave?'

Rob looked up, vacant eyed. 'What.'

'Did you contact Dave?'

He nodded, but I wasn't convinced.

I picked up the radio. 'Dave are you there?'

Dave came back immediately. 'Guv! What's up? I've been calling you?'

I looked down at Rob. He was deep in shock – unable to focus on anything other than the decapitated body.

'Did you call the police, Dave?'

'Yes, guv. They want to know the reason for requesting their attendance? Rob wasn't making much sense – something about a body on the railway line.'

I paused. 'Tell them – tell them there's been a murder.'

'Murder? Did you say murder, guv?'

'Yes, Dave. Did you tell them that there are four armed men on the permanent way between Manor Park and Forest Gate?'

'No, guv. Was I supposed to?'

I looked away from Rob as I spoke. 'Do it now. They might still be in the neighbourhood and if the Bill move quickly there's a chance of catching them.'

'Will do.'

Rob was shaking his head from side to side and I squatted down beside him.

'There's nothing we can do, Rob,' I said.

He nodded. 'How old do you think she was?'

'I only saw her for an instant. Mid-twenties at a guess?'

He shook his head, 'There were four of them.'

'Yes, I know.'

I took him by the shoulders and helped him to his feet. 'We'd best move away. It's a crime scene now.'

We walked back from the body into the shade of a trackside storage building and I immediately felt the change in temperature.

I knew I should call Dave again and get the trains stopped, but the image of the killer slicing through the neck and holding up the head kept invading my thoughts, distracting me. In the event Dave came back on the radio.

'Guv, where are you exactly?'

'Where are you, Dave?'

'At the junction of the main pathway into the cemetery and the tarmac path that you and Rob went down.'

'Thirty yards down that path there is a sunken track between the graves – it leads to a hedge. On the other side of the hedge is the permanent way. We're about fifty yards east of where the sunken track meets the hedge.'

'Got you. Do you want us with you or what?'

'No. Stay where you are and turn your blue flashers on.'

'Okay. Do you need anything – salvage sheet?'

'Not for the moment. Get back onto control. I want a priority message stopping all rail traffic between Forest Gate and Manor Park stations.'

'Will do – hold up, guv. We've got company.'

'Company? Dave? Dave are you there?'

'There's a crowd of Asians coming through the cemetery gates, guv. They look well fired up.'

I closed my eyes. 'Get on to control fast and say I want the urgent attendance of the police to control a crowd.'

There was a pause. 'What do you want first, guv? The trains stopped or the police to attend?'

'The police first, then the trains stopped – and Dave?'

'Yes, guv?'

'Drive further into the cemetery, Let them see you, but keep well ahead of them. Stay in radio contact.'

'Got you.'

I was hoping that the crowd would head for the appliance, but the sound of raised voices grew louder and louder until there was no mistaking their intent. Then the first heads appeared at the gap in the hedge and they started climbing over the fence and dropping down on to the trackside.

'Let's keep it as calm as we can, Rob. Do nothing to provoke the situation.'

He nodded, but again said nothing.

They ran across the tracks towards us shouting and screaming, led by a heavy set bearded man wearing a topi – the cloth pill box cap worn by Muslims. I thought I remembered seeing him amongst the crowd in the Romford Road.

I positioned Rob and myself between the body and the crowd and hoped that I could keep them from swarming all over the crime scene, but then they caught sight of the mutilated body and went berserk.

'Move back slowly, Rob. Do nothing sudden,' I whispered.

With a rush they came forward and the body was lifted up

shoulder-high and shown to everybody. Feet trampled the crime scene until it I could no longer be sure where it had been.

But now my mind was fixing on a bigger problem.

With a hundred plus people on the tracks and no confirmation back from Dave that the trains had been stopped there was serious potential for a disaster. I had no choice, but grab the attention of the leader and hope to God that he understood the danger of the situation.

I pushed my way through the crowd and grabbed him by the arm.

'Listen to me – the electricity is still on,' I shouted, pointing at the overhead lines, 'If a train comes through you'll all be killed!'

He shook his head and seized the dead woman's arm. 'Who did this? Who killed this woman?'

The accent was thick and almost impossible to understand above the noise.

'It's dangerous to stay here,' I persisted. 'Help me get your people off the railway lines.'

If he understood me I had no way of knowing. He turned away and shouted something, then punched the air with his fist and the crowd erupted.

Suddenly I was pushed from behind and turned to see a dozen angry faces. At first I wasn't sure whether it was deliberate, but then a huge bald-headed man, maybe twenty stone, grabbed me and started shouting in my face.

I had no idea what he was saying, but he kept shaking me and pointing to the mutilated body. The crowd closed around me and they were screaming and grabbing hold of me.

The big man pointed his finger at me and then at the body. – There was no mistaking the inference. Someone seized my hair and then my shirt was grabbed and ripped.

It seemed to be a signal and punches came from everywhere.

I tried to call Dave Chase on the radio, but a massive fist struck me in the side of the head and the radio fell from my hand.

Two more blows hit the back of my head and I almost lost consciousness, but then I heard a loud voice and I was thrown to the ground.

The next thing I was aware of was the man in the topi pulling me to my feet and dragging me away.

A struggle developed between him and the big man who had grabbed me. I looked around quickly for Rob, but I couldn't see him anywhere. I hoped to God that he'd got clear.

Two youths got around the side and suddenly made a grab for me.

I tried to pull away, but the punches started again.

Ducking low, I protected my head and body by pulling my arms in to my sides and bunching my fists against the sides of my head in a natural guard. I started swaying from side to side, bobbing and weaving, trying to gain a percentage of safety by spoiling their aim.

More hands held me and heavy blows thudded into my arms and body. Instinct screamed at me to hit back, but logic was arguing that to do so would get me killed.

I saw a movement to my left and the man in the topi grabbed me and pulled, knocking hands away as did so. There was pushing and shoving on all sides, but somehow I was free and facing the crowd.

The argument raged between my helper and the big man who seemed intent on making me pay for the woman's death.

I kept stock still – aware that the slightest provocation on my part would see the beating start again.

The man in the topi turned to me.

'Go!'

I didn't move.

'Go!' he repeated

I backed slowly, avoiding eye contact. Then, out of the corner of my eye, I saw Rob.

He was half-turned away from me holding his hands to his face. Blood was pouring from his mouth and nose and his T-shirt had been ripped off him. Deep, ugly looking scratches ran the length of his back.

I took a chance and grabbed him.

'We're going. Don't look back. No matter what happens keep walking.'

3

It was just over a quarter of a mile to Manor Park station, but it took us fifteen minutes to make it.

I ached in a dozen different places. My right eye and the side of my head were throbbing the whole time and when I put my hand up I could feel the swelling starting to distort the side of my face, but it was the ballooning ankle that slowed me.

The beating seemed to have snapped Rob free of shock, but he was only managing one-word replies to my inquiries about his injuries. Not that he needed to explain much, his nose was slanted across his face like a washed up boxer.

I wondered what had happened to Dave and Mike and whether they had raised the alarm now that we were out of contact. I swore at myself for losing the radio in the mêlée and hoped that Dave had got through with the message to stop all trains.

A hundred yards out from Manor Park station I got my answer.

Two policemen were assisting railway staff evacuate a train. When they caught sight of us they came running over.

'Who are you? What the hell are you doing on the line?' shouted the younger of them.

I quickly explained what had happened and who we were, then insisted that they inform their CID. He in turn confirmed that the power had been switched off and all trains stopped between Liverpool Street and Stratford.

'All we heard was that there was some people trespassing on the line. We were sent to cut off any at this end,' he said.

I fought to keep the exasperation from my voice. 'Well you've a murder scene that is being trampled into the deck as we speak and a corpse that is being paraded around by some very upset people. Did you see anything of the four men who came this way?'

He shook his head.

'I had a message sent.'

He looked blank. 'I've heard nothing about that.' He looked at the other copper, an older, fleshy-faced man, who now took charge.

'Look,' he said quickly, 'let's get you off this track and into the station. I'll arrange for CID to meet us there.

They led us through the people walking alongside the train and took us on to the platform. Passengers who had just de-trained and those waiting to find out why the services had stopped, milled around. As Rob and I emerged from the platform staircase into the station foyer just about every head turned in our direction.

The older copper looked at Rob and then me. 'If we have you taken to hospital we can get the CID to meet us there.'

I caught Rob's eye. 'Hospital?'

He shook his head slowly. 'I'm fine.'

'Sure?'

'Positive,' he replied, though he avoided my eyes as he said it.

I turned back to the older copper. 'We'll stay.'

'An ambulance then – no harm in being checked over.' He let the words hang.

He was right to pose the question. Rob was too quiet and I had a sharp pain in my chest when I breathed. It might have been just heavy bruising, but could have just as easily been a cracked rib. Between that, the ankle and the state of my knees, refusing a check over didn't make sense.

I nodded to the older copper. 'Call an ambulance.'

As we waited I took the opportunity to ask the rail station manager for the use of his phone and put a fire flash call through to Lambeth control, asking them if they'd been in radio contact with our appliance.

The female control officer said that Foxtrot 801 had sent a message about a possible disturbance on the permanent way between Manor Park and Forest Gate and that they had lost contact with Rob Brody and me.

'Can you get on to them and have them drive to Manor Park rail station?' I asked.

'Will do.'

'And can you get a senior officer to attend here as well. The CID are going to interview us – about a murder.'

There was a pause at the other end and sure enough she made me repeat it.

Then we waited.

I could hear a series of two-tones in the distance – probably police en route to either the protest or the incident on the track. Two more police cars pulled up outside the station and judging by the expressions on the faces of the new arrivals and the amount of radio traffic being received by the older copper, things seemed to be getting worse.

Then the Pump Ladder arrived.

Dave Chase and Mike Scott initially looked relieved, but when they saw the state of us up close they pulled off the first aid bag. The station manager offered the use of his office and as Mike cleaned up Rob, Dave went to work on me.

Quietly I filled him in on what had happened.

He looked around. 'Bit of a three-ring circus around here, guv. Are you sure you and Rob wouldn't be better off going to hospital?'

'And sit in Casualty for four hours – no thanks. I'd rather talk to the Bill then go back to the station and get cleaned up. I'll send Rob home.'

'Fair enough, guv.' But he didn't sound convinced.

Twenty minutes later Bob Grant, Hornchurch's Station Commander, turned up and I repeated everything.

He listened intently, not interrupting. When I finished he sighed and shook his head.

Bob Grant was one of the ablest officers I knew. A large man with permanently amused eyes that missed little. Although not someone I socialised with, I nevertheless considered him a friend, certainly an ally.

'What were you doing way out here, Steve?'

'Interview with Mad Maurice.'

He frowned. 'What about?'

'Sandy.'

Bob had been at the Heathway fire and had been supportive throughout its aftermath. He knew me better than most and had fought my corner on more than one occasion since.

'Was it a discipline interview?'

'Sounding me out about a no-blame inquiry.'

He thought about that for a minute.

'It could be a good thing.'

'Could it?'

'You need to move on, Steve and it might provide a process.'

'Or label me for the rest of my career.'

He smiled grimly. 'How have you been recently?'

'Does it still haunt me, you mean?'

He shrugged, 'Does it?'

'Yes.'

He laid a hand on my shoulder. 'Not everybody thinks you screwed up.'

'But a lot do, Bob. And I'm not so sure that I'm not one of them.'

'You're bigger than that, Steve.'

'Am I? Sometimes I wonder.'

'How *was* Mad Maurice?'

I shook my head. 'Is there anything so dire as the village idiot trying to be avuncular?'

He gave a flat smile. 'Probably not. What are you going to tell the police?'

'Exactly what happened?'

There was a tightness around his mouth.

'Problem?'

'No,' he said carefully, 'don't say any more than you need though.'

'Why?'

'This has every chance of turning into something very serious.'

'Doesn't get more serious than murder, Bob.'

'It can. Did you hear about that Muslim imam that the police tried to arrest last night?'

Yes.'

'Well he died in Newham General about an hour ago.'

'Jesus!'

'A message has been sent out to all stations to expect possible civil disturbances in the Forest Gate and Upton Park areas.'

'A touch tardy.'

'He shook his head. 'The protest at Forest Gate police station was about the arrest. I'm pretty sure that the news of his death hasn't reach the street yet.'

With the innate speed of a sloth I put it all together. 'And now the woman.'

'Precisely.'

The rail station manager put his head around the corner of the door.

'Would any of you gentlemen like a cup of tea?'

We all did and he smiled and closed the door.

Shortly after that an ambulance arrived and the paramedics

gave Rob and me a thorough examination. They seemed pretty sure my rib wasn't broken and that Rob's nose was. Everything else, though messy and painful, was superficial.

They agreed that if we went to A and E we'd be triaged and would probably have to wait three or four hours to be seen. Their final words were that we should see our GP and get a week's sick leave.

We waited an hour and still the CID didn't show. Bob wasn't too impressed and took the decision to drive us back to our fire station, telling the older copper what was happening. Dave and Mike were to follow in the Pump Ladder.

Just as we got up to leave the station manager's office the older copper reappeared and informed us that a Detective Inspector had turned up.

The dark-haired athletic woman in her early thirties who entered the station manager's office made adrenaline shoot through my body.

Anne.

For a second, an impossibly long second, I stared at her – then I noticed the all too obvious differences and felt foolish.

The likeness was superficial – the shape of the body, the colour of the hair. Perhaps even to some extent, her smile. But it wasn't her, couldn't be her and the disappointment burned my cheeks.

She wore a white blouse and grey pencil skirt that were sufficiently stylish to make you miss her profession.

'I'm Detective Inspector Gordon, Jo Gordon,' she said.

Bob Grant did the introductions and hands were shaken all round.

'Look, I know you've been kept hanging around, but if you don't mind I'd like to wait for two members of the Homicide Assessment Team. They're only a few minutes behind me,' she paused, looking from me to Rob. 'Have you been seen by a doctor?'

'Paramedics,' I said.

'Right.'

And then she turned her head and the adrenaline threatened to cut loose again.

I looked at my watch – it was a quarter to two. The day had lost shape. It seemed only minutes ago that the Asian woman had been killed.

Had it ended there, had the day slowed and resumed some semblance of normality it would still have been a major punctuation piont in my life – the day I saw a woman slaughtered and was ambushed by a ghost – but the day wasn't done with me yet. There was still one more surprise.

Someone once said that good luck is when opportunity meets planning so that makes bad luck what – blind chance?

The two officers from the Homicide Assessment Team that Jo Gordon was waiting for turned out to be the two coppers I least wanted to see; Detective Sergeant Neil Menzies and Detective Constable John Coleman.

Menzies was a sour ginger-haired Scotsman with grey-green eyes that refused trust. Coleman was in his twenties – surly, arrogant and spiteful – the perfect balance to Menzies' artful cynicism.

I'd met them around the time that Sandy died. The loathing had been mutual and fast out of the blocks. Events had borne out my prejudice – I couldn't speak for them.

I'll give Menzies his due, you'd never had read any animosity in his greeting, but that only served to make me doubly wary. Coleman on the other hand wasn't quite as subtle. His face hardened on seeing me, but I don't think anyone else in the room caught it.

DI Jo Gordon asked me to go through what had happened and I went through it all again, occasionally looking at Rob for confirmation. When I'd finished she asked me a simple and very loaded question.

'Were the people who attacked her white?'

'Yes,' I said simply.

She looked at Rob and raised her eyebrows. He nodded in confirmation.

'And you actually saw the face of the man who cut her head off?'

'Yes.'

Everyone in the room seemed to go still, but Jo Gordon's voice didn't alter.

'Clearly? Did you see him well enough to be able to identify him, Steve?'

I thought about that. 'I think so. Maybe.'

'And what about you, Rob?' she continued.

'No. I saw what happened, but it was a blur – they were white though.'

She turned back to me. 'Steve, are you up to viewing suspects today?'

I wasn't thinking straight. 'You have suspects?'

She smiled. 'If there's a racial motive then we might have him on file.'

'Right.'

A looked passed between Menzies and Coleman and I felt a flush of anger. I didn't need this.

At that point Bob Grant intervened. Out of the corner of my eye I saw him look at Jo Gordon and shake his head.

'I appreciate that you have a murder to investigate, In-spector, but I think that both Steve and Rob have been through enough for today.'

He was right, but I couldn't help thinking Bob was being more protective of me than he normally would. Like a prat, I looked at Menzies to see if he'd caught the significance of the exchange and the bastard smiled right through me.

Jo Gordon nodded at Bob and I though that was going to be that, but then she suggested something else.

'You're right, Bob,' she said. 'I wonder though if Steve would take time out to help us identify the exact crime scene? It shouldn't take more than say half an hour.'

'Is it not still dangerous down there?' asked Bob.

She shook her head. 'It's still kicking off in the Romford Road, but away from there I've had the area secured. That's why we were so long in responding.'

'You've not been down there yourself?' I said.

She shook her head. 'No.'

'There's no need for Rob to go as well then?' asked Bob

'No. We'll take get a statement tomorrow though. If that's all right?'

Bob studied Rob, who looked visibly relieved to be out of the loop and stood up quickly. That seemed to be the cue for everyone to move.

'Okay then, Steve. The sooner we get this done the sooner you can go as well,' said Jo Gordon.

Bob Grant took Rob back to Wells Lane fire station with Dave Chase and Mike Scott following in the Pump Ladder. Before leaving, Bob made Jo Gordon promise to keep it as short as possible and to arrange for me to be driven back to Wells Lane immediately afterwards.

Menzies and Coleman went ahead and Jo Gordon took me in her car. She used the journey back to the cemetery to probe me, but not on the murder.

'How do you know Neil Menzies, Steve?'

I sighed. 'Do you know of the Sheldon case – the murder of Robin Sheldon?'

She paused, 'Yes. Not too much, I wasn't involved.'

'Well I got sucked into it.'

She thought for a moment. 'Right. Wait a minute – there was arson involved as well wasn't there? And a woman was rescued by a fireman at some point?'

'Yes,' I said flatly.

'And that was you?'

'Yes.'

'So that means you were instrumental in catching the murderers?'

'That's not the way Menzies tells it,' I said.

She turned to look at me. 'You don't like him?'

'Does anybody?'

She gave a brief shake of the head, 'Not many. He's a good copper though.'

'It depends on what you mean by good.'

'He's not afraid of getting his hands dirty.'

'I bet.'

4

We drove to the cemetery via Capel Road to avoid the ongoing trouble outside the police station. As Jo Gordon steered one-handed she flipped open a packet of cigarettes and offered them to me.

'I don't,' I said.

She nodded. 'D'you mind if I do?'

'Go ahead.'

Without taking her eyes from the road she drew a cigarette, inserted it into the corner of her mouth and lit it from a cylindrical gold lighter.

Perhaps a little too obviously I studied her.

Her complexion was dark and her eyes almost black so that I wondered if she was of Mediterranean origin and Gordon was a married name. There was no ring to support that, but it didn't rule it out either. When she spoke she had a slight huskiness to her voice, which may have been natural or the product of too many cigarettes.

She came across as professional with the aura of 'bought' dispassion that seems to shroud career policewomen, but there was also an underlying sensuality to her – something in the movement – and I realised that it was this that reminded me of Anne.

'Are you married, Steve?' she asked suddenly.

'I live with a partner.'

She gave a single nod. Then said, 'Children?'

I paused. 'One on the way.'

She turned towards me. 'What do you want – boy or a girl?'

'Either,' I said quickly.

I don't know why the question made me uncomfortable, but it did and she looked at me. Intuition or experience – either way she picked up on the vibe.

We reached Tylney Road and as we slowed to turn a police car rolled back to let us through. Further on two more police cars blocked off the Balmoral and Sebert Road approaches to the cemetery and there was a heavy police presence, including some in riot gear on the crest of the humpback bridge.

The police standing around looked tense and most of them had their attention firmly on the Romford Road end of Balmoral Road.

Beyond them, out of sight on the other side of the bridge, I could hear the shouts and screams echoing off the buildings. It was evident that as the afternoon had worn on the news of the murder had spread and probably by now the death of the imam as well.

One death on the face of it was a tragic accident, the other outright butchery, but asking an angry crowd to make the delineation was always going to be an empty exercise. The ever-brittle concept of 'community policing' was about to go through some serious torque with every chance it would completely disintegrate.

How the police responded would decide much. Going in too hard could lead to meltdown, going in too soft would hand the hotheads a gift – and firmness and delicacy had a tendency to cancel each other out.

And when does a civil disturbance become a riot? Who decides it's out of control?

I watched Jo Gordon closely. She didn't seem fazed, but there was an intensity about her that was evident from the first. I'd have bet money that she was ambitious – and I wondered how that sat with Menzies and his familiar.

'How bad is it? Do you know?' I asked.

'In the Romford Road? It's been escalating for the past hour. But no one will get down here, Steve.'

'And those on the railway lines?'

'Gone.'

There was something strange about the way she said that – not forced away or moved on – just gone. I began to feel uneasy and it didn't help that I couldn't pin down why.

She brought the car to a halt forty yards short of the cemetery gates, where the evidence line had been established. Menzies and Coleman were standing next to the tape, waiting for us.

I looked in vain for the black Audi and Jo Gordon turned to me, reading my thoughts.

'We haven't found the car.'

'Right.'

'Or the body.'

'You searched . . .'

She held her hand up to stop me. 'When we get out I want you to talk me through everything – from the minute you saw the veiled Asian woman right up to when you reached Manor Park station.'

'Okay.'

'Neil Menzies and John Coleman will be with us, but I want you to ignore them unless they ask questions.'

We climbed from the car and I pointed out where the woman had flagged us down.

'Show me,' she said.

I walked up to the tape that stretched across the road and indicated that I needed to go across the line. Jo Gordon nodded and we all dipped under the tape.

I took a minute to orientate myself and then pointed where I thought I had jumped down from the Pump Ladder.

'The Audi was there – both the driver and passenger side

doors at the front were open. She was wearing a black cover-all –'
I shrugged, '– a burka?'

'Hijab,' Jo Gordon corrected me.

I nodded. 'The veil was across her face and I could only see
her eyes.'

'From her voice,' asked Jo Gordon, 'how old would you say
she was, Steve?'

I took a moment. 'Hard to say – not young.'

'Thirty? Forty? Older?'

'Not thirty – older. Forty, forty plus.'

'And she spoke no English?'

'No. At least there was no recognition when I asked her what
was wrong.'

Off to one side I saw Menzies making notes. Jo Gordon
conferred with him and then asked another question.

'Which way was the car pointing, Steve?'

'At an angle to the gates, front towards them.'

Menzies fished in his pocket, produced a piece of chalk and
asked me to trace the car's position on the ground. Jo Gordon
waited until I'd finished then walked into the middle of the
drawing.

'And you say the engine was running?'

'Yes. I turned it off.'

She conferred with Menzies again. 'What did you do with
the keys, Steve?'

'Do with them?'

'Yes. You turned the ignition off so what did you do with the
keys?'

I stood and thought, then put my hands in my pockets and
brought out the keys; staring at them like a prize twat. Menzies
gave an almost inaudible sigh and reached forward to take
them from me. Coleman looked away.

'Sorry. I should have realised—'

Jo Gordon held up her hand and waved away the apology.

'It's what we're here for, Steve. Go on with what happened.'

'If I had the keys how did the car disappear?' I thought out loud.

Menzies shrugged as if sharing my bewilderment, but his glance to Coleman seriously pissed me off.

'It's an *Audi* key fob, guv,' Menzies said, holding the keys up to Jo Gordon.

His stress on the word Audi made the point that whatever I'd said before was not necessarily taken as the automatic truth. I understood that and the reasons for it, but I was getting the ache – as Menzies knew I would.

'What happened next, Steve?' Jo Gordon prompted.

I gave both Menzies and Coleman a stare, then turned back to her.

'She ran through the cemetery gates.'

'Show me.'

I led them into the cemetery and stopped at the tarmac side path where I'd told Dave Chase and Mike Scott to wait in the Pump Ladder.

'The woman was where at this point, Steve?' Jo Gordon asked softly.

I looked down the side path. 'About thirty yards ahead of us.'

She nodded and I started to walk down towards the sunken track. She stayed close to me but Menzies and Coleman hung back talking in low voices. When I reached the sunken path I stopped and looked around at them. Menzies's face was impassive.

I turned back to Jo Gordon. 'The woman in the hijab was going berserk about now. She was on her hands and knees pleading with us. We heard the screams coming from over there,' I turned and pointed, 'and we went towards the sound.'

'All three of you?'

'No. No – just Rob and me.'

'What about the woman,' put in Menzies, 'where did she go?'

'I don't know. The screams were desperate and we just took off after them. I don't remember seeing her after this point. I suppose she could have had another set of keys and taken the car, but . . .'

'But what?'

'But I got the impression she couldn't drive.'

'What makes you say that?'

'I don't know. Maybe the fact that she couldn't speak English and hadn't taken the car keys out of the ignition.'

He shrugged. 'So?'

I opened my mouth to say that I thought it was indicative of not being familiar with cars, but I realised that he'd lured me into speculation and I'd snapped at the bait.

He was enjoying this. There was no need for him to make a fool of me I was coping nicely on my own.

Jo Gordon now cut in, running a glance passed Menzies and Coleman as she did.

'Take us over the route you took through the graves, Steve.'

I nodded, but as I stepped on to the sunken track I noticed her drop back and shoot Menzies a look that he met with one of his own. I caught first his eye, then Jo Gordon's – what the hell was going on here?

I turned my back and led the way through the graves.

Jo Gordon caught up again and walked alongside me. Although I didn't want to over-read the situation it was hard to ignore the physical chess being played out. My head throbbed, my ribs ached and it had not been the best of days from any given angle. I didn't need this shit and a powerful urge was growing to tell Menzies to go fuck himself; her too, if it came to if.

I looked at my watch. They had another twenty minutes, then I was out of here.

Two uniformed policemen stood by the hedge that ran parallel to the railway lines and as we reached the gap where I'd jumped down on to the tracks Jo Gordon motioned Menzies and Coleman to close up.

I went past the policemen and stood between the bushes. 'This is where we saw the woman being attacked.'

All three of them moved in and peered down on to the trackside.

'Can you remember the exact spot, Steve?' asked Jo Gordon.

I thought for a moment. 'See that brick storage hut? It was about ten yards forward of there. To the left of it.'

'How do you know that, Steve?'

'We moved back into the shadow of the hut just before the crowd swarmed all over the tracks.'

'Take us through what happened once you saw them on the track.'

I turned back to the track too quickly and pain knifed through my head. I closed my eyes for a second and breathed out audibly.

'Are you all right, Steve?'

I paused, 'Not really. Let's just get this over, eh?'

She nodded and waited for me to continue. I took a deep breath and concentrated.

'When I looked through the gap I saw the four men attacking the woman.'

'How old would you say she was, Steve?'

'Twenties. Mid to late twenties.'

'You're sure?'

'I'm sure of nothing,' I said tersely.

'Go on.'

'I jumped down on to the trackside. One of the men – the tallest – drew a machete and hacked at her neck. I ran forward, but Rob Brody shouted at me and I leapt back just as a train shot in front of me.'

'Describe the men attacking the woman, Steve.'

'Dark clothing. The one who cut her head off wore a black hooded tracksuit top. Just before the train came through the hood slipped and I saw his face – but only for a split second.'

'And?'

I thought for a moment. 'Pale face, sharp features. Early thirties maybe.'

'Height?'

'Six. Six plus.'

'Broad? Medium?'

'Thin.' I stopped. 'He had fair hair, cropped short.'

'The others?'

'Smaller, but none of them short. One – the one with the baseball bat – was very stocky.'

Menzies wrote something down, and then said, 'You mentioned that the man who cut her head off ran away with the head?'

'I couldn't say for certain what he did with it, but Rob and I never saw it after that.'

He made a note. 'But they went down the track towards Manor Park station?'

'Yes.'

'You're certain of that?'

I didn't know if it was his tone or my headache-induced bad temper, but I felt he was on my case again. I looked at my watch and revised my patience level. They now had ten minutes – max.

Jo Gordon seemed pensive. 'Okay. Let's go on to the tracks.'

I lowered myself gently down the five-foot drop, careful not to take the weight on my swollen ankle. Jo Gordon followed and then Menzies and Coleman.

The scene of the murder had been churned up by the mob,

but I found what I thought were the remains of the sticky pool where blood had gushed from the severed neck.

'Sure?' asked Jo Gordon.

I glanced back at the brick storage hut. 'As much as I can be. Certainly within a few feet of here.'

Menzies marked the spot and then turned to Jo Gordon. 'We'll need to keep the lines closed and have forensics go over every inch of trackside from Forest Gate to Manor Park, guv.'

She nodded slowly, then turned to Coleman. 'John, get on the radio and get that organised. I want the whole area taped off fifty metres either side of where Steve has indicated. And I want another twenty uniforms down here – and ask where the scene of crimes officers have got to?'

Instead of moving Coleman looked at Menzies.

'Can we discuss this, guv?' said Menzies.

Her face didn't change.

Menzies went over to her and his voice dropped. She turned and began walking up the track with him. I couldn't hear what was said, but I thought I caught a slight shake of the head.

Menzies stopped walking.

This was nothing to do with me. I was a witness that was all. But logic was about to get carelessly kicked aside.

I saw Jo Gordon turn away from Menzies and walk up to Coleman. This time he made the radio call.

Jo Gordon came over to me.

'Is there anything else you can think of that might help us?'

'No.'

'Something might come to you later. Here's my mobile number.' She gave me a card. 'You're on duty tomorrow?'

'Nine till six.'

'I'll be down about ten. I'm going to get a patrol car to drive you to back to Romford. Thank you for all your help, Steve.'

Again I caught something, a feeling that something was

eating at her and that somehow Menzies was at its root. I looked at him as I spoke to her. 'Is there a problem?'

Her eyes softened for a moment, an almost involuntary admission. 'I'll see you at ten tomorrow, Steve.'

5

It was gone four when I was dropped off at the station.

Throughout the entire journey a deep pulsing headache had forced me to keep my eyes shut as I fought the urge to vomit. When finally we turned into Wells Lane fire station I opened the car door and virtually fell out.

The watch, led by my Sub Officer John Blane, came out to greet me, but all I could do was lean on the car with my head down. As they got near I glanced up and saw John Blane's expression change as he realised the state I was in, then I felt his hand on my shoulder.

'D'you need any help, guv?'

'Just give me a minute, John.'

I took a deep breath and turned to face the watch. They'd obviously been primed by the return of Dave Chase and Mike Scott and my appearance must have underlined the drama of it all. I looked from one to the other, nodding slowly in confirmation of what they'd heard. There was concern on some faces and curiosity in others. I looked for Rob Brody, but I couldn't see him anywhere.

'Bob Grant's here, guv. He held on to talk to you,' said John.

I half expected that he would, but the last thing I needed now was to rehash it all. I just wanted to down some painkillers and close my eyes.

'Where's Rob, John?'

'Bob sent him off-duty. Rob was well shaken up by what you saw.'

John's implied question of course was how did I feel?

'I've a splitting headache, my ribs hurt when I breathe and I've an ankle like a football, but other than that I'm coping, John'

'Sure?'

'Not totally, but I'll get by.'

As I hobbled towards the appliance bay the watch parted to let me through. Harry Wildsmith tilted his head to one side and raised his eyebrows as if to say here we go again.

I knew what he meant – coming off the back of Sandy Richard's death and the bomb incident a couple of months ago. It seemed I was destined to live in interesting times.

I turned on reaching the appliance bay and told the watch that I'd speak to Bob Grant and then have a word with everyone in the mess. Together with John I walked through the foyer to my office.

Bob was on the phone as we entered and he motioned us to sit down. He looked pale and serious and was nodding as he listened, making notes.

When he put the phone down he gave an uncharacteristic sigh.

'There's a full scale riot in progress in the Romford Road. Stratford fire station and all Eastern Command staff have been evacuated,' he said heavily.

'Where have they gone?' asked John

'Staff have gone to East Ham – Stratford's crews and appliances have gone to Leytonstone.'

'How bad is it?'

'Bad enough, John. Bricks were thrown through the windows and a petrol bomb followed. The police advised us that they didn't have enough manpower to protect the station. Officially the situation is described as *fluid* and privately as deteriorating by the minute.'

'Guv? D'you want me to get some ice for that ankle?' asked John.

'Please.'

John disappeared and Bob took a long look at me and asked me how I felt. I shrugged and there followed a silent conversation between us. I could hear voices outside the office and John came back in carrying a pack of frozen peas.

'Best I could get, guv,' he said, then stopped, reading the atmosphere.

'Go sick, Steve,' said Bob. 'Go sick and stay sick – for a week, two weeks.'

'No. I can't. I have an interview with the police tomorrow, remember?'

He pulled a face. 'You're in no condition to be anywhere near a fire station.'

'I'm not going sick, Bob. Not now. It would look like I was hiding from Charnley's no-blame inquiry. I'll tape up the ankle. The rest is superficial.'

Again there was a silence. John busied himself in propping up my ankle and draping the frozen peas over it.

Bob Grant nodded. 'Then go light duty – at least until the ankle is better.'

'No, Bob. There's enough rumours out there as it is.'

He pulled a face. 'I'll tell staff that you're detached tomorrow. After the police have finished with you go home.'

'Cheers, Bob.'

John looped a triangular bandage around my ankle to keep the frozen peas in place. The cold compress made me realise how much heat there was in the swelling. I had a figure-of-eight sports support at home and if I was to walk anywhere tomorrow I would have to dig it out.

Bob then asked John to sit down and gave us both a complete update.

'A "civil disturbance in progress" message has been sent out to all stations. Leytonstone has been designated as the Forward Control, which is why they've sent Stratford's appliances there. A police escort will accompany all shouts to the Romford Road area. Control are in the process of sending a message round to all stations to check their riot shields.'

The riot shields were clear plastic protection that clipped inside the windows of the appliances and were therefore invisible to rioters.

The fire service has always had a policy of impartiality where civil disturbances were involved and it was reasoned that to use wire grids as protection was to invite missiles. Even the subject of police protection was thorny – it lumped us in with law enforcement and in certain circumstances that was perceived as working against the idea of being a service for the community.

I'm not sure how the police viewed this distancing – especially when they were putting their backsides on the line for us.

A wave of tiredness suddenly swept over me and I sighed and rested my head in the fork of my hand.

Bob leaned forward in his chair. 'Go home now, Steve. You're serving no purpose by being here.'

'I don't think I'm up to driving at the moment, Bob. I'll talk to the watch and then close my eyes for half an hour if you don't mind. This headache is creasing me.'

'Do you really need to talk to the watch, guv?' asked John, 'Dave Chase and Mike Scott told them most of it and I'll update them on all this.'

'They might want to hear it first hand.'

A look passed between John and Bob.

'They'll cope, guv. Anyway, it's been on the satellite channels since midday. They're probably better briefed than you.'

I looked at my watch. It was twenty-five past four. 'Call me just before five, John. I want to see the news for myself.'

I left them talking and went to my room where I swallowed

two strong painkillers and sank down into the armchair. The next thing I knew was John was shaking me.

'It's ten to six, guv.'

I blinked, 'Six?'

He smiled, 'I looked in at five and you were well gone, so I left you.'

I went to nod my head, but thought better of it.

'The watch are all upstairs, waiting for the six o'clock news,' he added.

I stood up and tentatively felt the side of my head. It was puffy and the swelling extended from my temple to above my right eye. The painkillers must have had some effect because the headache had reduced to a dull ache.

We went upstairs to the television room and found all the watch, plus a fair sprinkling of the Red watch and Bob Grant, gathered around the large TV set in the corner of the room.

Heads turned as I came in and the Red watch members didn't disguise their shock. Someone offered me a seat, but I declined and stood at the back with John.

The news opened with a vivid sequence of film showing the scenes outside Forest Gate police station, including a vicious clash between the police and several hundred rioters in which a number of police had been badly beaten.

All the day's events, plus the death of the imam, were then recounted at length.

An interview with a prospective parliamentary candidate for Stratford South, Mohammed Ali Rahman, was shown in which he was invited to comment on first the attempted arrest and subsequent injury to the imam and then the protest outside Forest Gate police station.

It was obvious that at the time of the interview the imam, and for that matter the Asian woman, was still alive and the protest in its early stages.

Mohammed Ali Rahman was dressed in traditional long

shirt and loose trousers and had a neatly trimmed beard. I put him down as about thirty-five with a handsome, sensitive face and Oxford English diction. The camera loved him and I figured that if he didn't make it in politics he could always switch to films.

The only thing that stopped me buying the whole package were his eyes, which shone with a disquieting intensity, but maybe that was because I was looking for something. And I have to hold my hands up and admit that I went with my fears, expecting him to make political capital out of the situation. I was wrong.

He was very still when he spoke and his voice was soft with an unforced authority.

He spoke of how Imam Hussein was a respected figure in the community – a man of peace and mercy – and declined to become involved in speculation about the nature of the arrest.

'It wasn't helpful,' he said, 'to prejudge what had happened.' He hoped that an inquiry would be convened to ascertain the facts.

Then, with what I thought was breathtaking understatement, he said that a man as devout and respected as the imam might be excused for being taken aback by being asked to perform a breathalyser test. It posed questions surrounding the general level of understanding about the nature and practices of Islam.

He went on to appeal for calmness and reason whilst the matter was investigated. All of this was said with such dignity, such clarity and control, that the Chief Commissioner for the Met must have been having a breakdown.

From where I stood Mohammed Ali Rahman was a man with a handle on reality.

Strictly speaking the interview had been overtaken by events and was no longer news, but whoever decided to show it understood the power of irony. When the news then went live to the Romford Road and a media heavyweight, Anna Baxendale, you knew the programme editor was having an inspired day.

Baxendale was broadcasting from the top of a building about two hundred yards from the police station. Film came by way of a camera unit with her plus a helicopter hovering above the scene.

Her first words were accompanied by the low throb of rotors in the background. The cynic in me didn't believe it wasn't stage-managed.

She stood with her back to the Romford Road, so that as she spoke the camera looked over her shoulder and down to the chaos erupting in the street. The riot may have been the reason they were there, but there was no mistaking that it was Baxendale who was the main event.

They went through the standard studio-location interplay with earnest anchorman questions met by wind-snatched sound bites together with fingers being run through hair and urgent glances over the shoulder at the street.

It was as believable as the shine on a second-hand car.

The immediate details dealt with, Baxendale improvised, comparing disturbances in previous years in other cities with large ethnic populations, irrespective of any casual links. It was poor rabbit-from-a-hat improvisation – from reportage to speculation in a seamless line of verbiage.

I was going to call it a day when, unnoticed by Baxendale, something seemed to be happening down in the street. As she talked on oblivious, the camera zoomed passed her and picked out a knot of people against the side of a building.

Then the view switched to the heli-camera and as it manoeuvred to get a clear shot of the cause of the commotion the rotor noise finally distracted Baxendale and made her turn.

There was the briefest flicker of shock on her face as she stared down into the street. The editor seized the opportunity and ran side-by-side images – one of the street and one of Baxendale.

A roaring noise nearly drowned the sound of the rotor as several hundred voices rose up and the heli-camera found the cause.

The group by the building had grown to twenty and they were running along the pavement towards the police station. At first it looked like they were going to try to breach the police lines, but suddenly they switched direction and ran to the centre of the road, directly underneath the helicopter.

The sound that echoed off the buildings was unnerving, part anger, part anguish, a howling that rose as they lifted something up. At first it wasn't clear what it was, but then the camera zoomed closer and the image became all too clear – they were holding up the headless blood-soaked corpse.

6

Jenny had never asked about Anne – her name – where we'd met – where she'd gone.

She had been scared of the answers.

She'd known – guessed – that I'd found someone, but had returned because of the pregnancy. There was an unspoken agreement not to explore the past or ask even if it was the past.

But if, initially, Jenny's relief at my return forced her to take a pragmatic view, the passing of time had created a measure of safety so that the urge to know was beginning to surface.

Jenny would never ask directly. Mood was her litmus paper. Mood and eye contact.

There had been a time when she had so much control over me, possessed so much sexual nous, that she could read my every thought, assimilate my every emotion. Now she sensed the gulf and knew that a barrier lay beyond.

Perhaps she thought I was punishing her? Perhaps she thought it was a childish game of one lover for another?

She might have been happy with that, might have peace of mind in knowing the game.

But Anne hadn't been a game or a crude attempt to get back at Jenny for her affair with Kris Mayle. Anne had been an attempt to fill the void. That it had turned into something else hadn't been by design. Anne had been unexpected – a love affair so sudden, so precipitious, it had sucked the air from my lungs.

Anne was not, could not, be a threat to Jenny – but her

memory was. It was the gulf. The barrier was the guilt I felt at not loving Jenny when she was pregnant with my child. So gulf and barrier were insurmountable, at least it felt that way.

I'd left home that morning in neutral; my emotional life with Jenny on autopilot, neither expecting nor wanting anything else. Since then I'd been stretched taut by the murder with emotions of all kinds writhing beneath the skin.

I hoped that she wouldn't choose tonight to probe me, because if she did she just might learn what she didn't want to know.

I slowed the Mondeo and turned into Prentice Street.

The block of flats where we lived was grey, our home basic – less than the flat I'd taken on when Jenny had left me and nowhere near the house we'd once shared.

The financial sinkhole of Jenny's business connection to Kris Mayle had nigh on bankrupted me so that current choices were few.

At one time that would have depressed me, but my expectations had undergone serious realignment in the past year and I was content to view it as merely a stepping-stone to somewhere better.

From close up, blindness, even wilful blindness, has the feel of pragmatism.

I was relieved to see a red and silver Shogun parked out front of the block and smiled as I slid in behind it.

Its owner, Alex McGregor, was my best friend, a rock of faith and probably the main reason I'd come through two bleak years with any vestige of humour remaining.

He was a loyal, family orientated ex-brigade Sub Officer with the face of a prize-fighter and cropped steel grey hair. Nowadays he ran a loss adjustors with his cousin Andrew.

His wife Margaret had died after a gruelling struggle with cancer, nursed by Alex till the last. His son Iain, reading for a doctorate in Maths at London University, was the very image of Margaret and the one source of pride Alex allowed himself.

At one time Alex and Jenny had little time for each other, especially when Jenny was putting me through the hell of the affair and its aftermath. She accused him of interfering, though never to his face. He condemned her, but not by anything spoken.

Communication was all done by subtle temperature change; ice forming whenever they were in the same room. It had remained that way throughout our brief reconciliation and inevitable separation.

Then Jenny had shown up and announced that she was pregnant. Alex, suspecting I might react on impulse, had counselled a DNA test and when it proved positive immediately cast himself in the role of benevolent uncle.

Barely credulous, I watched as his relationship with Jenny swung through a hundred and eighty degrees. The child, the family unit, the broad moral choice, had overtaken any other considerations.

Jenny, vulnerable, took the offered hand of friendship and years of mutual hostility disappeared.

I on the other hand had switched off, living day to day, telling myself that things weren't so bad. But it was a fraud because I was role-playing. And as her shape changed, so she felt increasing unfamiliar.

I no longer tormented myself over her affair with Kris Mayle. Post-Anne, the pain had disappeared. But the protracted dramas of our past life had left me exhausted and I couldn't go back, couldn't fake it. So I was relieved see Alex's Shogun, because he would be a distraction, a means of blocking Jenny's attempts at catching my eye, at trying to reconnect.

I sighed and edged myself from the car.

The ankle had started to swell again and I limped up the

stairs, preparing my replies to what would be an interrogation session.

As I opened the door Jenny was coming out of the kitchen. She gasped on seeing me and rushed forward to help.

'Oh my God – Alex!'

With Jenny's arm around my waist I hobbled into the passageway just as his head appeared around the side of the living room door.

'Stevie, what's happened?'

His thick Glaswegian rasp was somewhere between exclamation and inquiry.

It had briefly crossed my mind to tell them I had slipped over at work and spare Jenny the worry, but I wasn't in any shape to get inventive and they'd never have bought it.

Before I could say anything Jenny sat me down in an armchair and brought two ice packs, one for my face and one for my ankle. Alex took my coat, then propped up my ankle on the coffee table and slipped a cushion underneath it. I used the brief interval to consider just how much detail I should reveal.

In the event I told them nearly everything.

They listened without interruption, Jenny's face paling as I related an abridged version of what had happened on the railway lines. When I'd finished she said that she'd slept during the afternoon and hadn't seen the news. Alex had heard something on the radio earlier.

'Is it really that bad?' he asked.

I nodded. 'If it was bad before it must really be humming now. When they held that body up every Muslim in East London must have gone berserk.'

Jenny disappeared into the kitchen, leaving the door open so that she could still hear. Alex sat down in an armchair opposite me, his hands clasped in front of him.

'You said Mohammed Ali Rahman made an appeal for calm?'

'Yes.'

Alex nodded like it confirmed something for him.

'D'you know him, Alex?'

'Aye, I met him once, briefly.' He sat back and lit a small cigar, blowing the smoke above his head. 'Have you ever heard of David Khan?'

'No.'

'His real name is Daud Khan, but he's known as David. He's big in the Asian entertainment industry. A couple of years ago he started branching out into the mainstream market and began to spread his insurance load. Andrew and I were asked to look into his background, make sure he was a sound risk.'

'So?'

His eyes became shrewd.

'The Asian community is tight. Anyone who has clout, financial or political, knows each other. Andrew and I got invited to a reception to raise money for Mohammed Ali Rahman's political fund – Khan is a major backer.'

'And what did you think of Rahman?'

'I think he'll get elected.'

'Why?'

'Says the right things. He's a good-looking bastard too.'

'But?'

Alex shrugged. 'I have no buts. Within two years the man will be the member of parliament for Stratford South.'

'Which party is he in?'

He smiled. 'Well that's what's so interesting, he's an independent. All three major parties are sniffing around him. He's a winner and they know it. Doesn't hurt that he's Asian.'

'That's cynical.'

He drew on the cigar, 'It's the way the world is, Stevie. 'Ethic balance' is the new religion. Anyone not singing from that particular hymn sheet is a heretic – politically.'

'God help us.'

'God has nothing to do with it.'

'No, he hasn't. Don't get me wrong, I'm all for fairness, it's the shallowness of the thinking that pisses me off.'

'Well you'll get no argument from me on that one.'

The side of my face and ankle began to feel numb from ice packs and I shifted uncomfortably in the armchair.

Jenny reappeared from the kitchen and asked if we'd like a scotch before dinner. We both said yes and she poured three and passed them around. I caught her eye as she handed me the tumbler and she gave a tight smile.

Had Alex not been there she'd have definitely asked more questions. Although she was hiding it well, I could tell she'd been shaken up badly by my appearance.

I was grateful for her concern, but even more grateful that Alex was stopping to dinner. My injuries might otherwise have provided just the kind of bridge that she'd been looking for to close the gap.

'Do want me to switch the news on?' she said. 'There might be an update on the riot.'

I looked at Alex, who nodded. 'Please.'

Jenny reached forward then sat on the floor beside the armchair, handing me the remote. As she took a sip of scotch she squeezed my leg.

I flipped through the channels until I got the one I'd watched at the station.

Anna Baxendale was now standing in Stratford High Street with her back to a line of policemen, having had to abandon her previous position on the flat roof when rioters threatened to set fire to the building.

Breathless, she recounted the dash for safety that she and her camera crew had made out of the rear of the building and over the gardens of neighbouring properties.

She praised the courage and professionalism of her crew,

who continued to film throughout the escape – letting the viewer make the link from the camera crew to herself.

The anchorman in the studio asked her if there was any news on the identity of the headless torso.

Baxendale nodded as the question was being asked.

'At this moment Jim we have no information on that. The police say that no one has reported a missing person, but obviously normal channels of communication between the police and the community are disrupted.'

The next thing she said made me sit bolt upright and Alex shot me a look out of the corner of his eye.

'We believe that the murder of the woman was witnessed by some firefighters and that they have been interviewed by the police, Jim.'

'Do we know what station they're from, Anna?' asked the anchorman.

I went still and felt Alex and Jenny tense.

'No, Jim.'

Jenny placed her hand on my knee and Alex shook his head.

'That's not going to do you any favours, Stevie,' he said.

I swore softly.

'How did they find out?' Jenny asked.

'I don't know.'

'Who knew?'

'Anyone! Anyone in the police, anyone in the London Fire Brigade and anyone in the crowd that stormed on to the railways lines – plus their mates, relatives and passers-by. How the fuck do I know!'

The simmering anger that had built all day was coming out now that I'd stopped fighting it.

Jenny's face changed. She got up and said quietly that she needed to check the cooking.

Alex waited until she left the room and then raised his eyebrows.

'You bastard,' he said evenly.

'I know . . . sorry.'

He snorted, 'It's not me that you have to say sorry to.'

'It's been a hell of day, Alex,' I said lamely.

'Well imagine what it's like for her seeing you walk in here in that state.'

I took a deep breath. 'You're right. I'll deal with it.'

'Well, your manners aside, you're going to have to be careful now,' he said firmly.

'You think so?'

'Aye, I do. You've witnessed a murder, Stevie, and from what you've said you're the only witness that can identify them. The last thing you need is the press digging to find out where you work.'

I frowned. 'You think I'm in danger?'

'Don't you?'

Jenny came back into the room and Alex changed the subject. Jenny avoided my eyes and quietly laid the table. She didn't speak, even when I tried to catch her eye several times.

She smiled at Alex though – which made me feel great.

'I came around to ask you if you were going boxing tomorrow evening. Obviously that's not going to happen.'

'I'll come to watch,' I said.

'Right. Well ring me tomorrow around five and confirm that will you? I've got a feeling you'll have something else on.' He looked sideways at Jenny.

Alex left soon after dinner, using his early departure as a way of saying make good the damage.

Jenny went tactical and remained quiet after Alex left, leaving me to close the gap. I blew it totally. I drank too many scotches and then made a fumbled attempt at affection that was as transparent as it was clumsy.

I joined her on the sofa and placed an arm around her waist

and squeezed, waiting for the response. She gave me such a look of distain, such utter understanding of where I was, that I withdrew my arm and closed my eyes.

That night we slept with a gap between us and for the first time it was Jenny that imposed the distance.

7

I got up early and slipped from the bed to avoid disturbing Jenny.

The bathroom mirror revealed that the swelling on the side of my head had shrunk under the ice pack, but that a vivid yellow-brown bruise now covered half my face. The ankle wasn't too good either. I could stand on it, but it felt thick and unlikely to take much abuse. On the good side, my ribs were merely sore.

We'd gone to bed about an hour after Alex left, which suited me fine because I was just about at collapsing point and Jenny's monosyllabic conversation, though justified, was one more pressure I didn't need.

As a consequence I missed the late night news update so after shaving and showering I made myself coffee and sat in front of the television to watch the seven o'clock news.

The riots, unsurprisingly, were the top item.

They had spread across East London, with parts of Ilford and Tower Hamlets seeing scuffles and fights breaking out between youths and the police. In East Ham two cars had been set alight and shop windows kicked in.

At one point the Ilford and Forest Gate disturbances had briefly joined up, before the police had fed in extra manpower to force the rioters apart.

Sporadic clashes had occurred throughout the night along 'the strip' – a corridor with a high Asian population that ran from Ilford to Forest Gate and on to Bethnal Green. It hadn't quietened down till dawn.

Then a film was run without commentary, showing the Romford Road littered with burnt out vehicles and the scattered debris of street furniture. The camera moved at walking pace, picking out the detritus, the bloody smears on paving slabs and the sad shattered shop fronts.

It was hard not to be moved.

The camera zoomed into the damage inflicted on Forest Gate police station; scorch marks discoloured its red brick facade and the windows on the ground and first floors were broken.

People on their way to work stopped and stared at the aftermath and the camera moved from face to face, capturing the disorientation, the absorbed bewilderment.

It amounted to painting with a lens; the programme editor holding their nerve by refusing to allow an intrusive voice-over. The impact was the greater for it, the extent of the damage needing no more eloquence than its own image.

I don't know what the footage did to other people, but it scared the shit out of me.

Only now, in the sharp light of a new day, would the full implications sink in. Something had changed. East London was waking up from a nightmare, a violent communal hang-over and the unspoken fear had to be that it wasn't over.

The bulletin held me for scene after scene, until finally the images gave way to sterile studio debate.

With a sigh I turned the set off.

I had slept restlessly and could have done without going into work, but the interview with Jo Gordon at ten wasn't negotiable and, as Bob Grant had said that I needn't hang around after that, there was no pressure on me to work the whole day.

Also, if I was honest, I wanted to find out more about the murder.

Something about the killing drew me. Fascination? Horror? Simple intrigue? I wasn't sure, but I felt part of what had happened and needed to know more.

It wasn't lost on me that my therapist in Wales would have suggested that my motivation was deeper. That my inability to stop the killing of the Asian woman had triggered a relapse – making me assume the guilt was mine.

There might be some truth in that, but either way it didn't matter. I wanted to know more and the underlying reasons weren't important.

As I fetched my grip bag for work I glanced down the hallway towards the bedroom. I had no intention of waking Jenny. I told myself that she needed the sleep, but it was cowardice plain and simple.

In the event she woke just before I left and came out to see me off. Sleepily placing her arms around my neck and kissing me.

She was warm to the touch and as her lips brushed mine I had a moment of weakness – a flight of fancy that it was Anne. But then the small bulge of Jenny's belly pushed into me and I stood back and forced the image away; anger colouring my face.

Jenny pulled me into her and kissed me again. Reading my anger as being left over from the previous night.

'I love you,' she murmured and searched my face.

I nodded dumbly and placed my lips against her forehead.

'I'll be home early, not sure when, but probably sometime early afternoon.'

A pale smile of insecurity formed on her face and she nodded.

'Bye.'

I closed the door on her and made my way down the stairs and into the street.

Away from the flat there could be no pretence. My timing, as usual, was lousy, but that was no excuse for not facing up to what was happening.

The schism was growing wider.

It was no longer a case of not loving, but of being unable to love. The drift was accelerating and just as she needed me most I was unable to hold her. It was a mess. A mess of my own making.

I had no solutions, because deep down I didn't want solutions. I felt a complete shit – and in these matters I was rarely wrong.

Once in the car I turned on the radio and listened to a music station, not ready to cope with anything more cerebral. I came in just as they were playing an Aretha Franklin track, 'Ain't no way.'

The irony of the words and the intense musicality of her voice sent shivers down my back. I reached out to change stations, but told myself I was being stupid and put my hand back on the steering wheel and so was forced to listen to the words as they kicked holes in my conscience.

When I'd had just about all the penance I could stomach I switched the radio off, but by then it was too late. The song continued to bounce around inside my head for the rest of the journey, punishing me for daring to think the unthinkable – how to leave Jenny.

I pulled into the station yard and saw that both the appliances were out on a shout.

Out of habit I walked straight into the watch room and checked the teleprinter to see what they had picked up. It was a road traffic accident just off the A12. They'd been called about twenty past eight, fifteen minutes previously.

Three cars were involved with reports of a person trapped and one of the cars alight. A priority message had been sent by

Doug Leadbeater asking for an ambulance to attend a woman suffering multiple injuries.

Then I noticed the earlier message on the printer roll.

At nine o'clock the Pump had been ordered to stand by at Leytonstone fire station – the forward control point for the riot in the Romford Road.

At half nine the Pump Ladder had been ordered to stand by Ilford fire station – the forward control for the riots in Ilford Broadway and Dagenham's Pump had been stood by at Wells Lane as fire cover.

Neither our Pump nor Pump Ladder had returned to Wells Lane before half seven and then they'd pulled the road traffic accident about an hour later. They'd be slaughtered and they had another night duty to face in nine hours.

I went through to the mess to see if the teapot was still warm and found Dave Chase in the kitchen cooking toast.

'Morning, guv . . .' he stopped, catching sight of the bruise on my face, but then smiled, 'the camouflage ain't working. I can still see you.'

I smiled. 'Morning, Dave. Anyone else about?'

'Just you and me. The Red've had a night of it.'

'So I see. Think it'll continue?'

'Fuck knows.'

'I can see you're torn by the social implications.'

He took the toast from the grill and buttered both slices, offering one to me.

'Nothing I can say will alters things, guv. As usual it'll be our arses that are on the line if it all kicks off again.'

'That's what I like about this place, incisive comment and a sound grasp on reality.'

He poured a cup of tea for the both of us and pushed a cup towards me.

'Something wrong, guv? Other than the bruises that is?'

I nearly told him. It nearly all came flooding out, but instead I shook my head.

'Didn't sleep too well; ankle's giving me a bit of gip.'

He nodded and smiled neutrally. 'I'm surprised you came in, guv. Rob Brody's gone sick.'

'I won't be on the run. The police are picking me up at ten. I've got to make a formal statement.'

'Right.'

Through the kitchen doorway I saw John Blane climbing from his car on the far side of the station yard. He held up his hand as came towards us and as he reached the kitchen doorway he gave a rueful smile.

'Morning, guv, Dave. Have you seen the news this morning?' he said.

'Not good, was it?' I replied.

'I couldn't believe how quickly it spread,' said John. 'The Romford Road looks like a battle zone.'

'Let's hope the storm has blown itself out, eh.'

He nodded. 'Can I have a word with you in your room, guv?' asked John.

I saw Dave Chase turn away.

'Sure, John.'

We went through to the station officer's locker room.

'Did Dave tell you about Rob Brody, guv?'

'Going sick you mean? Yes he did.'

'Right. Did he mention why he went sick?'

I paused, only now aware of how tense John was.

'Go on.'

'I had to hang on for about an hour last night, the Red's new guv'nor . . .'

'Doug Leadbeater.'

He nodded. 'Well, he was stuck in traffic around Woodford, probably backed up as a result of the riots . . .'

'I'm listening.'

'Just before we went off duty Rob's wife rang. His doctor has put him off sick for two weeks – with stress.'

'Yeah, well he was shaken up.'

John tilted his head and pulled a face. 'Well he was shaken up all right, but—'

'But what?'

'Well, his wife seemed upset as well.'

'I imagine she was, seeing Rob come home in a state like that.' I paused. 'You're not convinced, are you, John?'

'No, guv.'

'Tell me.'

He sat down on the arm of the easy chair and sighed.

John was a big man with subtle ways and a wealth of common sense. I often felt that he drew his strength from his home life. He was very much in love with Sarah, his wife, and they seemed to have found the secret of loving each other a little deeper each year.

It wasn't an overt love, just seemingly casual looks and almost insignificant touches, a squeeze of an arm or a kiss without thought. The word passion didn't fit – at first – but I'd learnt that there was passion real enough, just below the surface.

'Rob's not been too sharp lately.' he began. 'You'd have missed most of it by being away in Wales. I was going to talk to you, but you've had enough problems on your plate.'

'Well I'm a hundred per cent now, John, so tell me.'

'Rob's been – distracted, guv. Doesn't want to go for a drink with the lads after work, doesn't join in the banter, doesn't laugh much.'

'So he's offish. Why?'

'Well it's been going on for some time.'

I nodded. 'How long?'

'Five months – roughly.'

'Sandy?'

John's face was apologetic. He knew the guilt I carried and was embarrassed at bringing the subject up.

'I think so. Rob's fought to keep it under control, but gradually it got to him.'

For the thousandth time I relived the moment of the back-draught and of how Mike Scott and Rob had entered the building immediately after the building erupted in flames and dragged Wayne Bennett, maimed but alive, to safety.

Rob was a tough man of twenty-six years who had been born in Romford, but had moved to Pitsea in Essex when he got married. He was a man who did his work without complaint and was a solid fireground hand with bottle and sense in equal measure.

If he was buckling under delayed stress from Sandy's death then I should have noticed, should have seen the telltale signs. Instead I was so wrapped up in my self-inflicted dramas that I'd missed it.

Had I known, had I been switched on, I would have got Mike Scott to come with me when the incident blew up with the Asian woman.

I shook my head in irritation as the most obvious of questions only now occurred.

'Are any of the other blokes having trouble dealing with the aftermath of Sandy, John? Like, say, Mike Scott?'

'Mike? No, guv.'

'Why did I miss the fact that Rob was struggling, John? Am I slipping?'

He shook his head. 'When you came back from Wales the wheels were coming off this watch and you turned it around.'

'Thank you, but you still haven't answered my question.'

He looked directly at me. 'No, you're not slipping, distracted maybe – before yesterday, I mean.'

'Right.'

'Don't take that out of context though, guv. Everybody was

scared that you'd never come back to full duty after Wales. We're a watch again now. If you don't mind me saying, you've a tendency to judge yourself too harshly. Nobody's perfect.'

'But I am the guv'nor and I should have sussed the situation with Rob.'

'Not necessarily. One or two of the lads think he has problems elsewhere.'

I weighed that. 'Like what?'

'You never know with Rob. He's private.'

'Have we no idea? Trouble with Linda maybe? She's quite a handful as I remember.'

'Linda? No. At least I don't think so.'

'Would you ask around for me – discreetly? I don't want to ignore it if there's something we can do to help.'

He got up to go, but then paused. 'You could try Dave Chase, guv. He's probably closer than most to Rob.'

'I'll do that.'

8

At nine the Red watch still wasn't back from the road traffic accident so instead of roll call the watch mustered in the mess. There was a strained atmosphere with an intense discussion about the previous day carried on in low voices. The unease was thick enough to cut.

At one point I saw John Blane have a quiet word with Dave Chase, who looked at me and nodded.

My bruised face drew comments, some sympathetic, some wickedly funny and for a few minutes the riots went on the back-burner. But all too quickly the conversation switched back to the previous day and the humour evaporated. The extent of the trouble and the levels of violence had shocked everybody.

'Once that imam died trouble was on the cards, but the murder of that woman was something else,' said Mike Scott. 'There'll be a backlash.'

'Backlash?' asked John.

Mike had the floor. 'Newham has two things in abundance – immigrants and far right nutters. This could go ape-shit.'

For a moment I was irritated that he'd said what he had, though the same thought had occurred to me.

'I hope you're wrong, Mike,' I said. I turned to John Blane at the end of the table. 'John, I want you go through the operational note on civil disturbance procedures immediately after Red watch get back and the appliances have been sorted out.'

'Yes, guv.'

'No doubt the Red watch are riding with the riot shields fitted, but just to make sure I want you to check that as soon as they show.'

'Will do, guv.'

I looked around the mess table. 'About yesterday – what happened to Rob and myself was nasty, but nowhere near as bad as it could have been. We were lucky. Now, it's very important that we don't suffer any more casualties so whatever happens with this situation on jobs you are all to consider firefighter safety as your priority. Clear?'

There were murmurs and nods.

'Moreover, if we get into any situations involving ethnic minorities, particularly Muslims, I want you to take great care not to inflame the situation – no comments, opinions or poorly thought out jokes. It needs to be professional on all levels.'

'Fair enough, guv,' said Harry Wildsmith.

I looked around the table again and the expressions were serious.

'I imagine that outside duties will be cancelled by CMC today, but if they aren't then I want you to cancel any inessential outside activities for us, John.'

'Fair enough, guv.'

'Any questions?'

'Do we know how Rob is?'

'Only that he's gone sick. I'll get hold of him sometime today. Who's the dutyman?'

'I am, guv,' said Dave Chase.

'Right, Dave, book me detached for the day and when John has read out the op note on civil disturbances, write it in the log.'

At that moment I glanced through the mess room window and saw the Pump and Pump Ladder. I gave a nod and the watch dispersed to sort the appliances out.

Then I went through to the office, logged on the computer and spent thirty minutes or so going through my e-mail.

It never ceased to amaze me how much crap oozed from BHQ. Esoteric facts and figures, data on the banal and memos of the stunningly obvious were issued ad nauseam. Instead of being tools, computers had become gods that sucked time from the working day and patience from their users.

I was halfway through reading an e-mail – a communication that informed me that I could now electronically order china mugs, size 300mg, and setting out a two page aide-memoire on the process – when John interrupted me.

'There's a Detective Inspector Gordon to see you, guv, I've put her in your office.'

'Cheers, John.'

I logged off and went through to meet her.

Jo Gordon had reminded me of Anne from the first, therefore the likeness shouldn't have surprised me again – but it did. As before, the physical similarities were marked, but it was the sensuality that nailed me.

And the eyes.

'Hi, Steve.'

The use of my first name was merely a tactic to get me to relax. After all I was a witness not a suspect, but it definitely had an effect on me. I'd have to watch that – I was too vulnerable to let my hormones kick in.

'Would you like a cup of coffee or something, Jo?'

'Coffee would be nice.'

There were lines under her eyes, as though she hadn't slept too well, which in the circumstances was what you might expect from a person dealing with the fall-out of a politically sensitive murder inquiry, but it was more than that.

There was a vibe about her that I'd caught at the crime scene, just at the end; a vulnerability that shouldn't have been there and, together with the huskiness of her voice, it made all conversations seem intimate.

'How do you like your coffee?'

'Black, no sugar, Steve.'

I went through to the kitchen and hunted out a cup and saucer rather than the mugs that we tended to use. Dave Chase and Harry Wildsmith were lurking in the mess room and couldn't resist a comment.

'Looking after our guest, guv?' said Dave with a grin.

I looked up and shook my head.

'Good looking woman, guv,' said Harry, neutrally.

'She is. Haven't you two got work to do?'

'Allo? The guv'nor's a bit touchy, H. A long line might be in order.'

Harry frowned. 'Why?'

'A long line and some wax for his ears . . .'

Harry smiled. 'Tie him to the mast, you mean?'

'That's exactly what I mean. Italian by the look of her.'

'Sirens were Greeks, weren't they?'

'I don't suppose he minds, H.'

'If you two don't disappear I'll get John to find some work for you.'

'Come, H, I know when we're not wanted. Oh, and the nice cups are in the top cupboard – if that's what you're looking for, guv.'

I swore under my breath and Dave grinned fiercely as he linked arms with Harry and went out into the station yard whistling loudly.

I found the cups, sorted out two that weren't chipped and made the coffee. When I took them back to my office I found Jo Gordon looking at the station honours and awards board pinned up behind my desk.

She turned and smiled. 'Who is Alexander McGregor?'

'My ex-Sub Officer.' I placed the cups of coffee down on my desk. 'He was awarded a Chief Officer's Commendation for saving a man in a collapsed trench incident. It was a disgrace. He should have got a gallantry medal, but someone up the road didn't like him. Alex was too outspoken for the delicate souls at BHQ. He made enemies of the wrong people. Or as he put it, the right people.'

'What did he actually do?'

'We got called to a trench collapse – persons buried, Whalebone Lane, Dagenham. On arrival we found three persons involved. A bulldozer had strayed too near the edge of a trench and it collapsed.'

She studied my face. 'Go on.'

'I organised a rescue team of two men in breathing apparatus attached to lines. The plan was to try and dig out the two men whose head and shoulders were visible. The third was completely buried. Unfortunately, as the rescue team were donning BA there was a further collapse of the trench wall. Alex reacted out of instinct and threw himself down the trench to shield one of the men with his body.'

'What happened?'

'The two men who had been visible, plus Alex, were buried alive. We got Alex and the man that he'd shielded, out. The man lived, but Alex was PU-ed with a back injury.'

She arched her eyebrows. 'PU-ed?'

'Permanently unfit. No longer allowed to stay in the brigade. Says that he swapped a pain in the arse for one in the back.'

'You still have contact with him?'

'Yes.'

She nodded approvingly. 'He sounds a character.'

'He's that all right.'

She picked up her cup of coffee and sat down, regarding me over the rim.

'And how are *you* feeling today?'

'Okay. Ankle's a bit fat, but I slept well once the headache cleared.'

She took a sip of the coffee and struggled not to pull a face.

'Sorry, we only have cheap instant in the mess.'

'It's fine,' she said waving a hand dismissively. 'You said you aren't married, Steve?'

'Live with someone.'

'And she's pregnant?'

'Yes.'

'It couldn't have been easy seeing you come home like that. How is she taking all this?'

'Coping.'

'You'll probably say no, but I can put the victim support group in touch with you, if you feel it might help.'

'We're both fine.'

'Sure?'

'Certain.'

'Okay,' she said slowly.

I wanted to say more, to say that the last thing either of us needed was a victim support officer. I wasn't a victim – just a prat and needed to stop being one. Jenny, for her part, needed a husband. But I had the feeling we were both going to be unlucky.

Jo Gordon put the cup back on the desk. 'I though it best, Steve, if I explained what we're going to do today.'

'I'm listening.'

'I want to interview you formally about yesterday and then get you to sign a witness statement.'

'Just you?'

She paused. 'Another Detective Sergeant will sit in on the interview – it won't be Neil Menzies.'

'Okay.'

'I read up on the Sheldon case last night,' she said slowly.

'So now you know?'

'Yes. Look, Steve, Neil Menzies and John Coleman are members of a Homicide Assessment Team from the Area Major Investigation Team. Their job is to make sure that all necessary protocols have been set up regarding the initial investigation. That's why they were there yesterday.'

'I see.'

'I'll do my best to keep you clear of them.'

'Whatever.'

Her head went back and she breathed out slowly. 'For what it's worth, Steve, I think they took umbrage with you becoming involved in the Sheldon case because it flew in the face of what they are meant to do – which is keeping things on track. I don't think it was anything personal.'

'Maybe not initially,' I said flatly.

'Point made. Shall we move on?'

'Okay.'

'There's quite a bit I'd like you to do today. After we've taken your witness statement I want to show you some photographs. Maybe you'll see someone you recognise and maybe not. If you don't recognise anyone I want you to help construct a likeness.'

'Whatever I can do.'

'If we get lucky I shall want you to attend an ID parade later.'

'No problem.

'Good.'

I looked at her virtually untouched coffee cup. 'Unless you'd like another I'm ready to go.'

'I'll pass,' she smiled and stood up.

I fetched my uniform jacket and cap and we went out into the station yard to her car. As I climbed in the passenger side I threw my cap on the back seat.

They say people buy cars that suit their personality or at least what they'd like to be. Well, Jo Gordon had a top-of-the-range black E class Mercedes with grey leather trim and a wooden dashboard. It looked and smelt new with just the faint odour of tobacco.

'Yours or the job's?'

She spoke as she looked over her shoulder, reversing the car. 'Mine. One of the perks of being single.'

She'd mentioned it so I felt I could ask. 'Ever married?'

The wheel spun back and she drove forward, out of the yard. 'Yes.' It was said flat with an unspoken please-don't-ask quality.

I ignored it. 'It's just that the surname is . . .'

'My ex-husband's.' She paused. 'My maiden name was Braganza.'

I smiled. 'So Jo is short for what?'

'Josefina. My father was Portuguese.'

'Right. But you've kept your married name?'

There was a smile then, a realisation that perhaps I wasn't just being nosy.

'I can see why you don't get on with Neil Menzies.'

'Do *you*?'

'No.' She smiled, but there was the merest glimpse of hardness about both her and the reply.

I'd thought on first impression that she was ambitious, now I was convinced. She had that stand alone quality that you see in high flyers – and an instinctive intelligence.

Her strengths made her a career natural, but I'd have bet there were bodies left in her wake, as well as the shattered egos of old-school police officers unable to accept or appreciate what she brought to the table.

Her very existence must thoroughly piss off Menzies.

It crossed my mind that the instant of vulnerability I'd witnessed was a ploy – a professional performance used to get close to people, close enough to climb inside their heads. But a more detached voice said that it was probably the effect rather than the intention.

Either way this was a complex woman – undeniably beautiful and very sharp.

And from the moment she'd arrived I'd been studying her – lips, eyes, the peach colouring of her skin and the curve of her breasts.

In my defence anyone would have looked twice, but I continued to look.

A flush of guilt hit me and I looked away, staring out of the passenger side window, feeling the soft insistence of Jenny's bulge reassert itself.

Had Jo Gordon arrived with another officer I wouldn't even have got on this line of thinking and had she brought Menzies the conversation would have been all together different – cold questions layered with barbed comment.

That she'd turned up alone had surprised me and if there was a reason it was yet to reveal itself.

At that moment she seemed to read my mind because as we turned out of Wells Lane on to the High Road she suddenly said, 'I came straight from home – I worked late last night.'

'Late?'

'Till three. If you saw the news last night you probably know that the body of the decapitated woman was dumped on Forest Gate police station doorstep last night.'

'I saw.'

'It complicated matters.'

'I bet.'

'As a piece of evidence the body is next to useless. It must be contaminated with the DNA of fifty different people.'

'Which now makes my evidence important.'

She shook her head. 'Which makes your evidence vital.'

9

We drove to Romford police station because Jo Gordon said that Forest Gate was best avoided. The feeling was that as the day wore on there were likely to be more street disturbances as groups of youths had again been seen gathering in Katherine Road just off Romford Road.

As we drove under the arch into the car park at the rear of the station she brought the car to a halt in a marked bay and told me to stay where I was. Then she got out the car and swiped a key-card through a door-lock and disappeared through a side entrance into the station.

While she was away I took the time to give myself a good talking to. The substance of which was 'stop staring'.

When she returned ten minutes later she had someone with her. I got out the car and Jo did the introductions.

'Steve, this is Detective Sergeant Proctor, he's part of my team on this investigation. Bill, this is Station Officer Steve Jay.'

Bill Proctor was tall, around six feet two, with a ready smile and a handshake that held nothing back. I liked this guy in the way that I'd disliked Menzies – instinctively.

'How are your injuries, Steve?' he asked.

'I've cancelled my wedding.'

He paused for a split second and then a smile slowly spread across his face.

'Right.'

As we went through the side entrance Jo Gordon went over the morning's running order again.

'Bill has arranged the use of an interview room for us, Steve. I'd like you to go through what happened again and then we'll take it down in a statement. Have you given a statement before?'

'For arson cases a couple of times.'

'Good.'

The side entrance took us into a corridor with rooms and offices on either side. Proctor led us to an interview room and Jo Gordon sat down opposite me with Proctor next to her.

The mood and the tone of their voices changed; they were all business now.

Both opened notebooks and Jo Gordon gave me a brief smile before nodding to Proctor. He switched on the tape recorder in front of them and spoke into it.

'Interview with Station Officer Steven Jay of the London Fire Brigade at 11.30 hours Tuesday 22 September. Detective Inspector Josefina Gordon and Detective Sergeant William Proctor are the interviewing officers.'

Then it started.

Over the course of the next thirty minutes they took me over the events of the previous day in minute detail; things I seen, done and said. Some questions were disarmingly simple – edges perhaps to the jigsaw? There was also lengthy questioning on the victim and her murderers.

Did I hear anyone speak? Did the murdered woman use any English? Clothes worn by the murderers? Height, weight, peculiarities of anybody and everybody?

Jo Gordon in particular repeatedly asked questions about the veiled Muslim woman that had flagged us down; voice characteristics, height, and colour of eyes. Then she asked a seemingly unanswerable question.

'Did you get an idea of her build, Steve?'

'Build? Hard to say under the clothing – thin if her hands were anything to go by.'

She made a note, 'Her hands were thin?'

'Bony.'

'Bony as in thin or bony as in old?'

I thought about that. 'The skin was shiny.'

'So old then?'

'I'd have to say yes.'

She flipped back a couple of pages in her notebook and then looked up.

'Yesterday you said forty maybe forty plus.'

'Some people are old at forty,' I offered.

Bill Proctor smiled and nodded as Jo Gordon wrote something down again. When she finished writing she passed the baton to Proctor.

'Steve,' he began 'I want you to concentrate now on the gang that attacked the victim.'

'Okay.'

'You said initially that there were four men.'

'Yes.'

'That's definite is it?'

'I saw four men.'

I was weighing each answer now, knowing the importance to them. Assumption had been questioned from the beginning. At first that had irritated me, now I recognised it as methodology – and common sense.

'Yet you also said,' he paused and Jo Gordon turned her notebook towards him, 'that you only saw the face of one of them. So how do you know that they were all men?'

I opened my mouth to say that it was obvious, but then realised that he would ask me to substantiate it. After a second I shrugged and said what I thought was reasonable – albeit an assumption.

'They had to be men. The build, the way they moved – everything about them.'

'But you only saw the one face?'

'Yes.'

'Previously you said that the weapons they used were . . .' another look at the notebook, 'a baseball bat and a machete?'

'Yes.'

'But the machete wasn't drawn until just before they cut her head off?'

'That's right.'

'Was there any reaction from the other attackers when the head was cut off?'

'Reaction?'

'Shock, anger, surprise?'

I shook my head. 'It was too quick. I was looking at the man who had the machete at that moment – then the train came past.'

'And the head of the woman – did he run off with it?'

I thought about the answer I'd given the day before and repeated it.

'I couldn't be certain of that. I saw him cut off her head and hold it up. After the train passed Rob Brody and myself ran across the tracks to the body.' I sighed. 'The head was gone.'

'And you chased after the killers?'

'Yes.'

He again looked at Jo Gordon's notebook. 'But fell and saw nothing more?'

'A hazy figure in the distance. It could have been anything.'

There was a pause and Jo Gordon looked at Proctor who shook his head. They both made further notes as I sat there feeling deflated, as though I'd let them down.

'Is there anything you can think of that you haven't mentioned previously? Anything at all?' asked Jo Gordon.

'No.'

'Okay, Steve, I want to take a statement from you now.'

Proctor switched off the tape recorder and we began drafting the three-page statement. When I'd finished I was asked to sign it at the beginning and the end.

I immediately felt a sense of relief and then irritation at myself. The process of giving a formal statement had spooked me, maybe because of its importance.

'Would you like a cup of something, Steve?' Proctor asked.

'Coffee, white with no sugar?'

'Sure.'

As soon as he left the room Jo Gordon softened into a different creature and I went back to staring. If it bothered her she didn't let it show.

'That bruise looks very painful.'

'It's tender.'

'Have you put anything on it?'

'Just ice.'

She stood up. 'I'll see if there's some witch hazel in the first aid box.'

'Thank you.'

She nodded and went to fetch it.

Alone, I reflected on what I'd told them. If I'd felt I had to justify myself to Menzies then with Jo Gordon and Proctor it was different; more like collaboration. It was, I was sure, merely a method of drawing out the interviewee and obtaining the best results.

What was more intriguing was seeing Jo Gordon switch off the second the interview ended. Here was the complete professional, knowing exactly where the line was drawn. Both sides of her drew me, but guilt snagged like a trailing anchor – no matter what my problems, I wasn't a free man.

She came back with the first aid box and was hunting through it when Bill Proctor returned with my coffee.

'Bill, would you set up the laptop for me?' she asked.

'Yes, boss.'

He placed the coffee down on the table in front of me and

left the room again. Jo Gordon came around the table and made me tilt my head.

Gently she dabbed at the bruise with a cotton wool pad soaked in witch hazel. A trickle of the liquid ran down the side of my face and she pressed her wrist softly against my cheek to catch it.

'You do that very well,' I said.

'I trained as a nurse.'

I was about to ask, when? But saw the look in her eye. I closed my eyes in acknowledgement. 'I deserved that for the wedding remark.'

'Yup.'

She smiled again and the anchor slipped its trace.

'Are you getting much pressure over this murder case?'

She gave a thin smile. 'You could say that.'

'The Met or political pressure?'

'Both. No one has said too much – just looks and the subtle distancing you get when you might go down and clutch for helping hands.'

I gave a tight laugh. 'I've been there. It's a dark country.'

She met my eye. 'Yes, it is.'

At that moment Bill Proctor came back in and said the laptop was ready. I moved to get up and felt the gentle pressure of her hand push me back down.

'Two minutes, Bill,' she said.

The door closed and Jo Gordon gave a final wipe of the bruise with the pad and screwed the top back on the bottle. She threw the used pad into a rubbish bin in the corner of the room and turned to face me. The professional slipped back into view.

'Can you picture the machete user in your mind at this minute, Steve?'

'I think I'd know him if I saw him.'

Her head went back. 'Yes, but can you see him now, in your mind's eye?'

I took a minute. 'Not clearly.'

She gave a short nod that might have been a sign of tension. I wasn't sure.

'Take a few minutes to clear your mind and then try to remember.'

'Okay.'

'We'll be outside when you're ready.'

As she opened the door to the corridor I caught a glimpse of Proctor. Then the door closed and I was alone.

It was a shrewd move on her part to do this, to let me take a moment to focus. It took me back to the therapy sessions in Wales; a process I'd been instinctively against, but one that had yielded positive results and might have yielded much more, had I stayed.

I settled back in the chair and closed my eyes, relaxing as best I could, then tried to recreate the face of the killer.

The scenes of the murder itself were vivid and the agonised face of the victim only too easily recreated, but that of the killer was elusive. I tried going through it all slowly, like a film shown frame by frame, but when it got to the moment when the tracksuit top slipped it became blurred.

I tried several times with the same result and then gave up. There was nothing more I could do except hope that I would recognise him if I saw his photograph.

I opened the interview room door.

'Ready?' said Jo Gordon.

'As ready as I can be,' I said flatly.

Proctor took us through to another room. In the centre of a table was a laptop computer, with the screen-saver on – a cartoon of a policeman and a bulldog wearing a police helmet, chasing a burglar in a striped jersey.

I was told to sit on the middle of three chairs. Jo Gordon sat on my left and Proctor on my right. Proctor clicked the left button of the mouse and the screen-saver disappeared and in its place were six photographs.

Below each photograph was a number. I scanned each photograph in turn and shook my head. Proctor hit the mouse again and another six photographs came on screen. Again I took my time and examined every image.

This process went on for some thirty minutes without success. Twice Proctor changed the CD, but the faces were all blurring into one. Then suddenly I saw the face of the killer. At least it looked like him. The hair was longer, but the eyes were the same. Jo Gordon read my reaction.

'Something?'

I looked at her. 'I think so.'

'Think?'

'I only caught a glimpse. It could be him. It's just hard to be certain.'

Another witness statement was produced and I had to write down that I had identified the person in the photograph, together with the photograph number.

Jo Gordon turned to Proctor. 'Bill, pull his record. I want everything on my desk inside an hour.'

'Right, boss.'

As soon as Proctor left, Jo Gordon turned to me.

'Thank you for your help, Steve. When we've spoken to this man I want you to try to ID him in a parade.'

'Okay. These people I looked at are all known racists?'

'Or linked to crimes that might have been racist,' she said precisely.

'Some of them look like bank clerks.'

'Some of them are bank clerks. Racists come in all guises.'

'I don't think the four that killed the Asian woman worked in a bank.'

'Probably not. Now listen to me, Steve. I don't want to alarm you, but it would be unfair not to make you aware of the potential danger that you could face by being an eye witness.'

'Funny, that's what Alex McGregor said last night.'

'I gave you my card yesterday with my mobile number on it.'

'I have it.'

'Good. Keep it close.'

10

I was driven back to Wells Lane Fire station by a patrol car.

The minute we turned into the yard I knew something was up. There were at least five serious-looking cars, including a Toyota Land-cruiser Amazon with tinted windows and a Daimler Jaguar, parked in the yard. Two Assistant Divisional Officers were standing nearby as though guarding them. Both looked uncomfortable.

I recognised one of them from a fire I'd attended some months back. He gave an uncertain smile when he saw me – conscious that I was a man under a cloud and that it might not be wise to be too friendly

'Afternoon, Steve,' he managed.

I caught his eye and held it for a second, wanting him to know how transparent he was. The other ADO caught the mood quickly and found his shoe needed lacing. Sighing audibly, I walked past them resisting the urge to ask who the visitors were.

As I made my way to the watch room I ran straight into Bob Grant and at the same time heard the murmur of voices coming from the mezzanine floor just outside the Station Commander's office.

'What's happening, Bob? Looks like the Motor Show out there.'

He raised his eyebrows. 'Let's use your office.'

As he led the way, I shot a questioning look at Harry Wildsmith, who was in the watch room changing the tele-printer roll. He saw me and raised his eyebrows.

Once inside the office Bob closed the door.

'Charnley's here, Steve.'

'I saw his car. Who owns the others?'

Bob hesitated. 'A local political figure, Mohammed Ali Rahman.'

I frowned. 'I saw him on television last night. What's he doing here?'

Again Bob took his time, as though weighing my reaction. 'It appears that Charnley contacted him this morning because of the riots. He'd decided that a little bridge-building was called for so he contacted Rahman and asked him was there anything the brigade could do help ease tensions in the community.'

'And?'

Bob breathed out slowly. 'Rahman asked to meet the fire-fighters who tried to help the murdered Asian woman and Charnley agreed.'

'He what?'

'Unfortunately it gets worse.'

'Go on.'

'The press are here,' he said softly.

'For fuck's sake! Has Charnley gone completely mad?'

'Calm down, Steve.'

It felt like I was being eaten alive. 'Bob! I've just got back from the police who have been at pains to tell me that I might be a target for the murderers – and Charnley flags up where I work!'

'I gather that bringing the press was Rahman's idea or rather his personal assistant's.'

'And I suppose Charnley didn't have the balls to tell them to go to hell.'

'In a word, yes.'

I sat down in my office chair, shaking my head.

'We can move you, Steve.'

'I don't want to move. I haven't been back that long.'

'It might be the smart thing, temporarily.'

I rounded on him. 'The smart thing, Bob, would have been not to let the press get involved!'

'This wouldn't be of my choosing either, Steve,' he said slowly.

Nobody was this stupid, not even Charnley.

'How long have they been here, Bob?'

'About fifteen minutes.'

'Have they spoken to the watch yet?'

'Rahman or the press?'

'Either of them.'

'So far Charnley's kept everyone in the Station Commander's room – drinking tea.'

Wells Lane was temporarily without a Station Commander and Bob Grant was filling in. We wanted him permanently, but the buzz was he was about to get promoted to Divisional Officer.

'So why aren't you up there, Bob?'

'I was waiting for you. Charnley had me ring DI Gordon and find out where you were? She said you were on you way back. So I hung around in the watch room to warn you about all this.'

I nodded. 'Sorry if I went off at you, Bob.'

'Understandable, given the events of yesterday. Unfortunately, I have to take you upstairs to meet Mohammed Ali Rahman – and the press.'

'No.'

'I know how you feel, Steve, but . . .'

'I won't do it, Bob. Charnley can go to hell.'

He stared at the floor. 'He won't like . . .'

'Fuck him!'

At that moment there was a tap on the door. Bob opened it and there stood a beautiful Asian woman of about twenty-five, dressed in a black business suit with a deep green silk blouse.

Bob stood back and she came in the office.

'Hello, I'm Zahra Asif, Mr Rahman's personal assistant. You must be Station Officer Steven Jay?'

The accent was middle-class English, with the suggestion of Urdu. The language was precise and the delivery direct, but warm, if only professionally so.

Out of the corner of my eye I saw Bob Grant watching me and fought the instinctive urge to stand up. But politeness won out and I got to my feet to shake the slender, perfectly manicured hand.

'Has ADO Grant explained to you why we're here?' Zahra Asif asked.

I regarded her for a few seconds, the counter-instinct now kicking in. 'No, he hasn't.'

Good move, Stevie, give the lady a hard time why don't you.

She smiled, revealing perfect white teeth and at the same time glancing at Bob, immediately picking up on the vibe.

'Well, then,' she said slowly, 'let me explain. Mohammed Ali Rahman is the prospective . . .'

'Parliamentary candidate for Stratford South,' I finished.

She looked at me, surprise in her face.

'You know of him?'

'A friend attended a fund-raiser.'

She smiled again, the almost black eyes dismantling the hinges of instinct and mood with alarming speed. *Sleep with Jenny tonight or you are going to make a fool of yourself sometime soon.*

'Your friend is?'

'Alex McGregor – he's a loss adjustor.'

She nodded, but didn't admit to knowing him.

'Mr Rahman asked Maurice Charnley if he could meet you and the men that tried to help the murdered woman. As I'm sure you are aware everybody is very concerned about . . . well everything.'

She looked from me to Bob and back again, confirming that none of this had passed us by. Bob and I nodded in unison and Zahra Asif clasped her hands in front of her, a tight smile of concern settling on her face.

Tiptoeing around racial division is a political rite of passage for people in the public eye, the rules are to play down glaring differences and seize on the common ground, but sometimes it's in the agreement that the gap is so sharply defined.

'My concern is the press,' I said. 'I don't want my name or my picture advertised.'

Bob coughed. 'I believe that SDO Charnley may have already released some details, Steve.'

Zahra Asif agreed. 'We want the message to go out that . . .'

'White men helped a brown woman,' I said bluntly.

I felt Bob stiffen, but Zahra Asif was a pro.

'Yes,' she said simply.

I folded my arms. 'Why wouldn't we?'

'Sorry?'

'Why, Miss Asif, wouldn't we help someone in distress? It's what firefighters do.'

'Not everyone would, Mr Jay. Believe me.'

She was right and I was being an arsehole.

I thought it through, then offered a belated bone.

'I'll meet Mr Rahman – without the press being present. I heard him speak on television yesterday. He seems . . . a considered man.'

She smiled at that and nodded at Bob, who thanked me. Though I suspected he wasn't best pleased.

'I'll let SDO Charnley know,' he said. 'The press will have

to settle for a handshake between Mr Rahman and the SDO. Shall I go and tell them?'

'Please,' said Zahra Asif. 'I'd like to talk to Steve for a moment.'

Bob went out the office, shooting me a 'behave' look as he went. Zahra Asif waited until the door was closed before she spoke.

'We seem to have got off on the wrong foot, Steve. I didn't mean to imply anything by my remark about your helping the poor woman who was murdered.'

'Forget it. I'm a bit touchy at the moment. A few aches and pains from yesterday.'

'Yes, I heard what happened. I must apologise for . . .'

'For what exactly?'

She paused. 'The misdirected anger of my community.'

'Right.'

My surliness was brought on by the feeling that I was about to be on the receiving end of some heavy patronising by either her or her boss. Which in the circumstances might be read as low-grade prejudice – in effect if not in intention.

'Mr Rahman is very wealthy. He would like to make a present to you and your colleagues.'

Bingo!

'Not possible. There are rules against it.'

'I see, of course.'

She came and sat down on the edge of the desk and I caught a wave of perfume. I moved my chair back a foot.

'Is there an official fire brigade charity to which he could donate some money?' she asked.

'Fire Service Benevolent Fund.'

'I'm still reading hostility off you, Steve. What can I do to reassure you that Mr Rahman is not a threat of any kind?'

I smiled. 'Quit politics.'

'I'm not sure what you mean by that.'

'Think about it.'

'Why don't you just tell me – then I'll know?' she said slowly.

'There's ethnic unrest in the streets, he's an ethnic political figure and shows up here to press the flesh with the media in tow. What am I supposed to think?'

She took a moment on that one. 'Mohammed Ali Rahman is an unusual political figure, Steve. He has a genuine wish to serve all, not just his community. He is not ethnocentric.'

'And the press?'

'He wants it known that there is good and bad in all communities – look at the bruises on your face. When he heard what happened to you and your colleague he was furious.'

I listened hard and if there was something to object to then I missed it. But logic wasn't the driving force here. Gut feeling argued that Mohammed Ali Rahman showing up was more to do with elections than a need to calm the mob or thank a group of firefighters for being in the wrong place at the right time.

Politicians are always politicians – it's not that they don't have altruistic tendencies so much as being ever aware of how best to utilise them. And if I pushed the cynicism I could make a case out for the riots being an opportunity rather than a problem.

The truth was a man quick on his feet and keen to show he wasn't ethnocentric could win big right now.

'You don't believe me do you, Steve?' she said directly.

'It doesn't matter one way or the other.'

She took a good look at me. 'Now who isn't being honest?'

If some people are an open book then I must be large print.

'Okay, let me ask you – does it matter what I think?'

'To me or to Mr Rahman?'

'Rahman of course.'

If she wanted to bristle then now was the time, but she didn't miss a beat. Jolting her out of her cocoon of professionalism was proving difficult so perhaps she was on the level.

'He'll like you,' she said softly, 'plain speaking matters with him.'

'Good.'

She stood up. 'Can I ring upstairs on your phone?'

I slid my chair forward and pushed the phone towards her. 'Be my guest. Just ring 21.'

She spoke quickly in English to either Bob Grant or Charnley, then switched to Urdu, presumably when Rahman came on the phone. There was an exchange lasting some minutes. Then she put the phone down.

'Mohammed will be down in a few minutes – alone. Apparently Maurice Charnley would have preferred to accompany him.'

'That doesn't surprise me. Still he daren't object.'

'Oh? Why?'

I smiled, 'Ethnic politician – a senior officer's nightmare. Fear of upsetting an uncontrollable force.'

'Wow, Steve. Now that really is cynical.'

'No, it isn't. It's the truth. And if you're in politics then I don't need to explain why, do I?'

'And rudeness is frequently mistaken for plain speaking and I don't need to explain why either.'

Steve Jay – man of glass.

'So now we know where we are?'

My reply was all front, I was bare-arsed and knew it.

'Well, we know where you are. For myself, I came to support Mohammed in his wish to thank the firefighters. There aren't any other agendas. At least not any that I'm aware of.'

She crossed her arms.

I was starting to regret my tone if not the words. She seemed genuinely hurt. I'd let my disquiet at their presence override manners and common sense, a habit I was falling into of late.

Before I had a chance to say sorry there was a knock and Mohammed Ali Rahman himself entered the room. Through the open doorway I caught a fleeting glance of another man, a sharply dressed Asian, aged about forty, who was holding a leather briefcase.

Then the door closed, shutting him outside.

Zahra Asif introduced Mohammed Ali Rahman and then spoke to him in Urdu for a few moments. She then turned, said goodbye with the thinnest of smiles and went out closing the door behind her.

If Mohammed Ali Rahman was impressive on television then in the flesh he was bordering on the charismatic. He was a little taller than me – six one, six two – and his features so regular that women must have shifted under his gaze.

'Station Officer Jay, I'm sorry if my presence has embarrassed or upset you. I came only to thank you for trying to help the victim.'

'I upset your PA – Zahra,' I said evenly.

He considered that. 'Perhaps you felt threatened.'

I nodded. 'I saw the murderers and I don't think it's wise that they learn where I work. The police would share that view I think.'

'Quite. In my eagerness to acknowledge what you and your colleagues did . . .'

'Tried to do,' I corrected.

'Yes, tried to do, quite. It was brave, brave and compassionate. For which you were beaten up.'

'The mob was angry and frightened. I didn't take it personally.'

He smiled then; a mixture of approval and recognition. I nodded back my acceptance and for a second I believe we understood each other perfectly.

He held out his hand and I shook it.

I took the opportunity to change tack. 'What do you think will happen now – about the riots?'

He frowned. 'They cannot be repeated, no matter what the provocation.'

'But if they are?'

'Zahra has arranged a number of radio interviews later today. I shall make the same appeal on each.'

'And if that doesn't work? Feelings are running high.'

'Then I will walk the streets and shame them until they stop, if I must. The riots cannot continue. There are too many people who would use the excuse to attack the Muslim community.'

All of this was said simply without any element of performance and was all the more effective for it. For such an imposing figure there was an air of gentleness about him, of real concern – and determination. Zahra Asif must have thought me a prat of the first water.

'I wish you luck – for all our sakes.'

He nodded. 'It needs people to do the right thing, to have the right instincts – like you and your colleagues.'

I didn't blush, but I should have. 'Thank you.'

Again he smiled. 'We will go now. Thank you again for what you did. I will speak to Maurice and hopefully you will get some form of official recognition for what you did.'

'I'd rather you didn't.'

'And I shall make sure the press don't print your name or indeed that of the fire station.'

'For that I thank you.'

He turned to go, but then paused, his gaze seeming to go right through me.

'Have you ever heard of Mevlana – the founder of the Whirling Dervishes?'

'No, I don't believe I have.'

'He once gave seven pieces of advice, last of which was,

"Either exist as you are or be as you look." He was I believe, a wise man.'

'As becomes a stubborn man confronted with kindness.'

'I am pleased to have met you, Station Officer Jay.'

'And I you.'

11

I left the station just after four, later than I'd planned, but necessary if I was to avoid the press. Bob Grant eventually got rid of them by saying I'd gone off duty.

I'd used the enforced wait to put an ice-pack on my ankle and then strap it with adhesive tape from the first aid box. It felt better for the treatment and I made the decision not to go sick, reasoning that operationally, with the added support from a fire-boot, the ankle would hold up.

With a final word to Bob and John Blane about my decision, I said goodbye to the watch and told them that I'd be in tomorrow, our first night duty.

It crossed my mind on the way home that I should bring a peace offering for Jenny, but artfully managed to convince myself that gestures are merely that and the root cause wouldn't go away by pretending it was some silly argument born of misunderstanding.

I had serious issues to deal with and further role-playing would only cause greater hurt in the long run. The choices before me were very simple; stay or go.

The truth was I wouldn't be living with Jenny now if she wasn't pregnant.

I'd been fostered when my mother entered hospital as a drunk and my father took his chance and disappeared. As a result I'd always had strong feelings about loyalty and had been possessive in relationships. Now that I was actively contemplating doing the same thing as my father the irony cut all too deep.

For the moment I chose responsibility, but knew that the urge to leave would reappear, because it was Anne's final gift to me.

In Anne I had found a love that had changed me and had enabled me to close the door on the past. Of all people Jenny would have understood that – had not the dilemma involved her.

My own beliefs had been shaped by first Jenny and then Anne, and it wasn't lost on me that I always seemed to be one emotion behind the game – one woman behind self-knowledge.

The urge to steer my life, to plan and achieve rather than react to its currents had been blocked by the pregnancy. Now the two emotions were in fine balance and I had no idea which way it would go.

One thing was certain; I was going to go to the gym that night with Alex.

All I had to do was get in and get out again without becoming embroiled in an argument or an attempt by Jenny to probe me on the reason for the increasing tension.

A clear-the-air discussion was coming, as it had to come, but not now, not until I knew my mind and had worked out the consequences.

I didn't doubt for an instant that my decision was selfish, but reasoned that it had to be, otherwise an explosion would occur and everyone would get hurt before I could devise a safety net that would protect us all.

I was beginning to loathe myself.

The drive home was hot with the sky empty of cloud and the sun cooking the asphalt until the rank smells of petrol and refuse mingled in the thick afternoon air.

I hadn't bothered to change. I never travelled to and from

work in uniform so the sight of me in white shirt with rank markings and dark trousers as I climbed from the car made one or two heads turn.

On my way up to the first floor I passed a neighbour, a fat scruffy man with lank hair and stubble, who studied me closely and then relaxed when he read the logo 'London Fire Brigade' on my shirt breast pocket.

He chuckled in amused admonishment at his own reaction and raised a hand to me in acknowledgement. I stared at him until he averted his eyes.

At the base of the staircase to the second floor I looked up and saw Jenny gazing down at me. She looked from the scruffy man to me, her expression telling me that she'd seen the exchange.

She smiled then, a pale smile of ambivalence and I tried to smile back, fighting the urge to turn around and walk. I didn't turn because it would have been weakness not a decision and my instinct was always to fight my weaknesses – when I recognised them.

'Hello.' Her voice was almost a whisper.

This time I managed a smile, knowing that she'd be alert to the smallest of signals.

'Hello.'

'I thought you'd be earlier.' There was a quiver in the voice.

As I reached her she stood very still and I leant forward and kissed her forehead. She responded by grabbing me and holding on tight. Instinctively I kissed her forehead again and she rested her head on my chest.

The scruffy man had stopped his descent and was watching us. Again I stared at him and he looked away and continued on down.

'Let's go inside, Jen.'

Maybe she misread that – maybe she'd spent the day worrying and in hoping for a positive sign mistook the softness of my voice, because as we got through the front door she closed it behind us and kissed me passionately on the lips.

'Jen . . . I . . .'

She pulled at my arm and led me down to the bedroom, a finger pressed against my lips.

For the next twenty minutes I put my brain in neutral and responded, physically. I stroked and touched, kissed, traced my tongue and bit softly, but I didn't say that I loved her and didn't respond when she said she loved me.

And always I avoided eye contact.

When it was over I lay staring at the ceiling, the sweat cooling my body and Jenny curled into me, half asleep, her hand entwined with mine, resting it against her stomach.

I'd never felt so bogus. If I had any resentment left over from her affair with Kris Mayle, I had just forfeited the right to it.

I closed my eyes and sighed. The next thing I knew the phone was ringing. I reached out for the bedside phone and heard Alex's voice.

'Stevie?'

'What?' I replied suppressing a yawn.

Jenny stirred beside me and kissed my neck.

'Are you training tonight?'

'Unlikely, wouldn't you say, Alex?'

'Come for the craic then – and a beer afterwards.'

I looked at Jenny out of the corner of my eye. She was listening to the conversation and mouthed 'go'.

'What time were you thinking of going?' I asked.

'I'll pick you up – say half seven.'

'I'll make my own way,' I replied.

'No problem for me to come and get you, Stevie. I'll be over at half seven sharp.'

I was probably wrong, but suspected him of wanting to see if I'd sorted things out with Jenny. If that was the case when he showed up he would see what he needed to see – Jenny relaxed, at least on the outside, and me smiling, if only because indirectly I'd bought some space. All of which made me feel like a snake, because I was now deceiving the two people most close to me.

Whatever the fallout I had to sort this and soon, before I grew too comfortable with the lie.

At half seven sharp Alex arrived and Jenny let him in.

They came into the living room where I was watching the news update on satellite.

'What's happened?' he asked.

'Sporadic trouble, bit of stone-throwing and a car set on fire in Bethnal Green, but so far nothing major.'

'Let's hope it's blown over,' he said.

'They've been commenting on the broadcast made by Mohammed Ali Rahman on the radio – feeling is that it may have taken the heat of the situation.'

'You met him today then, Stevie?'

I turned towards him. 'How do you know that?'

'I rang the station before I rang here. John Blane told me. What do you make of Rahman?'

I nodded. 'Different. I was pleasantly surprised.'

'Aye, well he must be special if he brought all this to an end just by a radio broadcast.'

'He's been in the streets as well. Katherine Road, Green Street, parts of Ilford – all the flashpoints.'

Alex smiled. 'Do I detect a hint of scepticism?'

'Before I met him maybe.'

'If I didn't know you better I'd think you were a closet racist, Stevie.' His grin was evil.

I stood up. 'Let's go before I change my mind.'

He chuckled and kissed Jenny on the cheek. 'Bye, Jenny.'

He watched as I followed suit and as we went out the door he turned to me.

'What's wrong, Stevie?'

'Wrong?'

'Aye, wrong.'

'Such as?'

'You look through her not at her . . . and if I can see it then Jenny can.'

I took a moment. 'I've had a lot on my mind. Yesterday didn't help.'

'That's logical, but hardly the truth.'

I sighed. 'Am I allowed any privacy, Alex?'

He stopped. 'Of course.'

I nodded. 'Well then.'

'Fair enough, Stevie.'

Inside the car Alex switched the subject to boxing. 'Paddy Ryan's got a new lad starting tonight. A right tearaway, name of Aaron Hardy.'

'Hardy? Why do I know that name?'

'His father, "Tug" Hardy, was a welterweight – good pro – beat the British Champion in a non-title bout.'

'Right. So what's the story with the son?'

'He was a good amateur. Schoolboy champion and was doing well in the seniors.'

I could feel something coming. 'But?'

Alex paused. 'He got in with the wrong crowd. Cocaine.'

There was an edge to his voice as he said the last word.

'And?'

'Tug Hardy beat the shit out of him when he found out and dragged him along to Paddy.'

I paused, 'That'll cure it, will it?'

'Aye, I'll grant you that it's not the usual method of rehabilitation, but Paddy's got a drugs support group involved as well.'

'Good for him. One down three million to go.'

'Jesus, Stevie, you really are pissed off with life at the moment.'

I considered that. 'Not life, Alex. Me.'

'It's a shame about that ankle. Some bag work and a spar might cut through that bile.'

'Boxing as therapy, eh? I think I've been there before.'

'You have that. So what does that tell you?'

'That my life is in constant crisis?'

He shook his head. 'That you need to train regularly.'

I laughed then, as the bastard knew I would.

'What is it with you?'

'Pain, Stevie, is God's way of telling you to think before you rush to judgement.'

'But the lessons cost a million brain cells a time, Alex.'

He chuckled, 'There or thereabouts.'

Paddy Ryan's gym was on an industrial estate just off the A13 at Dagenham. It had a brick-built, spray-can-embellished exterior with heavy iron bars on the windows and steel cladding on the doors. It was called the 1916 Club, after the famous Easter uprising in Dublin.

Alex had first brought me here about six months ago with the aim of giving my life some focus other than my troubles with Jenny. Since then the place had become a habit. In the training I found a level of satisfaction hard to describe to anyone who had not climbed into a ring.

Between the ropes there was only honesty.

Unlike most gyms the 1916 Club had more members over thirty than under, with a mix of ex-pros and amateurs who trained there for one reason only, Paddy Ryan.

Paddy possessed a lean, hard body kept in condition by constant training and fine tuned by sparring three times a week. Lithe, agile and fast, it was hard to credit his body was fifty-three years old.

If that wasn't enough, on top of his shoulders was housed a sharp brain and a philosopher's introspection, together with a tongue that cut through the thickest of skins.

If he'd taken this Aaron Hardy under his wing then he must have seen something in him, because he didn't waste his time. The 1916 Club was a harsh environment and Aaron Hardy was about to undergo a severe testing.

As we entered the gym I caught the smell of sweat and leather and heard the muffled thuds as serious-looking men hammered the row of bags along the back wall. The temperature was fierce, even with all the windows open.

Immediately I felt a prickling along my spine as I experienced the paradoxical emotions that swept over me whenever I enter this place.

The gym clock buzzed and suddenly everyone in the room stopped working.

Some walked around, hands on hips, breathing hard as steam rose from their bodies. Those who had been skipping used the minute interval to stretch legs and backs, ready for the buzzer to sound again.

At the centre of all this, in the ring, was Paddy himself. He was wearing focus pads and talking to a tall, broad-shouldered youth of about seventeen wearing bag gloves. The youth was sweating and the conversation seemed intense.

To one side of the ring stood a hard-faced man of about forty. He was so like the youth it had to be his father.

Alex nudged me. 'Tug Hardy.'

We stood watching as the gym clock arm swung slowly vertical and the buzzer sounded again. Paddy danced around calling out combinations and the youth chased him, hitting the focus pads as Paddy snapped them up and down like targets on a rifle range.

'Pivot! When you hook or uppercut, pivot!' shouted Paddy.

The youth nodded and curved his body behind the shots immediately increasing the impact.

'Move! Never, ever stand still, Aaron. Move your head, your trunk and your legs.'

Paddy swung the focus pads making the youth slip, duck and sway, before releasing the punches. Sometimes he walked forwards, forcing young Hardy to throw jabs on the retreat.

Every now and again Paddy stopped and held the focus pads on his chest as he bobbed and weaved before suddenly holding them up, requiring tight combinations from close range. And always the Irishman wanted one more shot, one more technique on the end of the combination.

He made the youth hit, move and think simultaneously, and the effort showed in his frown of concentration.

When the buzzer sounded again the youth looked relieved. I don't think the physical effort bothered him, he was fit enough, but he looked daunted by the mental stress Paddy was placing on him.

A look passed from the son to the father, who stared back impassively.

After two more rounds Paddy called a halt and told the youth to take a blow. Then he slid between the ropes, jumped down and went over to Tug Hardy.

The two men talked for a few moments and then Paddy turned and motioned Alex and me over.

'Tug, I'd like you to meet Alex McGregor and Steve Jay. Alex was one of the original sponsors of the gym and Steve works out here – when he isn't getting involved in scrapes.'

He looked questioningly at my face and I smiled ruefully. 'Got caught by a sneaky heavyweight, Paddy.'

Paddy grinned. 'Tug has brought his son Aaron here for a workout with some of the lads.'

'The stupid young bastard's been on the gear,' said Hardy simply. 'He's off it now, but I'm trying to find ways to keep him clean.'

'Good man,' said Alex.

'He's living with you now?' asked Paddy.

Hardy nodded, his face grim. 'I made him move back in

with me. He was living in Burnham Villas, Basildon, with his mother. The idle bitch never could do anything with him.'

'Burnham Villas?' asked Alex.

Hardy sniffed. 'They call it "Pueblo Escobar" – it's a shit-heap. Half the estate's on crack, the other half takes everything else from cider to solvents. If I hadn't got him out of there I'd've lost him for good.'

Paddy's tone was almost gentle. 'You did the right thing, Tug. But if I'm going to do any good, then he has to take that rehab programme *and* train here every night.'

'Don't worry, he'll be here, if I've to kick his arse the whole way.'

Alex and I stayed for another hour and watched Aaron Hardy spar a number of rounds under the harsh glare of his father and Paddy's incisive comments. When we left Alex turned to me and asked what I thought.

'Aaron you mean? I think the coming off drugs is hard, but coming off drugs with Paddy and Tug on your back is going to be harder.'

'Paddy reckons that under the surface Tug is at his wit's end. He found Aaron unconscious in the lobby of a block of flats. He nearly choked on his own vomit.'

'Hence bringing him to Paddy.'

'Aye.'

'I don't envy him, Alex. There's a whole generation on gear and at that age peer pressure counts.'

'Some say that alcohol's a drug.'

'Do they?'

'If I suggested a drink, would you be offended?'

'No.'

Alex and I drove to a quiet pub off the London Road, Romford, but after a couple of pints my headache came back with a vengeance so we called it a night and he drove me home.

It wasn't late, just after ten, but Jenny had got into the habit of going to bed early, so I was surprised to see her up.

The minute she opened the door I felt the chill.

'A woman rang for you about an hour ago.'

'Oh?'

'She said her name was Jo. She left her mobile number – in case you'd lost it.'

'Did she say what it was about?'

'No. She wanted you to ring her as soon as you got in.'

With Jenny watching me I picked up the phone and rang the number Jenny had scribbled on a sheet of paper by the phone.

It rang twice and then I heard Jo Gordon say hello.

'It's Steve Jay.'

'Steve, we've got him. Can you attend an ID parade tomorrow?'

12

Jo Gordon and Bill Proctor were waiting for me when I arrived at Romford police station.

I was met just inside the lobby area of the entrance and taken through a door into the station interior. Jo Gordon briefed me as we walked. Both of them had dark rings under their eyes and once again I thought I detected tension in Jo Gordon; nothing overt, just words clipped and a tightness in her shoulders.

'You'll view the parade through a mirror, Steve. They won't be able to see you. Take as much time as you want. Ready?'

I nodded and Bill Proctor led the way through the station to the viewing room. As soon as he opened the door I saw Menzies and Copeland standing at the back of the room. Next to them stood an older man, about fifty years old with wavy grey hair and dressed in a navy blue suit. Jo Gordon introduced me.

'Steve, this is Superintendent Howard. He's now in overall charge of the investigation.'

Howard shook my hand. 'Jo told me what happened to you and your firefighter, Steve. How are your injuries?'

'It could have been worse. We were lucky.'

He looked at me directly. 'Well obviously we have a murder

to investigate, but I'm going to ask you think about whether you want to press charges, providing of course that we can find the people responsible.'

His choice of words struck me as odd. Something in them seemed to be hinting that charges would be a complication. That was fine by me; I wanted to keep things simple.

'I can't speak for Rob Brody, but I don't want to pursue it,' I said.

'Good. Good.'

Howard looked around the room and there was a subtle mood change. Proctor, Menzies, but particularly Jo Gordon, were visibly relieved. It seemed I'd said the right thing.

Slowly, almost absurdly so, I realised why Howard had asked me and it thoroughly pissed me off. Political correctness never did sit easy with me. All too frequently it was the right sentiment for the wrong reason.

With public bodies like the police or fire brigade the well-spring was usually corporate cowardice; the innate fear of catching their arse on a hook.

'Can we get on with this?' I sighed.

Howard nodded to Bill Proctor and Jo Gordon moved next to me.

'Relax, Steve,' she said quietly, 'all everyone wants to do is help.'

I shot a look over my shoulder at Howard standing next to Menzies.

'Right.'

Proctor pressed a button and spoke to the uniformed sergeant on the other side of the mirror.

'Could you bring them through, please?'

Six adult males walked through a door to the left and turned to face the mirror. They were all around six foot. Three were slim, two were of medium build and one was stocky. All had short fair to blond hair.

I was drawn to one immediately, but there was something wrong – something that didn't shout jackpot! Perhaps it was because I didn't trust myself and was determined to test my reaction.

I was loath to make a prat of myself twice in front of Menzies.

The first and most obvious thing that struck me was that none of them were wearing tracksuits or even dark clothing. They wore a range of T-shirts and a mix of shorts, jeans and chinos. It threw me.

From a split second of eye contact more than forty-eight hours ago to a different environment with artificial lighting and the wrong clothing, I had to identify one of them. And, although my eyes kept coming back to the same man, I couldn't be certain.

'Can you get them to turn to the right?' I asked.

Proctor spoke into the microphone to the uniformed sergeant. They all turned to the right.

I shook my head. 'I'd like them to turn further away – so that they are half-facing the rear. And I'd like them to look over their shoulder at the mirror.'

He related the request into the microphone and again the line of suspects moved.

I could feel the tension in the room. Howard moved in behind me and even Menzies wasn't disguising his interest.

'You've seen him?' asked Jo Gordon.

'Third from the right.'

She blinked. 'Are you sure?'

I paused. 'Not a hundred per cent.'

'Put a percentage on it then,' said Menzies.

I ignored him and looked at Jo Gordon.

'Could you put a percentage on it, Steve?' she asked.

I studied the man again and stared directly into his eyes. I tried to match the image in my mind to the man that stood on the other side of the mirror; it was very close.

'Seventy-five per cent.'

'Seventy-five?'

'Without the tracksuit and in artificial light I can't be certain.'

I heard Menzies exhale behind me. 'What aren't you sure about?'

I looked from Jo Gordon to Howard. 'I caught a glimpse of the murderer – the clothes were different and there's something else I can't nail. But then again I settled on him pretty quickly. I can't explain it.'

Howard looked pensive. 'Seventy-five per cent you said?'

'Yes.'

'Okay, Jo, I want him re-interviewed and his alibi checked out. By that I mean drag in those that vouch for Vanzie and formally interview them.

Vanzie.

Howard glanced at me, knowing he shouldn't have mentioned the suspect's name in front of me. I looked at him blankly, as if I didn't pick it up.

'Thank you, Steve, for coming in so promptly,' said Howard, 'Jo, perhaps you can show Steve the way out and then come to my office.'

Menzies tilted his head.

'In fact,' said Howard looking at his watch, 'we'll all meet in my office in, say, fifteen minutes.'

Jo Gordon took me through the station and out into the yard. I tried making small talk, but she was mentally elsewhere.

'You look like you could use some sleep.'

She sighed. 'Working late again.'

'I thought you all went to the pub, unwound with a nightcap, then slept untroubled.'

'Only if your face fits,' she replied.

'And yours doesn't?'

'Not at the moment.'

'Something to do with Menzies?'

She looked at me directly and I thought she was going to answer, but then she said, 'You were reluctant to identify the suspect?'

'Yes.'

'Because of Menzies?'

'Because I made a prat of myself over those car keys, yes.'

'Menzies gets under your skin?'

'Under both our skins,' I said slowly.

She smiled then – and it wasn't Anne.

I met her eye. 'If circumstances were different I'd ask you if you fancied a drink with me.'

'Would you?' The smile she gave then was both enigmatic and open at the same time; a dark smile – with layers.

I opened my car door and climbed in, winding down the window. As she leaned forward I caught her perfume.

'You're going on duty now?'

I nodded. 'From six tonight till nine tomorrow morning.'

'Take care. I'll be in touch.'

'I'll ring your mobile if I'm in trouble,' I said softly.

She smiled and crossed her arms. 'You'll be late for work.'

'Bye, Jo.'

'Bye, Steve.'

The drive to the fire station was slow due to the start of the rush hour. As a distraction my mind turned to the identification parade and the man Superintendent Howard had called Vanzie.

I'd seen the murder, identified Vanzie – practically – but knew nothing about him.

And it was disconcerting knowing that he might be convicted or walk on my evidence alone. If Menzies could shake me, what would a barrister do? I hoped that Jo Gordon and her

team would find further evidence that would put the identification issue beyond doubt and that the whole business would
become no more than a matter of process.

At roll call all the watch, except Tom Reed, our oldest hand,
were present. John Blane called the roll and after I had checked
that everyone had their resuscitation packs and evacuation
whistles, he read out the latest teleprinter message from
Control.

'Last night,' he began, 'sporadic disturbances occurred
across parts of East London. Several cars were set alight
and several people arrested. Until further notice, at change
of shift, all stations are to ride with riot shields fitted and
selected appliances will stand by at the two nominated Forward Control Stations of Ilford and Leytonstone. Crews are
expected to be rotated at five hourly intervals and are to make
their own arrangements with regard to messing.'

I looked at Jimmy McClane, our mess manager.

'No problem, guv. I guessed that we might get a night of it
so I bought soup, steak, onions and French bread. It'll be quick
whether we have to cook it here or elsewhere.'

'Good one, Jimmy. I suggest that providing we aren't one of
the first crews to stand by, we eat straight away.'

Immediately I finished speaking the teleprinter bell
sounded. Doug Scott, who was the duty man, brought the
teleprinter slip out and handed to me.

'We're lucky, we've pulled the first stand by.'

I nodded and read out the message. 'The following appliances are to stand by at Ilford immediately. F41 Dagenham's
Pump – Watch Commander in charge, F38 Romford's Pump
and F45 Plaistow's ALP and F22 Station Commander. The
following additional appliances are to stand by at F49 Leytonstone immediately. F80 Wells Lane's Pump – Watch
Commander in Charge, F21 Stratford's Pump and F22

Poplar's Aerial Ladder Platform and F39 Station Commander. All crews to inform control when they are mobile and
when they book-in on arrival at the Forward Control Stations.'

Harry Wildsmith nodded slowly. He was driving the Pump.
The rest of the crew would be Dave Chase, the Leading
firefighter Gerry Mudd, and Simon Jones.

I looked at my watch. 'Ten minutes max, Pump's crew. I
want to be able to book mobile at 1815 hours. John, can you
get the Pump Ladder's crew to check the Pump over quick?'

'Will do, guv.'

I tested a BA set on the Pump and then changed into an old
pair of uniform trousers and T-shirt. Next I grabbed a cup of
tea in the mess with the rest of the Pump's crew while Jimmy
McClane wrapped up the steak, onions and packets of soup.

'Let's hope it's all a staggering anticlimax, guv,' said Dave
Chase.

'Amen,' added Harry Wildsmith. 'Either way I'd have
preferred Ilford to Leytonstone.'

Gerry Mudd nodded. 'The worse trouble seems to be at
that end. Ilford didn't cop much last night.'

'I listened to the news on the way in,' said Dave Chase,
'nothing's happened today.'

'So far, Davy,' said Harry, 'so far.'

'Ready?' I asked.

There were nods all round and we trooped out to the
appliance bay.

As we pulled out the station I informed control by radio that
we were mobile. In turn we heard the other appliances book
mobile, heading for the forward control stations.

The remnants of the rush hour traffic slowed our progress
as we drove through it to the A12, heading for the Green Gate,
Leytonstone. The early evening was humid and the sky
streaked with gold.

In other circumstances it would have been a great night to

find a country pub and drink the day to a close. Instead we were hot and uncomfortable, fighting the leggings that reached halfway up our chests and the heavy rubber fire-boots. We'd left our tunic jackets and helmets off – the clinging heat was bad enough without them.

'It's riot weather, guv,' said Gerry Mudd, 'you can feel it.'

I turned in my seat, but Dave Chase beat me to it. 'You, Muddy, are as thick as a blind cobbler's thumb.'

'Riot weather,' repeated Gerry Mudd, unabashed.

'Can we drop him off somewhere, guv?'

'Sadly, he's along for the voyage,' I said.

'Pity,' said Dave.

I looked at Gerry Mudd. 'Dave's got a point.'

We were just past the link road at Wanstead when we heard the message come over the radio.

'F441 from M2Fe, order your Pump Ladder to a fire at the Asian Cinema, Green Street junction of Oakdale Road, Forest Gate E7. F21's Pump and Pump Ladder are also attending, F441 over.'

'F441 received. Status two over.'

Dave Chase leaned forward. 'What d'you reckon, guv?'

'I don't know, Dave. Let's hope it's nothing, eh?'

At that moment control came back on the air. 'M2Fe to F802 over.'

'That's us, guv,' said Gerry Mudd.

I picked up the handset. 'F802 go ahead over.'

'M2Fe, order your Pump as additional attendance to the Asian Cinema, Green Street junction of Oakdale Road Forest Gate E7, further calls being received, over.'

'F802 received. Status two over,' I replied.

I looked at Harry who hit the two-tones and switched the blue flashers on before swerving around the car in front of us and hitting the accelerator.

The traffic ahead heard us coming and slewed left and right, opening up a corridor for us through the middle of the lanes. Harry read the road perfectly, allowing for the slower-reacting drivers and gunning the engine the second he could see some space ahead.

We rigged properly now, pulling on tunic jackets, flash-hoods and helmets, only to sweat the instant the tunic jackets were zipped because the flash-hoods effectively sealed the neck opening, trapping the heat inside the jacket and choking off air circulation.

At the Green Gate roundabout Harry threw a left and took us down towards Woodgrange Road.

'I'm going to chuck a left into the Romford Road and then a right into Green Street.'

He shouted above the noise of the two-tones and the roaring engine and I nodded back as I switched on my hand-held radio, hoping to catch any messages between the first crews to arrive. Just at that moment Stratford's Pump and Pump Ladder booked in attendance.

We went over the hump of Forest Gate rail station bridge doing forty-five miles an hour – not fast in a car, but fast enough for a twelve-ton machine snaking through traffic. As we hit the Romford Road the main radio burst into life.

'M2Fe from F212 priority over.'

'M2Fe go ahead over.'

'F212, from Station Officer Hurd. Make Pumps eight, persons reported, further traffic, over.'

'M2Fe go ahead with further traffic, over.'

'F212, from Station Officer Hurd. Approximately one hundred persons involved, cinema complex smoke-logged on all floors – search by breathing apparatus crews in progress.'

13

We turned right into Green Street at the police station and immediately saw the pall of smoke.

'Sets on, guv?' asked Gerry Mudd.

'Let's see what they need first,' I replied over my shoulder.

Fifty yards further on I saw the stream of Asians, mostly men, but some women and children as well, running down towards the smoke.

'Guv!'

'I see them, Dave.'

The traffic was backing up now, unable to get beyond the fire. Harry swung the appliance left and right, trying to find a way through and then turned violently so that we were driving half on the pavement and half in the road.

'Jesus!' shouted Simon Jones, 'let's keep *some* of the wheels on the ground.'

Harry ignored him, his face was set in concentration as he bumped off the kerb and back again, avoiding lampposts and trees and scattering the running crowd.

It was fast and furious driving and if it were any other driver I'd be reining him back.

A large van was parked tight into the kerb and Harry swore, then swung hard right, taking us back down the centre of the road as the cars separated to let us through.

Up ahead a thick black cloud of smoke lay across the width of Green Street and climbed slowly in the heavy evening air. Shops and stores flashed by as Harry stole every possible inch of room and kept his foot pressed down hard.

As we drew near I saw Stratford's appliances for the first time, their blue flashing lights contrasted against the smoke.

'There it is.'

The last hundred yards were a blur. Harry brought the appliance to a halt on the opposite side of the road and twenty yards short of the cinema.

That's when I took in the scale of the incident.

Heavy, viscous smoke was erupting from the cinema and dozens of people were staggering out into the street, coughing and retching uncontrollably. Many collapsed on hitting the fresh air and others, horrifically burnt and screaming in pain, cried out for help.

I couldn't see any ambulances in attendance and all the firefighters were doing three jobs at once. Everywhere I looked men were laying out hose, dragging ladders and equipment off the appliances or rigging in breathing apparatus.

It was chaotic.

'Stay with the machine,' I yelled. 'I'll find out what they want. And keep an eye on that crowd.'

I jumped down from the Pump and ran forwards just as an elderly Asian man fell into the road directly in front of me. His face and clothing were soot-streaked and thick, carbon-coloured dribble discoloured his beard as he gasped for air.

For a second our eyes met and he held out a hand to me.

I turned back to the appliance and pointed at him. 'Resuscitator!'

Gerry Mudd nodded and I turned back, hunting for the Incident Commander.

More and more casualties were emerging from the entrance. I saw a youth lying in the centre of the road, moaning in agony; seared skin hanging from his face and hands. And a man, so badly burnt that the skin had peeled from his back, exposing the flesh beneath. He was running in circles, blind and howling like an animal.

It was chaotic, frightening and already threatening to lurch out of any kind of control. But I ran on, fighting my instincts, knowing that was there was a different task for me, a larger picture – if the greatest number were to live.

All three appliances of the initial ordering were in attendance and I found Stratford's Pump driver hastily making out the Incident Command Wallet at the rear of the appliance.

I pulled at his shoulder. 'Where's Station Officer Hurd?'

He pointed across the road to a group of firefighters. 'At the entry control point – he's briefing a BA crew.'

'Thanks.'

I ran across the road, leaping the lines of hose that snaked up to the entrance of the cinema. The entry control point was on the corner of Oakdale Road and Green Street – the most logical place – free from the viscous smoke that poured from the mouth of the cinema. At the centre of the huddle of firefighters I found Hurd; deep lines of stress evident in his face.

He had an enormous responsibility. The fire was well developed, casualties were growing by the second and there was no way of knowing precisely how many people were still inside the building.

If he used all his training and experience and luck was with him, it still wouldn't be enough. But he just might limit the toll.

'Steve Jay, Well's Lane,' I shouted above the noise. 'What do you need?'

His first question was the most obvious. 'Are you on your own?'

'Yes. We were en-route for Leytonstone when we got ordered on as additional.'

'I've got my Sub Officer around the back,' he said. 'I think we've upwards of a hundred people involved and the smoke is

down to floor level in there. I've got two BA crews in already
and this crew are about to follow. They're rescuing people
from the foyer – just inside the entrance. It's choked with
casualties, but I'm blind as to what's going on beyond that.
Once the foyer is cleared I may have to pull all crews out.'

'Why?'

He turned and pointed down an alleyway at the side of the
building and for the first time I saw how far back it went. The
place was huge.

'It used to be an old-fashioned cinema, but there's been
some conversion work done – now there's hidden voids at the
back and on each side of the public areas. I think the fire's
spreading through them.'

'What's your plan?' I asked.

'If I could be certain that it's safe beyond that foyer I'd flood
the place with as many BA crews as I could, but I don't want to
commit them into trouble. Will you take a crew in for me
beyond the foyer and lay a guide line?'

'Me?'

'Yes. It needs a serious dynamic risk assessment if I'm going
to commit that many men. Make sure one of your team has got
comms on their BA set so that you talk directly to me.' He
grabbed my arm, impressing the urgency on me. 'I need to
know the full strength of it.'

'Will do. Are eight pumps going to be enough, d'you
reckon?'

He shook his head. 'I'm about to make them ten.'

'I'll take a three-man crew. Do you need water?'

'One of my driver's is helping East Ham set into a hydrant –
if you could get one of your blokes to do the radio for my entry
control officer that would make life easier.'

'Right.' I turned to run back to the Pump, but then stopped.
'Have you seen the crowd coming this way?'

He shook his head. 'Problems?'

'I don't know, but I'd keep an eye on it if I were you.'

'I'll add it to the list,' he said heavily.

The distant sounds of two-tones carried as the reinforcing fire appliances, police cars and ambulances fought the traffic en-route to the fire. All around the pavement was filling as the crowd reached the scene.

A firefighter was running traffi-tape from one side of the road to the other, encircling the area and trying to keep the crowd back, but it was obvious that we were struggling to cope with the numbers of injured and dying and people were ducking under the tape, trying to help them.

We were going to lose this. There was too much to do and too few resources in situ. It was starting to slide, to go beyond our reach. Hurd was being overwhelmed, the whole incident teetering on the edge of meltdown.

I closed my eyes and thanked God that for once I wasn't the officer in charge. Hurd was experiencing the fire that would define him, that would make or break his reputation and there was nothing he could do except try.

I willed him to keep his nerve.

'Guv?'

Dave Chase was running towards me. 'What's happening, guv?'

'We're going in. We're to ignore what's going on in the foyer and lay a guide line to carry out a dynamic risk assessment, because he's going to throw in as many BA crews as he can – if we say it's safe.'

'Safe? Have you seen the side emergency exit.'

Dave pulled me and pointed down an alleyway at the side of the cinema. A set of fire exit doors had been forced open and people, burnt and smoke-blackened, were spilling out into the alleyway in a heaving mass.

'Okay, I've seen them.'

Dave's mouth opened, but he didn't speak.

'We've other work to do, Dave,' I said flatly.

He nodded and we both ran back to the Pump where the others where waiting.

Gerry Mudd had handed over resuscitation of the elderly Asian man to the first ambulance crew on scene and was standing with Harry Wildsmith and Simon Jones.

'We're to supply a three-man BA team to lay a guide line.'

'Who's going in, guv?' asked Harry.

'Me, Dave and Gerry. I'll take the guide line, Gerry take the comms set, Simon, I want you to be at the other end of the comms, so get a radio, switch it on to the BA channel and find the BA entry control officer. He's over on the corner of Oakdale and Green Street – to the right of the cinema as you look at it.'

'Right, guv,' said Simon.

Suddenly a great tongue of flame flared from the roof of the cinema and a scream went up from the crowd. They broke through the tape and rushed forward crying and screaming. Some tried to help the casualties on the ground, while others tried to fight their way in through the smoke at the main entrance.

Two policewomen and a firefighter tried vainly to stop them. There was pushing and shoving and I saw one of the policewomen go down.

'Jesus wept, guv, we need some serious police support or this is all going to turn to rat shit,' said Harry.

I nodded. 'Find Hurd. Get him to send a message asking for major police back-up. Better still, Harry, tell him that you'll send it in his name.'

'Will do, guv.'

Dave Chase, Gerry Mudd and I rigged in breathing apparatus and made our way over to the entry control officer and Simon Jones.

Gerry tested the Barrie communicator, the breathing apparatus radio – known as comms for short. Communications with Simon Jones revealed no problems.

'You've no emergency crew,' I said to the ECO.

'We're still at stage one control, guv,' he replied, showing the entry control board to me.

There were now three crews of two men working the foyer area. Our crew of three would make nine BA men in total. He was allowed to control up to ten personnel before the BA control went to stage two – requiring a Sub Officer to be the ECO and allowing for more than one point of entry into the building.

'Even so, I'd like you to get me an emergency crew as soon as possible. Stage one or no stage one.'

'My guv'nor said that he's going make it stage two as soon as the other machines get here. Wherever the fuck they are,' he said tersely.

He was right. I'd heard their reinforcing appliances some minutes ago, but they still hadn't arrived. I suspected that diverted traffic was clogging the area.

'They'll be here. Just make sure it's a priority. I don't want our arses hanging out to dry.'

He looked at me, deadpan. 'As soon as I can, guv.'

I handed him my tally, bearing my name, set number and the amount of air I had in my cylinder. Dave and Gerry did the same and Simon Jones tied the 'running end' of the two hundred foot guide line to a handrail beside the main entrance.

For deep penetration work guide lines are essential.

They are carried in a pouch attached to your BA harness and have sets of tabs – lengths of thin line – one five inches long and one two inches long. The short tabs show the shortest way out of the building, the longest show the way in. Each set was eight feet apart so that, providing you kept in touch with the line, you feel for the tabs and find your way out.

And like most safety features involved with BA procedures, they had been bought with the lives of other men.

I would lead, so Gerry unravelled the short length of his BA personal line, a line used to link individual crew members together, and clipped on to me. Dave clipped on to Gerry and then finally a firefighter handed me a charged high-pressure hose-reel; for self-protection not firefighting.

The crowd were still pushing forward and shouting, but we forced our way through and finally they moved for us when they saw that we were going in.

Linked together, we walked upstairs and went through the double doors to be instantly swallowed by the smoke. Immediately the noise and drama of the street vanished.

Firefighters outside a building move quickly, speed is all, but BA crews move with studied care.

Unable to see your hand in front of your face, you perform a continual slow pass of the hands in front of your body, using the backs of your hands in case you touch an electrical cable.

You have no idea what you are treading on, how solid it is, whether it will suddenly give way and plunge you into a basement or shaft, so you test your weight before moving forward.

Every sense, except sight, strains for information, trying to build a mental picture of what's around you. Not for the first time did it cross my mind that the Dutch were wise to send their firefighters to blind school.

It was red hot inside the foyer and I was already starting to question how far we should go in.

I found the right-hand wall inside the entrance and made my way slowly forward, testing and feeling as Gerry and Dave shuffled along behind me. Gerry pulled the guide line from the pouch attached my BA harness and tied it off at intervals; waist-height if he could, for ease of locating it.

Almost immediately I heard noises off to my left and took a step towards them before reaching out to feel another BA air cylinder low down to my left. I tapped it so that the wearer knew we were there.

He stood up and grabbed me. 'Who are you?'

His voice was distorted by the facemask and the sucking sound of his demand valve. Even right up close with my torch shining directly at him I could barely see his shape.

'Wells Lane,' I replied. 'We're laying a guide line.'

'Laying it where?'

'We're supposed to go through the foyer and into the cinema to see if it's safe for the crews that follow.'

'If you keep to this wall you'll come to a wall at right-angles to it. To the left there's a set of double doors. They're locked, but if you keep going there's another set that leads into a corridor. I think you can get to the theatre section from there, but we haven't been beyond them.'

'Thanks.'

'Listen, this smoke is getting thicker by the minute and the heat's increasing all the time. I intend to take my crew out with the next casualty that we find and I intend to tell the other crews the same.'

'Where are they?'

'They're about fifteen feet off to my left. There're bodies everywhere around here. We're trying to sort the dead from the dying. Take care if you're going beyond the double doors. The heat is blistering the paint off them.'

'Will do.'

I briefed Dave and Gerry on what had been said.

'This is heavy shit, guv. If those crews leave and there's no emergency crew we could be in dead lumber,' said Gerry.

'Tell me about it.'

'There aren't many places where I can tie the guide line off either.'

'Do what you can, Gerry.'

I found the wall again and set off along it. All the time I

could hear the other BA crews over the other side as they searched and removed casualties. The smoke was so dense that even the survival of rescued casualties was doubtful.

The back of my gloved hand touched the wooden doors and they gave slightly, but didn't open. A blast of hot air jetted under the doors. I stopped and told Gerry to stay where he was then edged past him to Dave.

'Dave, tell Hurd that we've reached the locked double doors and are making our way along the wall. Tell him we're trying to locate the corridor that leads to the theatre. And tell him it's red hot.'

We waited as Dave sent the message, taking the opportunity to do a swift gauge check on the contents of our air cylinders. Gerry read Dave's gauge for him while he was sending.

'Guv, Station Officer Hurd says that once you get into the corridor, let him know.'

The wall felt hot though my gloves and as we moved slowly along it I started to make some decisions. I'd go into the corridor and if it was bearable I'd continue on into the theatre, but only after checking with BA entry control that an emergency crew was standing by.

As I moved forward again the hose-reel snagged and we stopped while Dave freed it. You could feel the heat band mushroom down from the ceiling, so we crouched down and continued.

I found the next set of double doors about twenty feet further on and went down on to one knee. Dave and Gerry came close and I briefed them.

'We've reached the doors. Now it's well hot on the other side, so I intend to crack the door open and have a good squirt around before we move forward. Let's move slow and careful, but tell Hurd where we are first, Dave.'

'Got it, guv.'

Dave spoke into the comms and we waited to hear what the

reply was. He spoke several times and then crouched in close again.

'He says that things outside are turning nasty, guv. He thinks it's because he withdrew the other crews. He's got a three-man emergency crew now, but he says if you think it's too dodgy to go on then we can withdraw.'

'Tell him we'll go into the corridor and then we'll contact him again.'

Dave passed on the message. 'Hurd says that Bob Grant is now the Incident Commander, guv.'

I pulled a bight of hose-reel and laid it out off to my left. 'Right. Let's do this by numbers.'

Gerry Mudd lent past me. 'Ready, guv?'

'One second, Gerry.' I opened the hose-reel momentarily to check it was working. 'Okay – just edge it.'

Gerry Mudd pushed open the door and a blast of hot air swept over our heads. I fired two pulses of water through the doors and upwards. Gerry let the door swing closed.

'Again, Gerry.'

He pushed on the nearest door and I gave another two pulses and once again the doors were closed.

I knew that with so much heat we could be going into a flashover situation where the surfaces of the building become so reactive that they all ignite simultaneously. The pulses of water were to drop the temperature and prevent that happening.

'Once more,' I shouted.

The doors were eased open and this time I sent four pulses into the corridor. The wave of heat that came out wasn't significantly cooler, so we gave it another three sequences of opening and closing; sending four pulses each time.

'If the theatre doors are open that heat could be coming from beyond the corridor, guv,' yelled Gerry.

'If that's the case then we're on the wrong end of some

pretty big flame,' I called back. 'This time I'll give it some longer bursts.'

As the doors moved I opened up the hose-reel and sent the water in six sustained bursts. The change in the heat was small, but enough to encourage me.

'It's working. Again.'

Gerry pushed and I opened the hose-reel and again there was a small drop in temperature.

'I'm going in this time. Unless I see flame I'll change the jet to a spray.'

As he opened the doors again I flattened out on to my stomach and wriggled in under the heat band. Crawling to the right I worked the spray in figures-of-eight in front of me. Gerry tapped my boots to let me know he was following and I moved further into the corridor as Dave let entry control know what was happening.

I found one body in the corridor. It was hard and crispy to the touch and I moved passed it.

I found the far wall of the corridor and the heat started to increase again. I thought I saw the beginnings of a neat flashover – flame in the fume cloud – and changed the spray back to a jet, sending more pulses upward.

We were all inside the corridor now. Gerry and Dave were tucked in behind me, still connected by their short personal lines and in physical contact. The pulses were having less and less effect here and the heat was climbing again.

I found another set of double doors on my left and pushed them. They barely moved, but the heat that came out made me turn away quickly and change the jet to a protective spray again.

For maybe a minute I washed down the doors and sprayed the general area, trying to drop the temperature. Then sent two more bursts upward, conscious always of the danger.

'Something's blocking the doors,' I shouted.

'They must open towards us as well, guv, if they're exit doors,' answered Gerry.

I gave him the hose-reel and knelt on one knee.

'When I pull it open give it a serious burst, Gerry.'

The edge of the door was blisteringly hot. I pulled it and it barely moved. I pulled again as hard as I could, but nothing happened. I got to my feet, immediately feeling the difference in temperature and had to crouch low before taking hold again. This time I threw my weight back and the door gave way violently.

Immediately I was struck by something tremendously heavy and went down under the weight with the wind knocked out of me. I gasped, but my diaphragm must have gone into spasm and for a few seconds I couldn't breathe.

A huge weight was crushing my chest and I couldn't move. Panic engulfed me, prickling my skin. I couldn't even scream.

Then my diaphragm relaxed and I sucked air greedily through my demand valve, but the weight was still on my chest, restricting my breathing.

I turned and raised my shoulder then turned the other way and just managed to pull my right arm free. I cursed and swore, fighting not to be smothered. Then with strength borrowed from fear I pushed with everything I had. The weight on my chest moved a fraction; enough for me to reach my torch.

Tilting my head forward, I angled the torch beam and shone it at the weight.

I found myself staring at a man with his face completely burnt away. Then to my right I saw a woman's arm, another head and legs smashed and broken.

I was buried beneath a mass of corpses.

14

It took every ounce of will to prevent panic seizing me again. They were dead and couldn't harm me. But my reaction was primitive and emotional and I screamed out to Gerry and Dave.

Nothing.

Then I hit my ASDU – distress signal device – but still there was no answering call. Where were they? Trapped?

The piecing noise of the ASDU was hurting my ears, shooting bolts of alarm through my body.

Keep with the programme, Stevie. You've got to get out of here. Think – get your chest free first. One problem at a time.

I placed my right hand against the corpse with no face and pressed hard, wriggling for all I was worth. The top half of my chest came free. I pushed and wriggled again. More movement. I made the rhythm work for me; push, wriggle and breathe.

Each time I stopped I drew heavily on the demand valve. *Watch your air, Stevie!*

A compressed air breathing apparatus set will last you around forty-five minutes – providing that you work steadily – but its duration can be cut drastically by heavy work. I'd known a man under stress exhaust the contents of a full cylinder in barely ten minutes.

I looked at my gauge. I had sixty-five bars – it was two thirds empty and close to the red zone on the gauge.

'No more exertion. Work steadily, be measured,' I said out loud.

Against that logic was instinct, which screamed at me to fight for my life.

I managed to get my left arm free and push the faceless corpse down to my hips. I could feel that there was another body at an angle by my head, bearing down on the faceless corpse. It was this that was making things so hard.

To my left a corpse was wrapped around me and there was another lying across that. Cranking my body to the right I pushed down with both hands and pulled my right leg free. Again I sucked at the demand valve.

I was working through an equation and if I got it wrong I wouldn't be leaving, but equally if I didn't get free soon I'd run out of air anyway.

Keep cool.

Placing my heel into the mass of bodies, I kicked hard. They moved slightly and instantly a blast of scorching air hit me. I screamed out and kicked again trying to break free.

Another wave of super heated air swept over me.

'Jesus!'

I pulled the body back on top of me and stopped moving.

The corpses must have formed a human dyke against the reservoir of hot gases being generated within the theatre and that heat was now escaping through the doors – the bodies that I was pinned by were also protecting me.

Fighting the compulsion to gulp air, I laid still and weighed my options. That's when my low-pressure warning whistle sounded.

I groaned.

There was no choice now, it was get out and get cooked or stay and asphyxiate. I pushed away the body on top of me and was suddenly bathed in spray.

'Gerry? Dave?'

There was no answer, but I felt another body being dragged off my left leg and then someone seized my arm and pulled. I kicked against the last bit of weight as I was dragged back-wards under a water curtain.

'Guv? Guv, can you hear me?'

It was Gerry's voice shouting above the roar of the fire.

'Are you all right, guv?'

'I'm functioning – which'll do for now.'

I felt him move alongside me. 'Is that your whistle or mine, guv?' He grabbed my pressure gauge and read it. 'It's yours. If we move fast you might have enough air to get you out of here.'

'How's your own air?'

I saw the muted light of his torch beam move.

'I'm not much better off than you, guv. We'd best not hang around.' He patted my shoulder. 'Roll over on your stomach. We're going back down the guide line. Here.' He put the line in my hand and I felt for the tabs. 'You go first, guv, I'll keep the fire off our backs.'

I turned and looked behind to see a red glow rolling across the ceiling. With the double doors to the theatre open, the fire was raging out into the corridor with flame licking from the fume cloud.

'It's going to flash, Gerry!'

'Just go, guv!'

I crawled away on my belly while he pulsed water into the fume cloud, buying us time. Twice I pulled the hose-reel to stop it kinking as Gerry moved back on his belly, following me. I could hear the hiss-pause-hiss of the hose-reel as he fought the fire in textbook fashion.

The fire was going to take the building. It was going to rage along the corridor in an all-encompassing fire that would react off of every surface in what would be a classic flashover.

The trick was to make sure it didn't take us.

From the dark a hand suddenly seized me.

'Dave?'

'The double doors are just to your left, guv. Go through them and wait for us.'

'But the line's still attached to me and Gerry's personal line snapped when I was buried up.'

He put his mouth against my ear. 'I've clipped the long length of my personal directly on to Gerry. Don't worry about him, just go.'

I pushed at the double doors and went through. Minutes later Dave and Gerry came through them together. Dave detached the main guide line from my harness and tied it off on a radiator pipe.

'We're all low on air, guv. I'm going to tell them to send the emergency crew in for us,' shouted Dave.

'Do it as we're moving.'

'Right.'

I tried to stand up, but my ankle collapsed and I went down hard.

'Christ, guv! Are you all right?' said Gerry.

'Ankle. I might need a hand.'

They lifted me up. Dave took one side and Gerry the other. Dave was still clipped on to Gerry and I clipped on to the guide line.

'Let's go.'

The double doors from the foyer to the corridor stopped the worst of the heat, but it was still red hot and because of my ankle we were forced to stand upright and move slowly.

Even through our fire tunics and flash-hood protection it was punishing. My body was washed in sweat and I had no choice but to suck air and make as much headway towards the entrance as I could.

All our whistles were sounding now and, together with my ADSU, the noise was deafening. It took an effort to think clearly. Movement was clumsy with the three of us linked together and me being practically dragged along in the thick hot smoke.

My skin felt like it was being pricked by red-hot needles and sweat ran down my back. There was no talking now, just moving as quickly as possible, hoping to reach the entrance before our air ran out.

Then suddenly Gerry shouted. 'There's a torch – it's the emergency crew.'

A bulky figure loomed close and took hold of my harness. 'Are you F803 – the crew laying the guide line?'

'Yes and we're struggling for air,' I shouted back, 'all of us.'

'Right. Just stand still,' came the reply.

Several BA men moved in front of us and then the air-line from my facemask to my cylinder was grabbed. I heard the whoosh of air as he broke the air-line connection and reconnected it on to the Y-piece adaptor of his own BA set.

'You're done,' he said. 'Put your arm around my shoulder.'

I did as he told me and on either side of me I was aware that Gerry and Dave were exchanging air as well. The emergency crew were slick and professional and performed all three exchanges of air rapidly.

Later, I found out that they were from East Ham's Fire and Rescue Unit.

'Right,' said my helper, 'we're done. Now let's get out of here.'

All six of us made our way as a group towards the entrance. It wasn't fast as the air-line connections were short, but we moved steadily, always conscious that the fire could break through from the corridor any minute.

I could hear something now, a sound I couldn't identify, but that reminded me of bees in a hive. It grew louder, but I couldn't tune into it. Gradually it changed until it sounded like the sea breaking on the shore.

As we emerged out through the main entrance on to the steps of the cinema the noise hit us like a concussive wave.

It was the crowd.

At first I thought that they were cheering our rescue, but a volley of stones slammed into us. Dave Chase was hit on the shoulder and an emergency crew member took half a brick full in the face, smashing his BA facemask. He went down clutching his face and screaming.

There was blood everywhere. Then a second volley struck.

It seemed to be the signal and bricks, bottles and stones came from every direction. I threw myself across the emergency crew member, trying to shelter him and everyone huddled together for protection.

A group of policemen ran over and formed a wall around us with their riot shields – and then the world went mad.

Wave after wave of improvised missiles filled the air as the crowd screamed its indignation.

I realised then that there were no other firefighters around the cinema. Appliances, hose, ladders had all been abandoned and a fire helmet and fire boot lay in the centre of the road.

I yanked off my facemask. 'What the fuck is going on,' I yelled.

'They think that you're abandoning the people still trapped in the cinema; that you're running away,' said a police inspector. 'While you've been in there the situation's started veering out of control.'

I glimpsed between the riot shields and saw that the crowd were surging forward, pushing back a double line of policemen and women. Fights were breaking out everywhere and mounted policemen stood with their long batons drawn ready to move in.

'Let's get you out of here,' said the police inspector.

He spoke into his radio and another half a dozen policemen in riot gear ran over and extended the shield wall.

'When I say go, we are all going to make for that van,' said the inspector.

A police van with steel griddles on the windows was backing up towards the cinema steps. It caught the crowd's attention. They now had two targets and took full advantage of it.

'Go!'

The mounted police charged forward at the crowd and we took our chance. Some ran, I hobbled with my arms around Dave and Gerry's necks, while four policemen carried the injured firefighter.

The air was thick with missiles and we reached the van taking more hits on the way.

The rear doors were thrown open and all the firefighters scrambled inside. The doors were shut and then with a lurch the van accelerated and sped off down Green Street with a stream of objects thudding into its sides and roof.

The bewildering speed and ferocity of the crowd's attack, coming on top of the desperate firefighting, just about finished me. I pulled off my fire helmet and lay on the floor of the van with my chest heaving and my body crying out for a moment's rest.

I closed my eyes and tried to shut out the nerve-jangling sound of the ADSU.

'Guv?'

I opened my eyes and saw Dave bending over me.

'Are you okay, guv?'

I looked at him. 'Give me a minute, Dave.'

A series of drained faces looked down at me. Gerry in particular looked aghast.

'What?' I asked tersely.

Then I realised why they were staring.

My fire helmet, BA facemask, tunic and gloves were all burnt – I looked like I'd been char-grilled over a brazier. Gerry and Dave were scorched and blackened as well, but my fire gear was all but destroyed.

It had saved my life.

I ached all over, my ankle was swelling in my boot so that I
doubted I'd get the thing off, but I didn't have so much as a
burn blister.

'Dave?'

He knelt down next to me.

'Do me a favour, please.'

'Anything, guv.'

'Take that bloody ADSU off my set and fling it out the back
of the van.'

He grinned, unclipped the small blue distress signal unit
and sat on it, muffling the sound.

'Thank you,' I said and closed my eyes again.

I lay there for a few moments with my brain in neutral, until
a groan from behind distracted me. I propped myself up on
one elbow and looked around.

It was the firefighter who had been hit by the brick. He had a
massive blue/black lump where his cheek should have been
and his jaw was broken and hanging to one side. One of the
emergency crew was bent over him, talking softly.

'See what you can do to help,' I said to Dave.

He nodded.

A few minutes later the van stopped.

Gerry opened the doors and Dave helped me out, while the
other two members of the emergency crew lifted out the
firefighter with the broken jaw.

We were in Forest Gate police station yard and it was full of
other firefighters, paramedics and ambulances. Harry Wildsmith came running over to us as four paramedics immediately got to work on the injured firefighter.

'Are you all okay, guv?'

'More or less, Harry. What the hell happened when we were
in there?' I asked.

He looked from one to the other and then back to me. 'Are
you sure you're okay?'

'Superficial stuff. Looks worse than it is. You were saying?'

He nodded. 'It was a nightmare, guv. The crowd knew that there were lots of people inside the cinema and when the crews clearing the foyer came out and didn't re-enter, it went mental. Two firefighters from Stratford got beaten up badly and Bob Grant got the police to evacuate us.'

'And left us in there? said Dave in disbelief.

Harry shook his head. 'He kept some blokes back. They should be with you.'

At that moment another van pulled into the yard and the gates were closed behind it.

It stopped and Bob Grant got out, along with the entry control officer, Simon Jones and six other firefighters, three of whom were rigged in BA.

Bob searched the yard and when my hand went up in acknowledgement he gave the briefest of nods and then looked beyond me, counting. His gaze settled on the paramedics working on the injured firefighter, then he came over to me.

'How bad is he, Steve?'

'Took a brick in the face, Bob. His jaw's badly broken and the cheek's smashed in. It was pretty hairy.'

He ran a glance over me, as though only now absorbing the state of my fire gear. 'You and your people?'

'We're okay. It was close though, we nearly got caught in a flashover and were on our whistles when the emergency crew found us.'

He closed his eyes and sighed the tension from his body. I believe it was the most graphic display of emotion I'd ever seen from him. I gave him a moment and then told him what I'd found.

'There's something else, Bob.'

His eyes opened. 'Go on.'

'We got into the corridor and reached the theatre exit doors.

When we pulled the doors open there was a heap of bodies on the other side.'

His face was wary now, hearing the preparation in my voice.

'I'm listening.'

'The doors were wedged shut, Bob. It was murder – mass murder.'

15

The next day the media ran it as 'The night the East End burned'.

In Green Street, Katherine Road and the Romford Road shops, houses and cars were set on fire indiscriminately. In the surrounding neighbourhoods police cars, fire appliances and ambulances were stoned and petrol bombed while bitter clashes between the police and mobs of youths broke out in a dozen different places, leaving scores injured and many hospitalised.

The cinema itself was razed to the ground and newsreel after newsreel showed the same heli-camera shots of the gutted smouldering building underscored by a subdued commentary. The precise death toll was still unknown.

From this scene the disturbances had rippled out and ignited Asian communities as far as Ilford and Bethnal Green.

One reporter called it nothing short of a social earthquake – a seismic shock that had ruptured a genuine multicultural community, while another simply said that a wound had been inflicted that might never be fully healed.

The scale and the intensity left local politicians and community leaders struggling for words. No one trusted themselves to speak out; fear of being misunderstood imposed a rigid self-censorship.

For me, the aftermath was a blur.

All the firefighters and paramedics evacuated to Forest Gate police station were spirited away shortly after Bob Grant appeared. The fire crews returned to their base stations and new appliances were ordered to stand by at Leytonstone.

We arrived back at Wells Lane around half ten.

Dave, Gerry, Simon, Harry and I all came off-the-run for the remainder of the night.

We sat in the mess dazed and drinking coffee, switching between recounting our own dramas to the remainder of the watch and watching the news updates showing the madness that had taken over the streets.

After I'd drunk my fourth cup of coffee and answered a thousand questions, I retired to my room, where I performed the neat trick of showering the sweat and carbon from my body whilst balancing on one leg.

I'd nearly phoned Jenny, but didn't.

I was certain she'd have been watching the television and worrying, but to lift that phone would be to invite her near and I was too emotionally drained to perform the nuances of manoeuvre which that would inevitably entail.

Once again my cowardice and logic ran parallel.

Instead I got my sleeping bag out and lay down, running the cinema fire through my head like a tape on a loop.

My view hadn't changed from what I told Mohammed Ali Rahman – that the Asian community was scared and lashing out and that we'd just got in the way. I had to believe that or else admit that any form of racial harmony was a façade, a political illusion necessary to keep the lid on the pot.

I had no doubt also that in time 'thin' characters, unburdened by any form of humanity, would emerge from the shadows to point fingers and claim the riots were un-British, a manifestation of the way immigrants behaved.

Morass didn't even come close.

Sleep claimed me sometime after two and sucked me into a dream that I couldn't remember, but that woke me two hours later wet with sweat and uneasy. After that I dozed fitfully.

Next morning Harry gave me a lift home and Dave followed up with my car. Jenny played it clever and let me go to bed without either explanations or fuss, though it was obvious she was close to tears.

Exhausted, I slept until early afternoon when I was woken by the persistent ringing of the phone. Only half awake I lifted the receiver. The voice at the other end sounded only marginally less tired than I was.

'Steve? It's Jo Gordon.'

I fell back on the pillow and sighed heavily. 'What can I do for you, Jo?'

'Sorry, Steve did I wake you?'

'Yes.'

'I'm sor . . .'

'What is it, Jo?'

There was a pause. 'Can we re-interview you this afternoon at Romford police station?'

'No.'

'Is there a problem?'

I explained all that had happened and that I was off work sick with my ankle.

'I can't drive at the moment.'

'In that case can I come and see you?' she asked.

'If you must. What's wrong, Jo?'

I heard her take a breath, but then she said, 'When I see you.'

And with that she put the phone down.

I got out of bed, pulled a tracksuit on and limped out into the living room. The room was hot and stuffy and I opened a window and left the door ajar to get a through draught.

Jenny didn't like the windows open. She said it made the place stink of street.

She was out and had left a note saying that she'd gone shopping and would go to her parents afterwards, hoping to be

back around four. I may have been wrong, but I felt she'd gone
for advice, which meant the showdown was looming into view.

Let it.

I was so flat I could only deal with one thing at a time and Jo
Gordon's phone call had gained what little attention I had.

In an attempt to wake myself up I splashed my face and
chest with cold water and drank three cups of coffee. Then sat
in front of the television and listened in wonder at reporters
vividly describing scenes that they had been nowhere near.

Computer graphics of the cinema fire with a 'probable'
origin and progression were shown, complete with analysis
from a university lecturer.

Maybe it was me, but you just got the feeling that the nearest
he'd ever been to a fire, any fire, was a garden barbecue.

But I still watched.

Flipping backwards and forwards from channel to channel
and pictures to text, I allowed them to flood my mind with
stark images and inane and sometimes surreal comment.

It was a media carnival and they gave it both barrels.
Anyone who thinks that television news isn't theatre simply
isn't paying attention. The more I watched the more it
seemed like a black comedy – only the actors weren't in
on the joke.

When the doorbell rang an hour later I was grateful for the
excuse to switch off.

'Hello, Steve.'

Jo Gordon was wearing a dark skirt and sleeveless white
blouse with her jacket slung over her shoulder; the shoes were
black with just enough heel to give shape to the calf.

I peered over her shoulder, looking for Proctor, but she was
on her own.

'Come in, Jo.'

We went through to the lounge and I offered her coffee.

'Black, no sugar, please.'

I hobbled off to fetch it and when I returned she was looking out the open window.

'We bought it for the view,' I said.

She gave a wan smile. 'Got to live somewhere.'

'That's my line.'

'How's the ankle?'

'Fat and painful.'

I motioned for her to sit and she chose the chair opposite mine and draped her jacket over it. Then sat with her legs crossed.

'So, you were at the cinema in Green Street last night.'

I stifled a yawn. 'Is that what this is about?'

She took a sip of the coffee, 'No, but the team investigating the cinema fire came to see me this morning. They have a report that the inner doors in the cinema were wedged shut – they thought that it might be of interest to me.'

'Connected to the murder, you mean?'

'Yes.'

'And is it?'

'Too early to say. There's nothing outwardly to link it.'

'Except racial murder.'

She gave a single nod of the head. 'Except *possible* racial murder.'

'Great life, isn't it?'

She smiled. 'The best.'

I caught her eye and held it. She looked like she was struggling under a huge weight. I knew from the second I saw her that she was tough, but only now saw the price she paid for it. The pain began at the point where the professional ended and the woman began.

As she drank her coffee I watched her every action, wondering why she hadn't brought Proctor with her. Eventually my curiosity got the better of me.

'Are you going to ask me about the cinema fire?'

'No. I've been informed for information purposes only. Unless something turns up to the contrary it'll be investigated as a separate incident.'

'Vanzie?'

'Vanzie,' she confirmed.

'Go on.'

She turned and reached into her jacket, taking a notebook from it. She flipped through the pages.

'At the ID parade you said that you were seventy-five per cent certain that Vanzie was the man you saw?'

'Yes.'

'You also said that part of the doubt in your mind was connected to Menzies – not wanting to make a mistake in front of him?'

'Yes.'

'Have you thought anymore about it?'

'Of course.'

'And?'

'I'm still not certain. What's happened, Jo?'

She paused, 'Our man has an alibi – and it's good, almost too good.'

'You want me to say I'm certain?'

She almost smiled. 'I'd love you to say you're certain, that way we could hold him longer for questioning, but that's our problem not yours.'

I took a minute and thought back to the ID parade, then the murder. It didn't help that I felt drugged and, try as I might, the images refused to focus.

'I'm sorry.'

'That's okay, Steve. If you can't, you can't.'

That was her cue to stand up and make her goodbyes, but she stayed where she was. Slowly I realised that there was something else.

'This visit wasn't just about Vanzie, was it?'

She shook her head and placed the empty cup on the floor beside her chair.

'We've identified the woman.'

'How?'

'Her husband came forward.'

'And?

'Her name was Shenaz – Shenaz Rahman.'

I went still. 'Rahman?'

'Yes. She was the wife of a prominent Asian, Mohammed Ali Rahman.'

My mouth opened, the implications tripping over themselves. I took a moment, then said, 'I've met him.'

She frowned. 'When?'

'Tuesday.'

She controlled it well, but there was still a tightening at the edges of her mouth.

'How? Where?'

'At the fire station. A senior officer thought it might help if the brigade was seen to be actively working with the community in the wake of the first riots. They had the press with them.'

'Before the ID parade?' she said in confirmation.

'Yes.'

'What was said at the meeting?'

'He wanted to reward me and the crew for trying to help the Asian woman . . . I know what you're going to say, Jo. It's going look very suss if the husband of a victim offers money to a witness.'

She closed her eyes and groaned, her shoulders slumping. When her eyes opened she stared at the floor, silent, still.

I gave her a moment. 'Jo?'

She looked up.

'There's more, isn't there?' I said.

The smile on her face was a combination of weariness and acknowledgement.

'You're going to hear it sooner or later today anyway, so you might as well hear it from me now. Someone has leaked it to the press'

'Leaked what?'

'Shenaz Rahman's body had enough cocaine in it to keep her awake for a week.'

16

Jenny showed up barely twenty minutes after Jo Gordon left.

I hadn't noticed perfume on Jo Gordon, but Chanel or pheromone, she left something in her wake because Jenny detected it right off.

I wasn't certain as to whether she'd read anything on me, but she patrolled the flat three times and each time came back to the living room with a silent question framing her face.

She didn't ask, so I didn't say, though it was interesting that I felt some guilt, even though there was nothing to feel guilty about. Perhaps there didn't need to be anything, perhaps desire is the primer for sin. Either way Jenny had sensed something.

'How's the ankle?'

I lifted it up. 'As it looks.'

She disappeared and came back with some ice inside a clear plastic bag.

'Here.'

I swung the ankle across and she draped the ice-bag over it, avoiding my eyes as she spoke.

'Are you going to tell me about last night?'

'There was a fire at an Asian cinema in Forest Gate. I don't know how many people were killed – well over double figures. The crowd stoned us because they thought we'd abandoned the people inside. It was arson. Someone wedged the inner doors to the theatre. The rest I imagine you know.'

She went pale, her voice small, almost distant. 'D'you know

what time I went to bed? Four in the morning. I wanted you to phone and tell me you were alive.'

'I . . .'

'You could have phoned first thing this morning even – seven o'clock, eight o'clock, sometime . . . anytime. Instead I had to wait until you came home, not knowing *if* you would be coming home, because the television said that firefighters were hurt – some badly hurt, burnt.'

'I'm sorry . . .'

Her face changed. 'Fuck your sorry! I'm carrying your child and you make me wait until you get home to know you're alive?'

This was it. I could feel it coming.

I couldn't even accuse her of calculation because, irrespective of our troubles, not phoning was inexcusable. No leverage, no answers – no right of reply.

Anxiety was radiating off her and I should have put my arms around her, but fear of hypocrisy stopped me. So I waited, telling myself not to duck the issue and that lying and evasion amounted to the same thing.

If this was when we split, then I owed her the truth and we both had to understand why.

This time there would be no route back because passion – the ultimate forgiver – had died. At least for me.

Her eyes locked on mine. 'If I wasn't pregnant would you be with me now?'

'That's hypothetical . . .'

'Would you?'

I took a deep breath and sighed it from me. 'Probably not.'

She gave a short nod of affirmation, then her eyes filled with tears.

'You bastard,' she whispered, 'you rotten, rotten bastard.'

'I'm sorry, Jen.'

'No. You're not. You're embarrassed, Steve, but you're not

sorry. You let me drag that out of you because you didn't have the balls to tell me.'

'I didn't suddenly wake up and decide this, Jen. Things have changed between us. We both know that.'

'And Anne?'

My instinct was to ask, 'Anne who?' But the promise was no evasions.

'You talk in your sleep, Steve. Who is she?'

'Someone I met. She's no longer around.'

'I don't believe you. Someone's been here today.'

'The police.'

She hesitated. 'Anne was a police officer.'

I closed my eyes. I'd been dreaming a lot of Anne.

'There's no one else, Jen. No one. I met Anne while I was in Wales. It lasted a few weeks. By the time you reappeared and told me you were pregnant it was over. That's the truth.'

She sat back, for the moment saying nothing; regarding me with moist, angry eyes. Eventually she said, 'What do you want to do, Steve?'

I took my time over that.

'I don't know.'

She coughed in disbelief. 'You don't know?'

'No.'

'You could at least have the balls to lie – say you're not about to abandon me.'

'Abandon is the wrong word.'

'Is it?' Her voice became soft, 'Then tell me what's going to happen. Don't justify it, don't play with words, just tell me. – Please.'

It may have been instinct, but her left hand went to the bulge of her stomach.

I felt a fool and a coward.

Then suddenly she got it. She studied my face and scored

the jackpot. 'I hurt you so much over Kris Mayle that I killed it between us, didn't I?'

I shrugged. 'It was the start, but other things have happened.'

'Anne?'

'Yes,' I said simply.

'But she's not around any more you said.'

'That's right.'

'*Are* you going to leave me?'

'I don't know.'

Her eyes became bright. 'Then you'd best think about it and let me know once you've decided.'

With that she got up and walked out to the kitchen.

For the rest of the evening Jenny was artificially calm. After dinner we sat and watched the news or rather I watched the news and Jenny watched me.

The naming of Shenaz Rahman and the cocaine in her body was attributed to an unnamed source. The anchorman emphasised that the police had refused to confirm the rumours about the cocaine, although the source was stated to be a reliable one.

There was a background piece on Mohammed Ali Rahman and they ran the original clip of him appealing for calm shortly after the imam went into a coma.

In case we missed the irony the anchorman spelt out the implications of 'a prominent and considered Asian voice' having to deal with the savage murder of his wife and 'the riddle' of her body pumped full of cocaine.

Why, I wondered, would anyone leak the information on the cocaine? In whose interest was it?

An hour after it was first broadcast reports of major rioting started to come in. The previous riots, though vicious, were small compared to what erupted that night. For the first time disturbances broke out in other cities with large Muslim communities and everywhere fire was the medium of their anger.

Jenny went to bed around ten and I stayed up, channel hopping, looking for reports on the fire brigade in East London and wondering where my watch was and what they were dealing with.

I finally went to bed at one in the morning and slept fitfully with the jagged images of the past three days invading my dreams.

Friday
25 September
1.20 p.m.

Jenny awoke the next day as though our conversation had never happened.

She cooked breakfast, cleaned the flat and disappeared for her pre-natal class after getting me to sign a cheque. She left me lunch in the kitchen.

I managed to get a doctor's appointment for eleven, where I was told to rest the ankle and take a prescribed course of anti-inflammatories. The appointment had been necessary to cover myself brigade-wise; the real treatment for the ankle would be carried out by Paddy Ryan, who was a great sports physio as well as a superb boxing coach.

When the front doorbell rang just after one I was sat in front of the television watching the news again.

I limped out to the hallway, peered through the spyglass and saw Dave Chase. I opened the door and he smiled; he was shattered.

'Bad night?'

'Chronic, guv. They didn't send us to Leytonstone or Ilford, instead we stood by at Dagenham half the night and were in and out like a fiddler's elbow covering the gaps. At three we picked up a four-pump fire in a car showroom on Ilford's ground. It had been petrol bombed and was going like a train.'

'The news said the riots were worse than the night before.'

He gave a grim nod. 'It was a fucking nightmare. Sorry! Is Jenny in?'

I shook my head. 'The clinic. Coffee?'

He rolled his eyes in relief. 'Tea, if that's all right.'

I made us a pot of tea as Dave related the previous night's drama in detail.

'Many injured?' I asked when he'd finished.

'Mainly old Bill, but an appliance from Stratford got hit by a petrol bomb; scorched the side of the vehicle and scared the shit out of the crew. A few crews were stoned, minor injuries mostly, but loads of premises were burnt out. Christ only knows what it's all costing.'

Dave carried the tea through to the living room.

'The ankle looks rough, guv.'

I sat down and propped it up on the coffee table. 'I'm icing it every couple of hours and resting it – not sure if I've done the ligaments.'

His mouth turned at the edges. 'I wouldn't hurry back to work, guv.'

'Four days of rest should see it okay. Now, why are you here?'

Dave placed his cup down. 'Couple of things. First, a woman from the press turned up this morning just as we were going off duty.'

'Local?'

He shook his head. 'One of the tabloids.'

'What did she want?'

'She asked for you by name. Apparently the woman you saw murdered turned out to be full of cocaine.'

'I heard.'

'John Blane told her you were off work sick and didn't know when you'd be back.'

'If she's from a tabloid that won't stop her.'

'That's what I thought.'

'What did she look like?'

He took a moment. 'Short blonde hair, slim, thirtyish; attractive in a severe-looking way. Sun glasses worn like a hair band – and she reeked of Gauloise cigarettes.'

'Gauloise – do people still smoke them?'

'She does.'

'I really don't need this.'

'John left a note in the handing-over book warning not to give out any information and I passed the word in the locker room.'

'Cheers, Dave.'

I stirred my tea and told myself not to let it bother me. All I had to do was go back to the doctor in a few days and say the ankle was still feeling iffy. He'd sign me off for a week, maybe two. By then maybe the circus would have moved on.

'You said that there were two reasons for being here, Dave?'

He raised his eyebrows. 'Rob Brody?'

Shit! 'I'm sorry, Dave, in the drama of the last few days he went right out of my head. I should have rung him. How is he?'

Dave shook his head. 'Not sure. Linda Brody rang me this morning.'

'Oh?'

'She was upset and wouldn't say why.'

'So why did she ring?'

'Well that was the odd thing, she just started going on about Rob not coming back to work.'

'I'm not with you.'

'He's quitting the fire brigade.'

'Quitting? For God's sake why? Is this about Sandy?'

'I don't think so, guv.'

'Well what then?'

He brought his hands together and interwove his fingers. 'Rob's not been right for some time – I thought I noticed a change last Christmas.'

'Before Sandy?'

'I'd say so, yeah.'

My reaction was shallow; I was off the hook and grateful.

'John says that you've been beating yourself up over Sandy, guv – truth is we all have. But this thing with Rob Brody is different. Sandy dying couldn't have helped, but there's no way that you're to blame for Rob's situation. Trust me.'

'What aren't you telling me, Dave?'

He studied his hands. Eventually he shrugged and looked up.

'We went for a drink one night after work a few weeks ago. Rob was down and I thought a beer would take him out of himself.'

'Go on.'

'He started to talk, first about Linda and how they weren't getting on, but if I read him right there was more to it – from what he said I think Linda had the ache about Rob's sister.'

'You're losing me now, Dave.'

He nodded and paused again. 'Look, you didn't hear this from me and whatever you do with this, guv it mustn't come back.'

'I'm listening.'

'Rob's sister, Maria – she's had problems for some time. Rob's been helping her out and Linda apparently is not too sympathetic.'

'About what?'

He really didn't want to tell me. His face, body language and tone all screamed ambivalence.

'Maria . . . Maria has a drug problem.'

'Bad?'

'Very bad. Rob's been trying to get her clean. At first Linda was supportive, but Maria has lapsed too many times and Linda is sick of it.'

'He gives her money?'

'Money and his time – subs her out, picks her up and runs her to the local drugs support unit, let's her sleep over – which Linda reckons is not good for the kids . . .'

'Well it wouldn't be, would it?'

'It's his sister, guv. He can't abandon her.'

'And now it's reached crisis point?'

'Something's happened. Linda's tough, but when she rang me she sounded well upset.'

'So what's all this got to do with him quitting the brigade?'

'That's what I was hoping you'd find out, guv.'

17

I promised Dave that I'd drop in and see Rob some time in the next few days – just as soon as the ankle would allow. He wrote down Rob Brody's address and phone number for me and then left saying he intended to sleep for a week.

I wasn't entirely sure that visiting Rob Brody was the right thing.

We weren't close and he did have a tendency to keep his distance from the rest of the watch. There was also the situation between him and Linda, which by the sound of it was tense.

The final reason was a cultural one.

Firefighters don't like senior officers checking up on them when they are sick and although I didn't strictly fit that description, under the circumstances it might be viewed the same way, so I decided that before I went I would ring. There was no sense in blundering into private grief.

I looked at the clock. Jenny was a long time at the pre-natal class, but I reasoned that maybe she'd gone shopping afterwards. I turned on the television again and caught the start of the two o'clock news.

The riots were top of the list closely followed by the Rahman story. Halfway through rehashing the background to Shenaz Rahman's murder they broke away to a police spokesman outside Romford police station.

Amid a press mêlée, the speaker, a freckled-faced man in a weather-defying suit, waited for some semblance of quiet before speaking. Superintendent Howard, in shirtsleeves but wearing a tie, hovered in the background. Behind him stood a grim looking Bill Proctor.

Photographers and film crews adjusted positions again and more pushing and shoving broke out. Realising that things were as quiet as they were going to get, the spokesman held up a prepared statement.

'As I'm sure you are aware,' he began, 'on Wednesday evening we arrested a man in connection with the murder of Shenaz Rahman. The man continues to help us with our investigations.'

Sweat ran down the side of his face and he dabbed at it with a handkerchief before continuing.

'No decision has been made to charge the man with any offence as yet and an application may be made to a magistrate to extend the period allowed for questioning, should that prove necessary.' He folded up the paper and looked to his left. 'Superintendent Howard is head of the murder investigation and will now take your questions.'

He stepped to the side and Howard moved into position in front of the bank of microphones, glancing over his shoulder at Proctor who moved with him. The camera tracked the look they exchanged. Something was very wrong.

When Proctor stopped moving Howard began.

'Good afternoon. I'd like, if I could, to add a brief statement to that which you have already received, which may obviate the need to ask some of the questions.'

He ran a fat finger around his shirt collar.

'The murder of Shenaz Rahman is one of the most brutal that I have encountered in twenty years with the Metropolitan Police. Rightly, the community is outraged and expects us to spare no effort in finding and prosecuting the people who did this. The murder team now comprises more than fifty police officers and more may be added if required. This morning I had a telephone conversation with Commissioner Mayfield and he has assured me that any and all resources that I consider necessary will be available to me.'

He paused to let them digest that. When he spoke again the tone was softer.

'The last four days have witnessed public expressions of anger at the series of events that have occurred, but I would ask the community to trust us and refrain from street disturbances. The riots over the past four nights have seen innocent people hurt, shops and homes burnt and the emergency services targeted. This can only distract us from our task and divert officers away from the investigation.'

A reporter started to ask a question, but Howard held up a hand to indicate he wanted to continue.

'At present, the murder investigation is being treated as a separate crime to the cinema fire. A team of officers helped by the Metropolitan Police Fire Investigation Unit and the London Fire Brigade is tasked with this investigation and, although there is at present no obvious link to the murder of Shenaz Rahman, we are not ruling it out.'

He was sweating freely now. Again reporters started to ask questions, but once more he held up his hand.

'With regard to the death of Imam Hussein on Monday, I can tell you that the two police officers concerned have been suspended from duty and an investigation is being conducted into the matter by officers from Norfolk Constabulary. The Crown Investigation Service has asked for a preliminary report. I will now take your questions.

The camera zoomed in on a fit looking man in an open-necked shirt.

'Simon Benjamin, BBC, could I ask you to comment on the report that several police officers, including a female Detective Inspector, have been moved off the case – and can you tell us why?'

Jo Gordon?

Howard's face didn't change. Proctor look liked he'd been stabbed.

'I cannot comment on individual officers, but I can confirm that as more specialised officers are brought into the team it has proved necessary to rotate personnel – and it may prove necessary to do so again.'

He ran his finger around the inside of his collar again.

Benjamin wasn't done. 'Can you deny then that the Detective Inspector has been moved from the murder team because of allegations of racism?'

Howard's face was gunmetal. 'To the best of my knowledge that is not true.'

Was that a no?

'So there's no question that politics have played a part in the reconstruction of the murder team?' persisted Benjamin.

'I'm not sure what you mean.'

'Well, are there any Asian officers on the murder team?'

Howard was marinating in his own sweat. 'Not as yet.'

'So the answer is no?'

At that point Howard took a breath and let it out slowly, as though he was having to explain the obvious.

'The answer is not yet.' He turned away from Benjamin and pointed to a woman reporter.

She smiled sweetly. 'Are you telling us that with a crime bearing all the hallmarks of a racial killing that you don't at present have one Asian police officer involved in the investigation? Not even as liaison?'

'I believe I answered that when I said that it may prove necessary to rotate personnel if a specialised need is identified.'

If he expected that to be accepted as a complete answer he was quickly corrected. Questions flew from all sides. What he came out with next was as telling as it was forced from him.

'We have identified an Asian Detective Inspector who will join the team sometime in the next two days.'

'Is this why you've removed the alleged racist officer from the team?' asked Simon Benjamin quickly.

'I cannot comment further – other than to reiterate that personnel will be rotated as the need is identified.'

There followed a barrage of questions, but once the subject moved off the murder team and on to the investigation proper Howard looked more comfortable.

The most important question came from a reporter from a satellite channel. She asked why it had taken three days for Mohammed Ali Rahman to notice his wife was missing.

Deadpan, Howard said that it was a current line of investigation.

The press conference over, I turned off the television and rang Jo Gordon's mobile. It was switched off.

It was conceivable that there was more than one female inspector involved with the case, but only just. It had to be Jo. But racism? Was that why she looked uncomfortable – why Menzies had given her a hard time?

I didn't believe it. Every instinct said that it wasn't credible.

Over the next hour I tried Jo Gordon's mobile number three times and got nowhere. Around half three there was a knock at the front door and for a second it crossed my mind that it might be her. But I couldn't have been more wrong.

It was Menzies and Coleman.

I took them through to the living room and sat down. Menzies glanced around as if to say he'd seen better. Neither mentioned my obvious limping, in fact they looked at me like I was a total stranger.

Menzies looked at an armchair. 'May I?'

I nodded. Having them in my home irritated me and it must have shown in my face. As Menzies and I sat, Coleman stood to one side and positioned himself perfectly so that he was just out of my peripheral vision. Despite myself I turned and looked at him, effectively handing him the brass key that fitted in the middle of my back.

Menzies was all business. For once I didn't sense the usual hostility; just coldness, but I warned myself to take nothing for granted.

'I'm not here in connection to the murder of Shenaz Rahman, Mr Jay.'

'Then why?'

'It's to do with the cinema fire.' He looked at me, then took out a notebook and thumbed through it. 'I've spoken to Assistant Divisional Officer Grant and he tells me that it was you that made the claim that the inner doors to the film theatre were wedged shut.'

'Yes.'

'Why?'

'Sorry?'

He glanced at Coleman and I resisted the urge to follow him.

'My understanding – from what ADO Grant has told me – is that the whole building was smoke-logged. Visibility was virtually nil.'

I adjusted my ankle and propped it up on the coffee table. 'That's right.'

'Did you see these wedges?'

'No.'

'Handle them – picked them up?'

'No.'

'Tread on them?'

'No.'

He paused. 'Then how do you know the doors were wedged closed?'

'The doors wouldn't open when I pulled them. I had to pull hard with both hands and it was only when I threw my weight backwards that the doors opened.'

'So the doors were stuck.'

'Yes.'

'But you said wedged,' he shrugged. 'There's a difference, isn't there, between being stuck and being wedged?'

'I thought I felt the wedges give as I threw my weight backwards. I . . .'

'But you saw no wedges, as such?'

'No.'

'So why tell ADO Grant that the doors were wedged?'

'Because I thought they were. Because it's the only thing that makes sense.'

He shook his head slowly. 'That can't be right, can it? There could be all sorts of reasons why the doors didn't open at first – distorted by heat maybe or –' he looked at his notes again, 'or maybe jammed by the weight of the bodies – you said to ADO Grant that there were lots of bodies?'

'I told Bob Grant what I thought had prevented the doors from opening. They stuck and then they gave way – like wedges being displaced.'

His face was impassive. 'So you didn't see, handle or tread on any wedges?'

I hated him. He was absolutely right and I could have kicked his teeth in because of it. But equally I remember the feel of the doors when they gave way and I'd have bet anything that they'd been wedged.

He flipped a page of the notebook. 'There were two fire-fighters in your crew?'

'Yes.'

'Did they see these wedges?'

'They were behind me and, as you said, visibility was practically nil. When I pulled the doors open I was buried under bodies. I was pulled clear by Gerry Mudd, my Leading Firefighter. I doubt that he could have seen much.'

'And this other firefighter, David Chase?'

'He was further back down the corridor than Gerry Mudd.'

'So none of you saw these wedges?'

Coleman edged into my vision.

'Can't speak for the others, but when you put it like that it doesn't seem very likely.'

'No, it doesn't, does it? So far the fire investigation team haven't found a cause of the fire and the only testimony that it might have been arson comes from you.'

'Something stopped the exit doors from opening.'

'I agree – something probably did.' He stood up. 'Forensics will go over that cinema inch by inch. If no wedges are found I may ask my boss to consider a charge of wasting police time.'

'What?'

'I think you heard me. We've got half of London tearing itself apart and you go around making wild accusations that could get further people killed.'

'The doors were wedged!'

'So you say. Don't get up, we'll see ourselves out.'

Coleman slid me a sneer as they left.

The second they were out the door I rang Jo Gordon's mobile again.

Nothing

I was convinced now that she was the Detective Inspector moved off the case. It bothered me and yet there was no reason why it should. I was a witness – did it matter who took my evidence?

All the same, I felt uneasy. Menzies' effortless pulling apart of my statement and implied threat seriously pissed me off. Yet in the volatile atmosphere of the past five days I could see why the police needed to sit heavily on anything that didn't stand up to scrutiny.

Yet the doors were wedged! I couldn't prove it, but they were.

I sat there for maybe half an hour, arguing with myself that it didn't matter what I could and couldn't prove. I was a fire-fighter, not a copper.

Yet the barb had gone deep.

When the phone rang I glanced at the clock, thinking it was Jenny saying why she was so late. Like the rest of my recent guesses I was out by just the mile.

'Steve?'

'Hello, Jo. Where are you?'

'At the end of your road. Do you still fancy that drink?'

18

The late afternoon sun shone with the same intensity that it had for the past ten days.

Jo Gordon was quiet and thoughtful as she drove north out of Romford and once or twice she turned and let her liquid brown eyes sweep over me. Something was coming, but I figured that whatever was on her mind she'd let me know in her own time.

We drove up Orange Tree Hill to Havering-Atte-Bower with the sunroof open and the windows down. Jo was wearing Ray-Bans with the collar of her blouse flapping in the slip-stream.

I expected her to be upset, brooding, but that wasn't the vibe coming off her.

A few miles beyond Stapleford Abbotts there was a sign for a hotel off to the left and she turned the car into the narrow approach road. Through a screen of trees I could see a hotel, a Georgian edifice with a small lake to one side of it.

The cars parked on the gravel semi-circle in front of the hotel would normally have been enough to scare me off – I know my value and here I was outclassed – but Jo's Mercedes would go unnoticed.

I looked from the cars to my clothes – chinos with T-shirt – and looked at Jo. She waved her hand.

'We'll use the patio.'

When Jo had rung me I'd slipped a figure-of-eight sports

support on my ankle, which was now cutting into the swelling, but was enabling me to walk, albeit very slowly.

We negotiated the small flight of steps that led up to the main entrance and went into the foyer. Jo flipped the sunglasses up on to the top of her head and led the way to an impressive gilded reception lounge, through a bar, and finally out on to a dazzling patio area overlooking the lake.

Beyond, in the distance, I could see a golf course.

There were a variety of people on the patio, business types, golfers and others in the kind of casual clothes you see in Sunday supplements; money, money, money. Somewhere I had to have a doppelganger; Gucci-shoed and Armani-suited, living the fat life.

My face must have mirrored my thoughts because Jo turned to me and said, 'No one cares, Steve. They'll think you're so rich that you're deliberately dressing down.'

'Right.'

Jo took a packet of cigarettes from her handbag, selected one and lit it with the gold cylinder lighter, blowing the smoke upward.

A waiter approached and said hello to Jo.

'I'll have a long G and T,' she paused and looked at me.

'Rum and coke, plenty of ice, please,' I said.

'And we'll have some olives, please, Charlie.'

'Yes, Mrs Gordon.'

As he walked away I raised an eyebrow. 'Regular watering hole?'

'Yes. How's that ankle?'

'Rebelling against the bandage.'

Jo leaned back in the chair and slipped the sunglasses on again. 'Tell me about the cinema fire.'

I hesitated, 'Is this official?'

She shook her head. 'Just curious.'

I started describing the events and had just reached the part where we entered the inner corridor, when the waiter returned with the drinks and olives.

'Charlie, would you be a dear and fetch me some more ice, wrapped in a cloth?'

'Certainly, Mrs Gordon.'

'Carry on, Steve.'

I continued with the story, careful to neither embellish it nor play it down. When I'd finished she nodded her head slowly.

'It sounds heavy.'

'Heavy enough.'

She selected an olive and ate it. 'It's a nasty business all round.'

'The riots?'

She selected another and offered to me. 'Everything.'

'Was it you they moved off the murder team?'

'Yes.'

'D'you want to talk about it?'

'No.'

'So why are we here?'

She smiled, 'For a drink.'

I lifted my glass and took a long bite of the rum and coke. It was as though I'd stepped outside of my existence, no brigade, no squalid flat in Prentice Road and no guilt. And Jo sitting three feet from me, looking beautiful.

She drew slowly on the cigarette and looked directly at me. 'How long have you been a firefighter?'

'Thirteen years.'

'How long a Station Officer?'

'Six or seven years. Eight if you include temporary rank. What about you?'

'Ten years next month. Eighteen months as an Inspector.'

'D'you like it – the job, the rank?'

'Sometimes. Not today though.'

'What are you working on now – if not the murder team?'

'I'm not. I'm on leave as of eleven o'clock this morning.'

'How long for?'

'Indefinite. Till the wind changes – till this thing goes away.'

'Will it go away?'

She stopped her glass halfway to her mouth, then said quietly, 'I don't know.'

Charlie brought the ice in a cloth and Jo rolled up my trouser leg and draped the ice over the ankle. I caught her eye and held it.

'Menzies visited me this afternoon.'

'Oh?'

'Said that he'd been moved to the cinema fire investigation. He gave me a hard time.'

'Sounds like him. What was the problem?'

I told her about the wedges.

She closed her eyes. 'They're running scared, Steve. Panicking.'

'Political pressure?'

'Yes.' She finished her gin and tonic and ordered another one. 'Same again, Steve?'

'I'll get these.'

'You're not allowed. Guests can't pay.'

'I thought it was an hotel?'

'It is, but you have to be a member to even get in the place.'

'In that case, yes please.'

She looked at the olives again. 'Have you eaten, Steve?'

'No.'

'Like to?'

I laughed. 'What have I done to deserve this?'

She shrugged. 'I'll ask Charlie for a menu.'

'So how come you're a member here?'

'I joined last year. Someone I knew suggested I apply.'

'Policeman?'

She shook her head. 'No.'

'It must cost money being a member here?'

'It does – so how can I afford it?'

'Well it would be too expensive for a Station Officer,' I said slowly.

'My father had money. I inherited. Try another olive, these are good.'

'Why the police, Jo?'

She thought about that. 'When I finished my degree I looked around and it seemed the only thing with both excitement and a career structure.'

'How's the career going?'

The smile was rueful. 'Pretty shitty, seeing as you ask.'

The waiter reappeared and Jo asked for menus. He went off and came right back with them.

'What's good today, Charlie?' she asked.

'The Beef Wellington, Mrs Gordon.'

Jo looked at me. 'Too heavy?'

'I'll go with your choice,' I replied.

Jo studied the menu briefly. 'Right, Charlie, we'll have the trout.' She looked up at me. 'You don't look a Chardonnay man?'

'I'm not, but I feel reckless.'

'Bottle of Chardonnay, Charlie.'

A man on another table caught Jo's eye and raised a hand. She smiled in acknowledgement.

'Do you know many here?' I asked.

She blinked. 'The regulars. Most are friendly.'

'I'll bet. What are you going to do with your leave?'

'Not sure. It wasn't planned.'

'Right.'

It felt easy with Jo; nuance of tone and brevity of sentence marked out the no-go areas and the little sideways looks and unclosed remarks flagged-up the free-zones.

I liked this, it was comfortable and the rum helped, but beyond the parameters I guessed that she was hurting and that I was probably here to be the balm to that.

This wasn't a get-to-know-you meeting, it was a sit-still-and-wait meeting – because anything might happen and because no decisions had been made. So we talked about nothing special and enjoyed the sun, drinks and surroundings.

And I looked at her.

I reasoned that that was allowed. Anyway I did and she knew it and didn't seem uncomfortable with it. After about fifteen minutes Charlie returned and announced that our table was ready.

'I've put you in the lake room, Mrs Gordon,' he added.

Jo ground the cigarette under her shoe and pushed the Ray-Bans on top of her head.

We got up and followed him through to a small dining room with just half a dozen tables and just two other diners; middle-aged men in business suits. We sat with our backs to them, at a window table looking out over the lake.

The trout was excellent and the chilled Chardonnay as dry as it comes. But either way it wouldn't have mattered, because the rum was hitting me and I was watching her.

Once, fleetingly, I caught her returning the look. A smile briefly lit her face and she tried to cover it by lifting her glass.

'What shall we drink to, Steve?'

'It's your toast.'

The smile faded. 'Yes, it is. Okay – to the truth.'

'Truth?

She gave a short nod. 'May it become fashionable again.'

'I thought I wanted truth, but lately I've been avoiding it,' I said softly.

'We all do. The trick is not to let it become a habit.'

'You sound like you're fighting that.'

'I'm fighting more than that,' she said with a sigh, 'I'm fighting memory – distorted memory, and cynicism.'

'Sounds nasty.'

'It's priceless.'

'Tell me.'

She shook her head. 'Too complicated. Everything's too complicated. And right now I want simplicity.'

'Do you?'

'Yes,' she said quietly. 'And you want me, don't you, Steve?'

'I . . .'

'Don't you?'

'Yes.'

Her head went back. 'Well then.' She reached across the table and kissed me. 'I'm booked in,' she said softly.

Then she took my hand and we stood up. In silence, we walked from the dining room, through the foyer and up a broad spiral staircase that led to the galleried first floor.

Her room was the fourth down on the left and once inside she closed the door and turned to me.

'Come here.'

The scent of her perfume hit me as she reached up and placed her arms around my neck. I could feel the tension in her body and brushed my lips gently against hers.

Her eyes closed and she shook her head. 'Not softly. I don't want you to make love to me – I want you to fuck me. I want you fuck me slowly, Steve.'

Her tongue found mine and I pulled at the buttons on her blouse. Beneath she was wearing a white satin bra that barely held her, the peach colouring of her skin contrasting with the material and the thin dark edges of her nipples just in view.

She undid the hooks at the front of the bra and let it fall to the floor. Then she pulled my T-shirt up over my head and pressed against me.

The feel of her skin against mine was incredible and her

breasts were heavy, silken. I cupped each one and kissed them in turn, running my tongue in small circles. I heard her gasp and she held my head and kissed my mouth then guided me back to her nipples.

Again she grasped my head and kissed me as I unhooked her skirt and let it fall to the ground. With quick movements her hands found my belt and undid it, pulling my trousers and pants to the floor. She started to kneel, but I shook my head and turned her towards the closed door so that her back was to me, then placed her hands against the wood.

Slowly I pulled down her briefs and tights.

She turned her head, but I pushed it back and ran my fingertips around her breasts, down her sides and then to the junction of the thighs, making her spread her legs.

I kissed the centre of her back and the sides of her neck as I touched and probed, allowing no other part of me to touch her, but lips and fingertips.

She started to writhe and I knelt and explored her with my tongue. Her breathing changed and I turned her towards me, but took her hands and forced them out to the sides, pushing them flat against the door.

'Close your eyes,' I whispered.

She stood there with her eyes shut and her arms and legs spread, while I ran the tip of my tongue in and around her sex and then up slowly to each breast, sucking and biting gently.

She brought her hands forward to take hold of me, but I turned her around towards the door and began again.

I could smell her. As my tongue entered she raised herself up on to her toes with her breath escaping in small gasps. With each entry and withdrawal of my tongue her hips moved and her hands clenched tightly.

Then I took hold of her hips from behind and barely entered her. She tried to push back, but I whispered, 'No'.

Slowly, rhythmically, I entered slightly and withdrew, as my hands went back to her breasts and cupped them.

Suddenly I plunged into her and she stiffened.

I thrust harder and harder, circling my pelvis and holding her waist from behind. Her hands gripped my wrists and she pushed against me. Immediately I stopped and turned her around so that she was facing me, pushing her hands out to the side. Then knelt and began again with my tongue.

I felt her start to build and stopped. She was trembling and I let her subside and then, my tongue barely touching her, started over again.

Each time I felt her tremble, I paused and each time she stopped I began.

Her eyes suddenly opened and her body quivered – on the very edge.

I stood and kissed her. Her tongue found mine and she seized my hands, pulling me towards the bed.

Pushing me backwards she lowered herself slowly on to me and then hugged me to her so that her legs were wrapped around me and we were sitting upright. She moved with a gentle rocking motion, her tongue darting in and out of my mouth. Then, closing her eyes, she changed to moving in small grinding circles, thrusting down on to me, clutching my head fiercely to her breasts.

She was in control now.

Taking my hands she laid them on her breasts as she kissed me, her tongue finding mine as she circled and pushed down, faster and deeper. For the first time a tremble coursed through me and she sensed it. We seemed to ripple in concert, each action sending waves of sensation through me to her and back again.

In an instant she lost the rhythm and ground her pelvis faster and faster as she felt me building. Her breath seemed to be forced out of her each time she pushed down until a long aching spasm shook her violently.

'Now!' she breathed.

I stopped any measure of control and drove hard into her until she clutched me frantically, her head going back in a final act of abandonment. Then I released.

We stayed there locked in an embrace, our bodies shaking, kissing softly.

19

Jo lay smoking a cigarette, blowing the blue/grey smoke from the edge of her mouth.

'How are you for time?' she said.

I looked at my watch. It was seven p.m. 'I'm fine for an hour or so.'

'Should you phone?'

'Perhaps later.'

She turned on her side and faced me. 'I'm not sure what happened today.'

'Oh?'

'I needed someone and . . . you wanted me.'

'When did you decide?'

'Pretty much as soon as I met you. You stared,' she smiled, 'you always stare.'

'Bad habit.'

'It can be little intimidating.'

I rolled on to my back and placed my hands behind my head. 'When I first saw you I did a double-take, you reminded me of someone.'

'Someone who's special?'

'Someone who was.'

She looked sideways. 'How much like her am I?'

'Looking at you now? Not much – but there's something, the way you turn your head, small gestures. It shook me up.'

'I see. And do I fuck like her?'

'We never fucked, we made love.'

At that she gave a small nod. 'You miss that?'

'Yes, I do.'

'No chance of you getting back with her?'

'Absolutely none.'

'But you're living with someone else?'

'So it would seem.'

'That not permanent then?'

'It's falling apart – too much history.'

She extinguished the cigarette and rolled over, lying across me. The feel of her skin against mine, her breasts as they fell against me, started to arouse me again and I kissed her.

'You said she was pregnant?'

'Yes.'

'That can't be easy.'

'For neither of us. But it's crumbling and I think it'll happen sooner rather than later.'

'That must be tough.'

'And what about you? Your ex-husband?'

She looked away. 'My dead husband.'

'Sorry.'

'Don't be, I'm not.'

'Tell me.'

She kissed my chest, almost absently. 'He was a copper, older than me and in many ways a stereotype. He drank with the lads and lived the life of a canteen copper. He seemed very masculine. It was a turn on.'

'The things we settle for.'

'We married and it took me all of six months to realise he was fucking around. It hurt. Within a year we were virtually living separate lives. Then he got himself into trouble.'

'Trouble?'

She nodded. 'He arrested a Jamaican. Terry was never overly tolerant, especially where ethnics were concerned.

The guy gave him some lip so Terry cuffed him and beat him up. The guy made a formal complaint.'

'What happened?'

'Terry was a Detective Sergeant, the guy was a known drugs dealer, small time. In an out of court settlement the Met paid him fifteen grand and Terry was demoted at a tribunal. He was lucky to keep his job.'

I propped myself up on one elbow. 'Is this the business about racism that got you moved off the murder team?'

She nodded. 'Guilt by association. Now, this will make you laugh – we were already separated when Terry beat the guy up.'

'So this doesn't really involve you at all?'

'Oh, it gets better. Terry was desperate to get back together. I wasn't interested, but he kept calling round. Then he started turning up drunk, usually when the pubs closed. One night he begged me to take him back. I said no and he hit me. After that I started divorce proceedings.' She sighed, remembering. 'A while later he got ill, very ill. Stomach cancer. It was out of control by the time they found it and he died within three months. I moved back in and nursed him up to the end and he cursed me for it. After his funeral it started.'

'What did?'

'The talking, the Chinese whispers – that I abandoned Terry when I found out he had cancer, that I put my career before my marriage, that it was me that was screwing around. It died down eventually, but never really went away. Couple of years later, when I went for promotion to Inspector, Neil Menzies was also up for it. I got it, he didn't and the whispers started again. It was Menzies, though I could never prove it.'

'Was Menzies a friend of Terry Gordon?'

'No. He knew him, the occasional drink, but friends? No.'

'This business with the murder team is connected to all that?'

She nodded slowly. 'Yes. But again I can't prove it. To call someone a racist is not only to remove them from the game – it damns them. That's the way it is now.'

'Howard knows all this?'

'Yes.'

'It stinks.' I said flatly.

'That it does. But even friends are backing away from me. In the current climate it's not wise to be associated with a racist. It's the new leprosy.'

'Couldn't you transfer somewhere?'

'It would follow me like a bad smell. No, the only thing I can do is tough it out and hope things change – that I can make them change.'

'And the murder of Shenaz Rahman? Where's the investigation now?'

She raised her eyebrows. 'In trouble the last I heard.'

'Is that because I couldn't positively ID Vanzie?'

Her hand stroked the side of my face. 'It's not your fault, Steve. Vanzie has a bloody good alibi. They'll struggle to hold him. The best they can do is release him on police bail and try to build the case before having another go at him – which means they'll probably re-interview you. And also that other firefighter that was with you.'

'Rob Brody,' I offered.

'Yes.'

'Look, Jo, I know you're out the loop now and that I can't prove it, but I swear those inner doors to the cinema were wedged shut. And that's murder, mass murder. That can't be ignored.'

'It won't be, Steve. But from what you've told me even you didn't see the wedges, so that makes it flimsy evidence.'

'Has the search of the cinema wreckage been completed?'

'I doubt it. They'll note what you say and forensics will go over the place inch by inch. If there's anything left to find they'll find it. There's a massive police presence down Green Street and the whole area is now sealed off.'

'So Menzies was just being an arsehole?'

Her head tilted to one side. 'No. I imagine he was trying to find out just how certain you are.'

'Because of Vanzie and my uncertainty over the ID?'

'Yes. I would have done the same. Differently, but with the same intent.'

'The press turned up at my station again. A woman from one of the tabloids.'

'Try to avoid her, Steve, and whatever you do don't talk to her. If they find out where you live they'll show up on your doorstep – and that I wouldn't recommend.'

With that she edged forward and kissed me.

'Again please,' she breathed.

It was gone eight when I arrived back at the flat.

Jo paid for a cab – it must have cost the best part of forty quid.

When I left she didn't say anything about where, if anywhere, we might take this. But she smiled and that was both a promise and a thank you.

I smiled back.

On the journey to Romford I thought of possible explanations to give Jenny, but they all involved half-truths and lies so I resolved not to go that route. I'd made my decision now and Jo Gordon wasn't a factor in that.

Jenny needed certainty as much as me and now that my feelings had come out it was better that we made some decisions. So when I entered the flat I was clear in my mind that the whole thing should not be turned into a slanging match, it would be painful enough without turning it into farce.

But the flat was empty.

I looked around in case she'd been and gone, but nothing looked disturbed. I decided to check the answer-phone and sure enough there was a short message from Jenny.

'I'm at my mother's. If you want to talk, you know where I am.'

And that was the end of Jenny and me.

There might be conversations, recriminations and perhaps an autopsy or two, but we were through and we both now knew it.

Congratulations, Stevie – another success story.

The flat felt airless so I opened some windows and a nerve-jangling backbeat of speeding traffic, shrill teenage voices and intermittent bass drifted in from the street. It underlined the feeling that I'd rolled into a hole.

I opened a bottle of rum, poured myself a stiff measure and turned on the television.

According to the newscaster, the riots had started again in the early afternoon, although they weren't as widespread. A Home Office spokesman made a plea for calm and was questioned on whether any racist murder team should have a prescribed number of officers of ethnic origin.

The spokesman wriggled like a snake on a stick and said that the composition of any murder team was a matter for the individual police force.

I was about to switch channels when they broke to Romford Police station where it had just been announced that the man held for questioning in connection with the murder of Shenaz Rahman had been released on police bail.

If Jo was right I'd be re-interviewed soon.

I went through half the bottle of rum and fell asleep in the chair.

It was gone midnight when the phone rang and by the time I'd reached it, it had stopped. I rang 1471 to retrieve the number, but whoever had rung withheld their number.

Jenny? Jo?

I went to bed only to have the phone ring again the minute my eyes were shut. I swore, dragged myself from the bed and limped out to the living room. Again the phone stopped before I got to it and again no number was left. This time I took the phone off the hook before I went back to bed.

The rum did its job and I slept through till eight; the best night's sleep I'd managed in weeks. I rose, shaved, showered and made myself breakfast, before placing the phone back on the receiver.

It occurred to me then that, although the late night caller had left no number, I hadn't checked to see if they'd left a message. I pressed 1571. There were two new messages; one at 12.13 hours and one at 12.21 hours.

I pressed to accept the first message and heard Linda Brody's voice ask me to ring her urgently. The second message was blank – no voice.

I dug out the number that Dave Chase had given me and rang it. There was no reply.

My ankle felt better for the ice-packs and, although still swollen, it had reduced in size. I figured I could drive if I used the ankle support again. Pitsea was only a forty-minute drive and, providing I took it easy, I'd make it okay.

20

Pitsea was a blister on the edge of Basildon.

A so-called new town when it was built, Basildon had all the vices of the East End, where most of its inhabitants had come from, and few of its virtues.

This was Metropolitan Essex, a malign concrete strip that ran parallel to the Thames – ninety-five per cent working class and five per cent underclass. The five per cent was all too frequently the image that prevailed, for Essex Man was supposedly the beast that stalked this land and he was reputed to be illiterate, foul-mouthed and hopelessly right-wing.

Or at least so the tabloids would have it.

I found Rob Brody's house in a cul-de-sac of neat tiled-faced two-storey semis. His car wasn't on the hard standing and I regretted not waiting until I'd managed to speak to Linda Brody first.

As I climbed from the car I thought I saw a curtain move. I rang the doorbell and waited. Almost immediately I heard footsteps, but the door didn't open.

I gave it a couple of minutes and tried again.

This time I heard a single thump, but again the door wasn't answered. Feeling like a bailiff, I looked through the letterbox and saw a young girl of ten or so looking back at me.

'Go away!' she screamed.

'It's Steve Jay, I'm Rob's boss from the fire station. Is Linda there?'

'Go away!'

Her eyes were filled with tears and she was trembling. It was time to back off. I closed the letterbox.

Reluctant to just drive back to Romford, I knocked next door. It was opened by a large red-faced woman in a crop-top with no bra.

'Yes?'

'I wonder if you know where Linda and Rob are.'

'Who are you then?' Two small boys with dirty faces appeared either side of her.

'I'm from the fire station.'

'Where?'

'The fire station – Rob's a firefighter.'

'Is he? I wouldn't know about that. We keep ourselves to ourselves round here. Especially if you have neighbours that are screaming and shouting at all hours of the day and night.'

'Right.'

'If you work with him you should tell him to watch the company he keeps as well.'

I was about to ask what she meant when she closed the door in my face. Suddenly Prentice Road, Romford didn't seem too bad.

It was hot and getting hotter and I didn't fancy sitting in the car for a couple of hours till Rob or Linda returned. Equally the thought of an empty flat didn't beckon too strongly either.

I found a phone box and rang Alex.

'I was wondering when you'd ring,' he said.

'I take it you've spoken to Jenny?'

'She rang me first thing this morning.'

'Go on then, give me some stick.'

'Well you know your own mind, Stevie. I just hope you haven't made a major mistake.'

'I don't love her anymore, Alex.'

'Aye, well, I didn't imagine you left her because you did.'

'We okay, you and me?'

'You haven't left me,' he said thinly. 'Are you at home?'

'No, Pitsea.'

'What're you up to now?'

'I'm visiting Rob Brody. He's got some domestic problems and his wife rang last night.'

'*You* have domestic problems. It might be an idea to sort those first.'

'Well, you've got me there.'

'Have you been to see Paddy about that ankle yet?'

'I'll ring him after I've seen Rob Brody.'

'Aye, well that's two of your own problems that are being put off for Rob Brody. I hope he appreciates it.'

'Speak to you later, Alex.'

I put the phone down and sighed. He was right.

I decided to go into Basildon town centre, grab a cup of coffee and then come back in an hour or so. If Rob or Linda weren't in then I'd drive home.

I'd tried.

The centre of Basildon is a soulless concrete box that some planner imagined might be a town square. It has a bright, well-designed shopping mall, but the square as a focal point has all the charm of an industrial park.

People deserve better than this.

The migration from the East End of London had been going on for years. People's dreams of finding somewhere green with places for children to play had turned into a hollow joke.

Basildon was now the East End in the country, but minus the community spirit or the character of the old place. From north to south and east to west it was a sterile council estate, or at least that's what it seemed to me as I limped around the square.

My mood was no doubt bleeding the colour from the landscape.

Over several coffees and the morning paper I planned the

remainder of my day. I would go back to Rob Brody's and, if he wasn't there, I'd ring Paddy Ryan and see if he could fit me in for a session on the ankle.

Then I'd ring Jo.

An hour and a half later I found myself outside Rob Brody's house again, but his blue Ford Mondeo was still not parked on the hard standing.

Alex's remark about sorting out my own domestic problems before other people's was dual-edged. It was a plea to get my priorities right and a point of irony that I should be even contemplating offering advice to Rob Brody when my own life didn't bear too close a scrutiny.

I knocked on the door and waited. Footsteps sounded beyond the door, but the door didn't open.

'Rob – Rob it's me, Steve Jay.'

The door was opened by Linda Brody. She looked pale and anxious.

'You rang me, Linda.'

She nodded and beckoned me in, looking past me into the street.

The house was small, but comfortably furnished, although I spotted the fragments of a broken vase in one corner, just below a stain on the wall.

'He's not here, Steve,' said Linda, reading my expression.

'Why am I here, Linda?'

'Sit down, please,' she said.

I sat on the edge of the sofa. The young girl I'd seen through the letter box came into the living room and sat next to Linda. Her eyes were wide and fearful.

'Can the fire brigade get us accommodation?'

'Accommodation? I don't know. We used to have some flats for recruits, but I don't think we have even those now. Why?'

'We need to move.'

I searched her face. 'Is this money problems, Linda?'

'No,' she said firmly, 'but we need to move away from here.'

'I can speak to brigade welfare, but I'd need to know a little of what it's about. Can you give me a clue?'

She closed her eyes and tears ran down her face. This wasn't the woman I'd met before. Linda Brody had always struck me as fiery by nature and tenacious by design. What I was seeing didn't fit the template.

'I . . . I can't tell you.'

'Look, is this about Rob's sister?'

'How . . . who told you about his sister?'

'A few people on the watch have had concerns about Rob for some time.'

'I can't tell you. He'll have to tell you himself.'

'Where is he, Linda?'

'I've just dropped him off at his sister's place.'

'Where's that?'

'Burnham Villas, Laindon.'

'Do you want me to go and speak to him there?'

'No! No, he'll be angry that I told you.'

I shrugged.

'Can you come back tonight, Steve? He'll be here after eight.'

I was about to say no, but her expression stopped me. I looked at my watch, it was nearly one.

'Ring me when he's here. I can get here in under three-quarters of an hour.'

'Thank you.'

I stood up. 'Linda, I'm not sure what this is all about, but taking a flying guess, let's say it involves his sister's drug problem. Between the social services and the police . . .'

'No! Not the police.'

'There are drugs support agencies that specialise in this sort of thing. They're the experts. I take it Rob's in touch with them?'

'Was.'

'Well if it's out of control then he's going to need all the help he can get. Loyalty won't be enough.'

I abandoned the plan to visit Paddy Ryan at the gym and instead drove straight to Alex's house.

He nodded when he answered the door, as though he was expecting me. It always irritated when he second-guessed me, especially when he was openly smug about it.

'I had no one else to visit, so I came here.'

'Coffee?' he grinned, 'or something stronger?'

'It'll have to be coffee, I've got to go back to Pitsea later.'

'Why?'

As he put some fresh coffee on I explained to him what had happened. He heard me out without comment.

'I'm not sure what to make of it, Alex.'

He puffed his cheeks out. 'Debt probably. If Rob Brody's sister has a serious drug problem then she'll have a serious money problem as well.

'We all have money problems. Linda's very frightened and so is the kid.'

'Maybe his sister owes someone and they're pressuring Rob for it.'

'That would fit actually.'

'So I'm a genius,' he said.

The more we talked the more I felt that Alex was on to something. Drug dealers don't take no for an answer where debt is concerned and their methods for retrieving what they're owed are not subtle. Which would explain much.

Eventually the subject came around to Jenny.

'It's over, Alex,' I said simply. 'It's been coming for a while. The truth is after Anne I don't see Jenny in the same way.'

'Understood, but it's not just about Jenny.'

'I know.'

'So?'

'So I move out the flat, support her, be there for the birth. If that's what she wants.'

He poured the freshly brewed coffee and passed me a cup.

'You loved her once. You couldn't get enough of her. It's natural that you should miss Anne but, for what it's worth, I think you have to stay with Jenny until the birth. You still care for her, I take it?'

I thought about that. 'Yes. How much of that is habit I don't know, but yes, of course I care for her.'

'Well then.'

'You think I should reach an agreement with her – about staying till the birth?'

He took a sip of the coffee and regarded me over the brim of the cup.

'Is there something you're not telling me, Stevie?'

'Probably, why?'

'Jenny said that she thinks you may have another woman.'

'What else did she say?'

'That not a "no" then?'

His eyes were hard, but then again they always were. It's just that they lit with a savage humour every now and again, and right now I couldn't tell what they were signalling.

I shook my head. 'You know better than anyone else what Jenny put me through. For six months she left me for that bastard Mayle and then when she came back to me she still couldn't keep away from him. I walked. I moved on, Alex. I told her where we stood and then got on with the rest of my life. Then I met Anne and, despite it being short-lived, it freed me from the past.

'I know . . .'

I held my hand up. 'Hear me out. When Jenny showed up pregnant I stood by her, but the truth is Anne wasn't out of my system and even if she had been, Jenny wasn't in my plans any more. I tried to do a three hundred and sixty degree turn to make it work, honestly I did. But now I can't do it anymore. I need to go.'

He put his cup down and folded his arms. 'You have got someone, haven't you?'

I sighed. 'No. Not quite. I've slept with her, once. Yesterday. I don't know if there'll be another time. I'm not totally sure I even know why it happened. That's it, the whole story.'

'Except who she is.'

'As a priest you don't quite make it, Alex.'

'Indulge me, I'm curious.'

'I bet you are.'

He put down his cup and topped it up, offering the percolator to me.

'Jenny thinks it's that woman Detective Inspector.'

'If you're determined to be a pain in the arse I'm going.'

He was relentless. 'Jenny is going to need more than financial support, Stevie. You're going to have to deal with this carefully.'

'And as soon as I see her, that's what I intend to do.'

21

I drove back to the flat still mentally sparring with Alex.

It didn't help that not for the first time he'd nailed the situation dead. Problem was that my emotional clock was running a little slow.

I'd get there.

My ankle was throbbing from overuse and by the time I'd climbed the stairs it was threatening to give way. So once I'd showered the sweat from my body I made myself comfortable and put a new ice-pack on the ankle.

I stayed that way for some time, letting the ice take the heat out of the injury and resisting the temptation to watch the news.

I checked the answerphone for messages, but there none. More importantly, there were none from Jenny.

With time on my hands until Linda Brody rang I searched for something to occupy me and for the first time in months opened my Steinbeck omnibus. The last time I'd done that was in Wales, when I first met Anne; when my life had gone through a curve.

I considered putting some Mahalia Jackson on the CD player, the phenomenal singer that Anne had loved, but that would have been to risk nostalgia and if I was sure of anything it was that the past was dead.

So I settled for James Taylor, which is the nearest to Joni Mitchell that a man should allow himself to get.

The clock crept slowly round to seven and by then, between

Steinbeck and emotional plectrum of Taylor's voice I was mellowed and ready for the world again.

I switched on the television.

The first thing I saw was Mohammed Ali Rahman on the steps outside Romford police station. Standing next to him was a suited Asian, aged about forty, whose face was vaguely familiar. Then I remembered he was the guy I'd caught a glimpse of through the open door of my office, the day that Rahman had come to the station.

The Asian suit was preparing to read a statement and as he shuffled with his papers a caption reading 'Iqbal Asif – recorded earlier' appeared under his image.

Rahman looked calm, almost detached.

'Mister Mohammed Ali Rahman has asked me, as his legal representative, to make a simple statement on his behalf.' Asif cleared his throat. 'This afternoon, following a request from the police, Mohammed Ali Rahman attended Romford police station voluntarily to assist with the investigation into the death of his wife. He has not been arrested and once again calls for calm in the community whilst these matters are dealt with and asks that no one should use this as an excuse to cause further street disturbances. Thank you.'

The news went live and cut to the studio, where the questioning of Rahman was described as potentially explosive. An ex-senior police officer, a commentary regular, remarked that whilst it was routine for relatives of a murder victim to be closely questioned, the formal manner of this interview suggested that the police were acting on information received.

Five minutes later the phone rang. It was Jo.

'Hi, Steve.'

'Hi, Jo. Have you seen the news?'

'I'm avoiding the television.'

I told her what had happened.

'And he attended with his solicitor?'

'Yes.'

There was a pause. 'Something happened. It's not going to help the situation on the streets, that's for sure.'

'Are you still at the hotel, Jo?'

There was a pause. 'You're alone?'

'Permanently by the looks of it.'

'Oh.'

'Nothing to do with what happened. Jenny left me yesterday morning and forgot to tell me at the time.'

'Sorry,'

'Don't be.'

There was another pause. 'Does that mean you're available for a drink?'

'That seems a nice idea. It'll have to be here though, I'm expecting a call.'

'No chance of being disturbed?'

'Unlikely. Where are you?'

'Romford. I can be with you in ten minutes.'

I opened the windows, tidied the flat and sprayed air-freshener around the place. I'd barely finished when there was a knock at the door.

Jo was wearing a pale blue halter-necked dress with a black clutch bag. Around her neck was a simple gold chain with a cut diamond cross. She looked stunning.

'Come in.'

'You sure this is okay?'

'Certain.'

As we went through to the living room her perfume side-swiped me and I think it showed in my face. Her smile could have healed the lame.

We sat on the sofa and I explained that I might have to drive to Pitsea later.

'Want me to drive you?' she said. 'Your ankle looks like it could use the rest.'

I hesitated, not wanting to tell her about Rob's sister. 'It might be difficult.'

'We could go back to the hotel afterwards,' she smiled.

'It's just that it's Rob Brody I'm going to see and it's a domestic situation between him and his wife.'

'Okay. But I could wait in the car up the street for you.'

'You sound keen.'

She leant forward and kissed me. 'Aren't you?'

'And you're happy to chauffeur me?'

'I think so. We'll have coffee now, go to Pitsea whenever and then go back to the hotel for a drink afterwards.'

'Sounds great.'

'Good.'

She came to the kitchen with me and stood talking as I made the coffee. I raised the subject of Mohammed Ali Rahman.

'Does it mean he's a suspect?' I asked.

'You're a witness, Steve, I shouldn't talk to you about it.'

'I'm asking you for an opinion, not to divulge evidence.'

Her eyes swept over me and I wondered what she was reading. 'No wonder you get up Neil Menzies' nose. Look, before I was moved off the team there was a lot of discussion about the time it took to report Shenaz Rahman missing and her death. Three days. It's a long time, Steve.'

'Not to mention the cocaine.'

'Exactly.'

We took the coffee back into the living room and sat on the sofa.

'What about Vanzie?' I asked.

'His alibi was too good, they had to let him go.'

'It's back down to me again isn't it?'

Her hand went to my shoulder. 'If you could positively say that it was him it might be a different picture,' she admitted.

'I've gone over it in my mind a thousand times, Jo, and I'm simply not sure.'

'Well he won't be let off the hook. One more piece of evidence against him and he's nicked properly.'

'What about DNA? I know you said before that the body is probably contaminated with the DNA of too many people, but the crowd that stormed on to the track was solidly Asian and if you could find Vanzies's DNA on the corpse it must make it very difficult for him to explain how it got there.'

'Not really. No one knows what happened to that corpse between the railway track and ending up in the Romford Road several hours later. He could claim he got caught up in the riot, anything. No, forensically the corpse is compromised. We need someone who saw what happened at the car. That's the missing piece.'

'The old Asian woman?'

She nodded. 'We've been doing house to house, leaflet drops, appeals on the community radios in the obvious language choices, but we've drawn a blank so far.'

'It was in broad daylight. Someone must have seen something.'

'The riots have seriously hampered us. No one wants to be seen to help the police right now'

'Perhaps Mohammed Ali Rahman might know who she was?'

Her eyes shone. 'Perhaps that's the reason he's been interviewed.'

I could be run over by a steamroller I was that fast. 'It must be painful for you to watch me get there.'

'Not really. You're not a copper, Steve. Personally I think you're doing fine.'

She kissed me again.

'So Mohammed . . .'

She put a finger to my lips. 'Enough. I'm on holiday.'

We kissed again and she laid back into the corner of the sofa, but just as my hand went to her thigh the phone rang.

She smiled. 'Go on, answer it.'

I reached over and lifted the receiver. It was Linda Brody. She was hysterical, barely making sense.

'What's wrong, Linda?'

'It's Rob . . . you come . . .'

'Linda? Linda?'

'Oh please help us, please!'

I could hear noises in the background; crying and someone groaning. Then the phone went dead.

Jo looked at me. 'Problems?'

'By the sound of it. I've got to go to Pitsea, now.'

She picked up her clutch bag. 'Then let's go.'

The Mercedes could really move and she drove north to A12 then to the M25 before turning on to the A13 and gunning it the whole way. It was the longer route and I wouldn't have chosen to go that way, but I didn't own a Merc and it meant she could hit seventy all the way to Pitsea.

We did the journey in twenty-five minutes

On the way it crossed my mind to offer the Brodys my flat, reasoning that I could ask Jenny to stay at her parents while I moved in with Alex. Then Alex's words about putting the Brodys' problems before my own bubbled to the surface.

Jo looked at me out of the corner of her eye. 'How serious is this domestic problem?'

'Rob's? Not good and it seems to have got a whole lot worse tonight.'

'Sure you don't want to tell me about it?'

'To be honest, Jo, I really don't know the full strength of it. I'd be guessing.'

She got that look in her eye again. 'Sure that's the reason?'

'I thought you were on holiday?'

'There are domestics and domestics. At one time if a man murdered his wife it was called a domestic.'

'It's not that sort of problem, Jo.'

'Okay.'

We flashed by a road sign saying Basildon Town Centre and Jo started to slow.

'Another mile up here. Just follow the signs to Pitsea,' I said.

She turned off the dual carriageway a minute later and I directed her through the side streets. The big black Merc drew eyes in a landscape otherwise populated with second-hand family saloons.

I asked Jo to pull up thirty yards short of the house and told her that there was an outside chance we might have passengers on the return journey. Her eyes danced with interest and, despite the claim to be 'on holiday', I knew she was switching on.

As I limped up the short path to the Brodys' front door I could see it had been smashed in. Suddenly Linda Brody appeared in the doorway and came running out to me, red-eyed and shaking.

'I didn't know who else to call, Steve.'

'What is it, Linda?'

She grabbed my arm and led me through the passageway into the living room. The whole place looked like it had been hit by lightning.

Furniture was smashed, carpets pulled up, crockery lay broken on the floor and a bloody smear down one wall ended just above the crumpled form of Rob Brody.

I knelt down next to him, and inspected his injuries. He was barely conscious and groaning. If I hadn't known who it was I wouldn't have recognised him.

His face was blackened and swollen with blood bubbling out of his nose as he breathed and he was shaking from shock. There was a huge purple bruise on his right forearm and the arm was distorted just below the elbow; obviously broken.

'Rob? Rob? Can you hear me?'

He opened one eye and mumbled something I couldn't catch.

Shock and anger hit me, making me fight for control.

'Who did this, Linda?' My voice was hoarse, breaking.

The daughter clung to her legs.

'I don't know,' she sobbed. 'He won't let me call the police or an ambulance.'

'Well we can't leave him like this. He needs a doctor.'

She wrung her hands. 'They'll hurt him even more.'

'Look, Linda, I've got a friend with a car outside. Where's the nearest hospital with an Accident and Emergency department?'

'Basildon. It's off the A13. Take the slip road at the Five Bells roundabout, then it's half a mile on towards Basildon Town Centre.'

'Have you got someone you can go to?'

'Friends at Canvey.'

'Go there. Write me down their phone number and address. I'll get Rob to hospital and ring you when I know what's happening.'

She hesitated.

'Linda, write down the details, get in your car and go! And write down Rob's sister's address as well.'

'Rob won't like . . .'

'Just do it, Linda.'

She scribbed on a scrap of paper and thrust it into my hand.

'Now, help me get him out to the car,' I said softly.

As we came out the house Jo brought the car up level with the pathway. She didn't ask any questions, just got out the car and helped Linda and me pile Rob on to the back seat.

I turned back to Linda. 'Lock the door and go now. I'll ring you as soon as I know anything.'

She nodded and ran into the house, then emerged again with her daughter and put her in the Mondeo. We watched them pull away and then I climbed into the back seat of the Mercedes and held Rob.

'Can you tell me now?' asked Jo over her shoulder, as we sped back down the A13.

'Later.'

22

They took one look at Rob in the A and E department and rushed him through to be seen straight away.

After ten minutes a doctor came out to the waiting room and asked who we were. I told him I was a friend and he asked if my ankle had been hurt at the same time as Rob got his injuries.

Both Jo and I had blood on us from where we'd carried Rob into the hospital and the vibe I picked up from the doctor was that he thought we weren't being straight with him.

Sure enough ten minutes later a police car turned up outside A and E and two coppers came in and went up to reception.

'They're here for us,' I said to Jo.

'Want to tell me a little of this before things get really complicated, Steve?'

As I gave her a précised version of what Linda had told me the doctor came out and spoke to the two policemen. They turned to look at us and walked over.

Jo opened her clutch bag and took out her warrant card.

'Mr Jay got a phone call about an hour ago from Mr Brody's wife. She was hysterical and we drove straight down.'

I explained that I worked with Rob and knew little beyond what they had already been told.

'Where is Mrs Brody now?' asked the taller of the policemen.

I had no choice but to tell him. The other policeman peeled away and made a radio call.

'From what the doctor tells me Mr Brody is in a bad way. Have you any idea why this happened?'

Before I could answer Jo spoke up. 'Mr Jay is Rob Brody's boss. He felt obliged to respond when Linda Brody asked him, but other than that he's in the dark about this.'

The policemen looked at me.

'That's right,' I said.

They hesitated and for a moment I thought they were going to question us further, but Jo's warrant card had taken the heat off. They made some notes and took down our addresses, saying that we might have to make statements later. Jo asked if we could go and was told yes. Outside I looked at her.

'You were economical with the truth,' I said.

'Bill Proctor used to be in Essex. I'll make sure that they get the full information through him,' she said.

'So we haven't lied?'

'They'll talk to Linda Brody and get what they need. All you know is what you've been told. That's hearsay – useless as evidence.'

'But Rob's sister needs to be checked out. She could be hurt as well.'

'Look, I've just extracted you from all this, Steve. Go looking for his sister and you cross that line again.'

'He's one of my firefighters, Jo.'

'He is, his sister isn't. There's something heavy going on here, Steve. You could be walking into anything.'

She was right, but the anger was boiling away inside of me, though I managed to keep it from my voice.

'I just want to check on his sister. Make sure she's okay.'

Jo crossed her arms. 'Do you know what she looks like?'

'No.'

'Well?'

'I want to knock at the door, talk to her if I can.'

Jo closed her eyes. 'If there is anything remotely iffy when we get there, then we back off and call Essex police.'

'Agreed.'

It took us ten minutes to get to Laindon and another fifteen to find our way on to the estate. I didn't expect much after Tug Hardy's description, but I still wasn't prepared for what we saw.

Burnham Villas was a soulless, needle-infested rat-hole that condemned its young from the moment they were pushed from the womb.

It was the type of 'concept' development once mooted as the future of urban housing and had instead become little more than burnt-out garages, disembowelled rubbish bags and urine-soaked alleys and walkways.

Each graffiti-scarred concrete wall, each abandoned car, helped suck the life from its inhabitants, so that they might be less than they should, so that they were robbed of the very nerve to try for something better.

'I'll go try the front door. I suggest that you stay mobile otherwise you'll attract the local wildlife.'

'Are you sure you want to do this, Steve?'

'I want to make sure she's okay. That's all.'

'I'll circle and meet you back here in fifteen minutes. Don't be late.'

I nodded and walked as fast as my ankle let me through an alleyway that led towards the estate's centre. A group of youths were crowded around a beat-up Vauxhall Astra parked next to a low concrete structure and the driver was revving the engine to no purpose. Several turned and watched me as I made my way past a block of flats.

A baseball-capped head appeared over a third-storey balcony and a heavy gobbet of spit smacked into the paving stones in front of me. The would-be anointer called out and waved at the group around the car and they shouted back. Although aimed, I judged the spit to be a world-view rather than personal.

Each five-storey block of flats was identical and arranged as part of a rectangle with each block facing a refuse-strewn mud strip that had originally been a lawn and trees.

The address Linda Brody gave me was 107 Burnham Villas. It was a second-floor flat in a block where all the lobby lights had been smashed and, with the light fading, the stairwell was gloomy and forbidding.

It told myself that it was depressing rather than threatening, but I felt off my patch and vulnerable with a suspect ankle.

The front door of 107 didn't offer hope for what lay beyond. Its original yellow was barely visible under a camouflage of dirt and gouge marks and the doorjamb was split near the lock; like someone had taken a boot to it recently.

There was no bell or knocker, just a set of four holes where the letterbox had once been and was now boarded up on the outer side by plywood.

I banged on the door with the side of my fist and waited. Nothing.

I banged harder and waited again.

Outside I could hear the mindless shouting of the youths as they amused themselves with the echo-effect off the flats whilst their cerebrally challenged mate revved the car engine louder and louder.

I thumped on the door again, but again there was no response.

I wanted to go then, to walk back to the Mercedes and the prospect of the night in bed with Jo. But Rob had put himself on the line for his sister and I felt I couldn't ignore that.

I eyed the damaged doorjamb and tested the door gently with my shoulder. It sprung open at the first push.

The first thing that hit me was the smell, a thick, musty smell that hung in the air and clung to the back of my throat.

The hallway itself was bare of carpet and there was just enough light to see that every door off the hallway was closed. I went inside and pushed the front door closed behind me, careful to use my handkerchief so as not to touch anything with my hands.

Opening the door immediately on my right I found myself in a grubby kitchen. There was a small Formica-topped table with two chairs at its centre with coffee and sugar granules scattered across its top.

Used crockery was lying in dingy water in the sink and the whole place stank.

I left the kitchen door open to borrow light from the window and went back into the hallway.

Next I tried the door on the left.

It was the living room, if you could call it living. There was an old stained sofa against one wall and a threadbare rug beneath a broken coffee table. A set of dirty net curtains masked the window and stopped anyone peering in.

But that was all.

I'd seen flops used by meths drinkers that had more comfort than this place.

I felt for Rob then and guessed at the burden that he'd been carrying for God knows how long. No wonder he didn't want to talk about this, no wonder he couldn't turn away. If this was how his sister lived, then she was a long way down a very dark road. Perhaps beyond help.

The next door I tried was a bedroom.

Again it was sparsely furnished. The double bed had a wrought iron frame and there were ropes tied to the bed-ends. A thin semen-stained duvet lay half on the bed and half on the floor, like someone had left in a hurry. Clothing was piled haphazardly on an old wickerwork chair and shoes lay scattered around.

I backed out of the bedroom into the hallway. The smell was stronger here. I opened the door on my right. The bathroom.

And froze.

Blood was everywhere; up the walls, pooled in the bath,

smeared against the window and splattered across the poly-
thene-covered floor. Small, shapeless pieces of flesh lay in the
bottom of the bath, the detritus of a butchered body.

And the smell – the smell was overwhelming.

A deep congealed puddle lay just inside the door contained
by the crumpled sheet of polythene and as the door edge
caught the sheet it ran in an obscene rivulet into the corner of
the room.

Vomit surged to the back of my throat.

I was panting from shock, my pulse racing, but then my
heart gave one tremendous jolt – the blood on the tile-sur-
round was still running down into the bath.

Get out!

My hands were shaking as I pulled the door closed and
turned to head back down the hallway. But a sound at the front
door stopped me.

They're back!

I opened the bedroom door and stepped inside closing it
behind me and wedging the side of my foot tightly against the
door; keeping absolutely still and listening.

I heard them walk down the hallway and go into the bathroom – two, perhaps three of them – then the sound of the
water rushing from the taps.

The sounds of splashing and movement went on for several
minutes; time to wash the blood away maybe, but not enough time
to remove all the DNA evidence – the splashes of blood that would
seep into crevices and slivers of flesh that would be impossible to
see, but would reveal themselves under forensic examination.

As a clean up job it was cursory, flawed.

Then the noise of water stopped and I heard a mumbled
voice. Through the door I couldn't make out what was being
said, but a single set of feet walked towards the front door.

Why had they not all gone? Final search of the flat?

I edged back from the door. If someone came in I'd hit as

hard as I could and then go past him, dealing with anyone else as swiftly and nastily as I could. I was in no condition to get into a running fight.

The low voice sounded again and then nothing.

The rush of adrenaline was making my body shake uncontrollably as my senses strained for the slightest indication that they were coming in the bedroom.

Instinctively my fists balled and a litany sounded in my head: 'punch the throat, kick their legs out from under them and stamp down hard – throat or shin.'

But instead I heard the muffled sound of footsteps moving towards the front door and then the door opening and closing. I stayed where I was, not daring to move, giving them enough time to clear the building.

The minutes ticked by and just when I thought it was safe to move I heard another sound.

At first I thought I'd miscounted; that one had stayed behind. Then I recognised what I was hearing and the first wisps of smoke crept under the bedroom door.

Fire – the ultimate evidence destroyer.

I bent down next to the door and put the back of my hand against the metal handle. It was cold.

More smoke was percolating under the door and I pulled it open slightly, keeping my head low.

The fire was just getting into the hallway with flames coming from the bathroom. If I tried to go past I might make it but would probably get burnt.

I closed the door again and went to the bedroom window. The drop was twenty-five feet. I'd survived, but would undoubtedly break my ankles – if I were lucky.

There had to be another option.

I looked around and saw the duvet. I pulled it off the bed and crouched down behind the door.

This time I opened the door wider and smoke billowed into

the room. I got down on my stomach and peered around the edge of the door; the flames were building and rising upward, starting to snake across the ceiling of the hallway.

It was now or never.

I wrapped the duvet around me, held my breath and got to my feet, bent over double. In a half-run, half-shuffle, I lurched out the bedroom into the smoke-filled hallway turning my back towards the bathroom.

Immediately the duvet burst into flames. I held on to it for four or five steps and then abandoned it, but it had done its job. Once beyond the flames from the bathroom I was past the worst, but the fast movement caused my ankle to give way and I fell heavily.

The smoke was mushrooming down from the ceiling and I was forced to crawl, face down, feeling the heat at my back and fighting to breathe.

I reached the front door and stood up, pulling it open and falling through the gap on to the landing.

Down the hallway the fire was building rapidly with the fresh oxygen from the open front door. I knew I had to close it and pulled myself upright using the banister rail on the landing. I reached out, closed the door and then hammered on number 109, the next flat.

A pale, fair-haired woman in her early twenties answered the door and looked shocked when she saw me.

'Have you got a phone?' I asked urgently.

'Yes . . . why?'

'Call the fire brigade and the police. There's a fire in number 107. Now!'

She looked past me and saw the smoke, turned and ran back into the flat. I hobbled up the stairs and banged on the door of the flat above 107 and then the adjoining flat, shouting at the startled occupiers and telling them to get out and to knock on all the other doors as they went.

The stairwell filled with people and I made my way downstairs and out into the fresh air. I took one last look up at the living room window; it was already starting to blacken as the fire took hold.

As the occupants of the block streamed out of the front doors, others from the estate made their way towards the excitement. I walked as fast as the ankle would let me, back to Jo in the car; the fear melting into relief and the anger into barely suppressed rage.

23

We spent over two hours at Basildon police station making statements.

Between the business with Rob Brody at the hospital and then his sister's flat they were less than impressed and made me go over the whole thing from start to finish half a dozen times.

Having Jo along was a mixed blessing.

There was some suspicion that she'd been working Essex police area without proper liaison or protocol. She had a separate interview with a Detective Chief Superintendent who was less than pleased to find her involved and far from happy that he'd been dragged away from a party to deal with a suspected murder and no body to show for it.

They kicked us out around half eleven with the promise of further interviews in the days ahead.

When we climbed back into the Mercedes I tried to apologise to her.

'I'm sorry that . . .'

She shook her head. 'What happened wasn't your doing and, as I told that anally retentive Chief Superintendent, if you hadn't been there there'd have no knowledge of the crime.'

'I don't know what to say.'

'Try saying that from now on you'll back off now and let the police do their job.'

I agreed, but was contemplating the opposite. I thought I was pretty used to just about everything the world could throw at me, but the thought of those bastards hacking Rob's sister to bits sent a cold and insistent anger shooting through my veins.

Jo gave a half smile. 'I think it's too late for that drink now.' She looked at her dress and at me. 'I don't think we'd get in anywhere in this state anyway.'

'Sorry.'

'And stop saying you're sorry.' Her voice softened. 'Are you okay?'

'Fine.'

'Are you sure, Steve? You may think you're fine, but it's been a hell of a week.'

'What d'you recommend?'

'That I take you home and you get some sleep.'

'Don't want to join me?'

'Not tonight.' She paused. 'What have you got on tomorrow?'

'Sunday? Nothing.'

'We'll go somewhere, away from any possible drama. Lunch in a pub maybe and back to the hotel.'

She was a diamond. 'That sounds good.'

She smiled then. Her eyes lit up and she leaned forward and kissed me.

'You're a complex man, Steve, and I suspect that you're always going to be one gear shift away from a car crash.'

'That a problem then?' I grinned.

'Fatal.'

When we arrived back at Prentice Road I kissed her goodnight and she said that she'd ring late morning to arrange a time for the pick-up.

As I climbed the stairs to the flat it occurred to me that I'd blown a night with a gorgeous woman and substituted it with a classic Jay screw-up. I told myself that I did it for Rob, but did I?

Candle flames and a boneheaded moth seemed more likely.

In the flat I rang Linda Brody and apologised for not ringing earlier and explained it away by saying the police had turned up at the hospital after which I spent a number of hours down at Basildon police station.

She said that she'd rung a couple of hours ago and Rob was unconscious. His condition was described as poorly. I'd apparently just caught her before she left for the hospital to stay the night.

I deliberately didn't mention Burnham Villas; she had enough grief without adding to the burden. It wouldn't take the police long to catch up with her and find out the full story, whatever that was.

I said that I'd ring tomorrow to find out about Rob.

Next I showered and threw my blood and carbon-stained clothes in the linen basket before making myself coffee and sitting down to catch up on the news.

The world hadn't stopped because of my adventures.

Disturbances were still breaking out in Muslim enclaves around London, particularly in the Green Street and Katherine Road areas of Forest Gate, but generally it was more sporadic with mainly youths rather than the community at large involved.

There was a piece on the Shenaz Rahman murder, but again there was little that was fresh. At half twelve I took the phone off the hook, fell into bed and slept like the dead.

Sunday morning brought a clear sky and more moderate temperatures, around the low seventies. As I made myself breakfast I reflected on Jo's attitude after the Basildon situation. She'd been more philosophical than I deserved and I wondered why.

At the hotel, when she'd told me not to make love to her but to have sex, I'd read at as 'don't come close'; now I wasn't so sure.

I didn't want to read too much into things – I barely knew

her – but my attraction to her was strong, and maybe hers was to me.

When the phone rang at ten I expected it to be her, but it was Alex.

'Stevie, you're a hard man to get hold of. Your phone's been engaged for hours.'

'Took it off the hook last night.'

'Why?'

'People keep ringing me.'

I chuckled as I heard him sigh.

'You've the makings of a first-class idiot, Stevie.'

'And I'm your best pal, Alex. What does that say about you?'

'Aye, you've got me there. Are you available today?'

'Not really. I'm out for the day.'

'I won't ask who with.'

'Good. What is it you want, Alex?'

'Do you remember me telling you how I first met Mohammed Ali Rahman?'

'At a fund-raiser for his political campaign. You were a guest of a chap called David Khan.'

'Well done. Listen, something has come up involving Khan. Could be money involved and if you're going to split from Jenny you're going to need every penny.'

'I'm not sure, Alex. Life has been a little too eventful lately.'

'Oh?'

I told him all that had happened at Basildon. He listened in complete silence. When I'd finished he whistled softly.

'They murdered his sister?'

'Looks that way. Between Shenaz Rahman, the cinema fire and now this lot I'm up to my arse in statements. I intend to stay away from drama for the foreseeable future.'

'Stevie, this will be very straight forward, I promise you. Come and listen to a proposal. We'll pay a fee just for the consultation. You could use the money.'

'And no doubt you and Andrew could use the business that will be coming your way.'

'Aye.'

'Can this wait till Monday, Alex?'

'Monday morning, my office, at say ten?'

'I'll listen, but that's all.'

'That's all I want. I'll ring if there's a change of time.'

The minute I put the phone down on Alex it rang again. Jo.

'Morning, sleep well?' Her voice was silky.

'Very well. You?'

'Well after I'd had a bath and a stiff gin I felt more human.'

'Sorry about yesterday.'

'You're doing it again, Steve. What happened happened. Are you still on for today?'

'Please.'

'I'll pick you up in an hour.'

The rest of that day was a marked contrast to the previous one.

We lunched in a North Essex pub in the centre of a village with a green and a ducking stool. Basildon it wasn't. Prentice Road it would never be.

Afterwards we went for a walk along a riverbank that ran by the rear of the pub. We talked, kissed and discovered a little bit about each other. Neither of us had lived the perfect life, clearly both of us were in some respects responsible.

The partners we choose, the lifestyle we lead, has more to do with us as individuals than the circumstances that life bestows.

Choice.

That was Anne's word.

Settling for what we feel we must rather than that which would promise more, but would equally lead us into a game of chance. Cowardice is the hidden shaper of many lives and all lives in some aspect.

There, with Jo, on the edge on a riverbank, I realised that life was offering me more – if I had the nerve to try.

When we got back to the hotel she was very quiet. No labels were attached to what we did then, no words of proscription, of safety. All I knew for sure was that afterwards we stayed in each other's arms and kissed long after the heat had passed.

I stayed the night and woke up with her pressed into me and the sensation of her skin on mine immediately aroused me.

I think that was the best then – no barriers and no inhibition.

We had breakfast brought up and talked throughout, stopping only to catch an eye, to hold a gaze and I swear at some point she blushed, though only she knew why.

Just after nine she drove me to Alex's offices in Upminster and we agreed to meet later. I would phone her mobile, probably late afternoon.

Alex ran a loss adjusters with his cousin Andrew in Station Road. The offices were on the first floor and as I climbed the stairs Alex was waiting at the top.

'You managed to get a lift I see. Nice car.'

'I'm starting to dread our conversations. It's like going to confession.'

'Much to confess then?'

'Yeah, I don't have any real friends.'

'We are sharp this morning.'

'I wonder why?'

He chuckled as he showed me through to his office. We looked in on Andrew on the way and said hello. Andrew gave me a weird look and my antennae extended to match it.

Once in his office the banter stopped and Alex was all business.

'Right, Stevie. Tell me about the cinema fire again.'

I went through it thoroughly and Alex listened and made notes. When I'd finished he stayed silent and thought, drumming his fingers on the desk as he did so. Eventually he exhaled audibly and shook his head.

'Stevie, I have a problem.'

'Go on.'

'David Khan is a client of an insurance group who retain us. He owned the cinema in Green Street that burnt down. You may remember me telling you that Khan has expanded recently into the area of general entertainment rather than just for Asian customers. He may be over-extended – not sure. However, what is sure is that the cinema was losing money. Asian youth is not apparently following in its parents' footsteps.'

'That's integration for you.'

'Andrew and I have been asked to look at his businesses. The insurance company feel that the motive for the fire is open to question.'

'Not racist?'

'Exactly.'

'So why am I being told this?'

'I need someone to dig around the edges, look into what Khan is and has been doing. Has he need of cash right now? You get the idea?'

'You want me to play detective?'

'Yes.'

'No.'

'No?'

'Yes.'

'Correct me if I'm wrong, but aren't you the man about to split his income into two households? You're already in financial trouble?'

'And you're being the Good Samaritan?'

'The provider of lucrative work.'

'I'm still waiting for the money to come through for the Sheldon case, Alex, and that was six months ago.'

'That'll come to court soon. Inside three months. When the convictions come in we'll all get paid.'

'I'm on sick leave, Alex. The fire brigade aren't very forgiving if you do part-time work while sick.'

'True. But you're not going to be sick forever.'

'I'm taking the next tour off. The ankle is still swollen and the past few days haven't helped.'

'Does that mean that when you're fit you'll take the job?'

'It means, Alex, that right now my main preoccupation is rest and recuperation.'

'But then you'll consider it – for the money?'

'Maybe.'

'Good.'

'I thought you said today was going to be a meeting with Khan?'

Alex looked at his watch. 'Khan is coming here at eleven to discuss the situation. A sort of preliminary interview. He is coming willingly and will be bringing legal counsel.'

'What!'

'Calm down, Stevie. All I want you to do is to sit and listen – and read him. You're awfully good at that. I think that paranoia of yours is a great bullshit detector. If Khan is crooked I think you'll sniff it out.'

'Khan here? With legal counsel? Jesus Christ, Alex, you get worse.'

'Relax. I'll introduce you as a consultant. You needn't speak.'

'I look like I'm dressed for a business meeting don't I? No wonder Andrew looked at me like I had two heads.'

He smiled. 'I think it's great that you're dressed casually. It'll throw up questions in his mind, make him uneasy.'

'That's the trouble when you live alone, you watch too many videos.'

'Do you want to borrow my electric razor?'

'Please.'

After I'd shaved Alex showed me a file on Khan. He owned two Asian cinemas and three restaurants and a partial interest in an import/export business. At first glance he was a rich man getting richer by the day.

Were any of his other businesses losing money besides the cinema that burnt down?

I glanced up to see Alex watching me.

'Interesting man isn't he?'

'You like Khan?' I asked.

'He's great company.'

'Doesn't mean he's straight.'

'No. It doesn't.'

Khan turned up at eleven sharp and arrived with his solicitor. Iqbal Asif.

Asif nodded to me and showed no surprise that I was there. Khan greeted Alex like a friend or, at least, someone he regarded as an ally.

Khan was a man pretty much in the same mould as Mohammed Ali Rahman, tall with a neatly trimmed beard and celebrity looks. Where he differed was the vibe that came off him. He was all smiles and flamboyant gestures.

How much of that was front I had no idea.

'Please sit,' said Alex to them. 'I asked Steve Jay to this meeting because he has expertise which may shed some light on what happened at the cinema.'

'Mr Jay and I have already met, have we not?' said Asif.

I nodded and shook his hand and then Khan's. So far it was all pretty laid back and no one except me was spooked.

'Right,' said Alex, 'perhaps we could start by asking you, David – is that all right – David?'

Khan held up a hand and smiled. 'Of course.'

'. . . If we could ask David about the cinema in Green Street?'

Khan nodded. 'Business was good up to about nine months ago. This year we've had a fall in profits, especially throughout the summer months.' He made a face. 'When it's hot cinemas don't do so well. When it rains or is cold, they do. The drop didn't worry me. We'll recover in the winter.'

'You've other cinemas?' Alex asked.

'Yes.'

'How are they doing?'

'Fine.'

'And your restaurants?'

'Fair to good.'

'What about your other interests?'

Khan was about to answer when Asif interrupted. 'All Mr Khan's businesses are healthy, as his tax returns show.'

'Except the cinema,' put in Alex.

'Of course,' Asif replied, 'but there is of course the situation in the area.'

'Situation?' queried Alex.

Asif looked at Khan. 'It's a largely ethnic area, racists are always active, looking for trouble. You must be following the news?'

'Of course. Is that connected to the cinema fire?'

'I believe it is a line of police inquiry.'

'Have there been any racist incidents prior to the recent ones?'

Again Asif interjected. 'Mr Khan has owned the cinema for only eighteen months. We have no knowledge of what occurred before then.'

'Personal enemies?'

Asif was going to speak again, but Khan spoke across him. 'No. At least not any of which I'm aware, Alex.'

'Any prospective business ventures meeting with problems?' continued Alex.

'No,' said Asif before Khan could answer.

'So what do you think happened at the cinema then?' asked Alex, looking directly at Khan.

'I don't know. I'd like to think it was an accident, but in the present climate who can say?'

'You are a friend of Mohammed Ali Rahman, aren't you, David?'

'You know I am, Alex.'

'Do you have any business connections with him?'

Asif cut in. 'What are you inferring, Mr McGregor?'

Alex looked at him sharply. 'You brought up the question of racism, Mr Asif. Wasn't Shenaz Rahman attacked by racists?'

Asif shot Khan a look and then leaned forward in his chair. 'That's a matter of a police investigation and doesn't in any way involve Mr Khan.'

'No. No, of course,' said Alex, 'but I was thinking that if racists were involved in burning down the cinema and racists were involved in the murder of Shenaz Rahman and given that you're a friend of Mohammed Ali Rahman . . .'

'I've no idea where you're going with this, Mr McGregor. Are you speculating or asking a question?'

'I'm not sure,' smiled Alex, 'thinking aloud maybe.'

'Have you any more questions for Mr Khan relating to the cinema?'

Alex thought about that. 'No. No, I don't believe I have.'

Asif and Khan stood up.

'But I might have after I've spoken to a few more people,' said Alex.

The handshakes going out were less warm than at the start, although Khan flashed a smile as he left.

Alex gave it a minute and then turned to me.

'Well? What did you think?'

'I think you deliberately tried to rattle them.'

'And?'

'And I think they thought that you'd stepped off a space-ship.'

'Wild idea then – the link with Rahman?'

'Off the wall from where I was sitting. Unless you know something that you're not telling me.'

He shook his head. 'And Khan? What did you make of him?'

'I read nothing either way. He could be a good guy and he could not. That Asif is sharp though.'

Alex smiled wolfishly. 'That's his job and very good he is at it.'

'Do you really think it's possible that Khan burnt down his own cinema?'

'I don't know, Stevie. I was hoping you'd help me find out.'

24

For the next fifteen minutes Alex tried to persuade me to take on the inquiry work and, as tempting as it was, I turned him down.

I also declined to take the fee for the hour's 'consultancy', because that would have meant I was a bought man, which was of course Alex's intention. But I hinted before I left that I'd keep my nose to the wind and, if I happened across anything, I'd be back and take the money off him quicker than you can say 'Stop, thief'.

There was no point in being perverse.

I looked at my watch and it was getting on for half eleven when I escaped Alex. He offered to give me a lift, but I knew he'd work on me during the journey so I said I'd grab a cab at Upminster Station.

The ankle was better as I walked the hundred yards or so to the station, but I still didn't fancy my chances of returning to work tomorrow, Blue watch's first day duty. Anyway, a week off and the company of Jo seemed preferable to limping around the station on light duty.

Paddy Ryan had said to wait for the swelling to go down before I went for treatment on the ankle and now seemed as good a time as any to give him a call.

When I got back to the flat I rang Paddy who said that he'd be down at the gym from two p.m. onwards.

I debated calling Jo and asking her to meet up earlier, but instead rang Basildon Hospital, told them I was Rob's boss and asked how he was. They declined to answer, but said that I could speak to Linda if I wanted.

Linda came on the phone and she sounded exhausted.

'Hello, Steve.'

'How is he, Linda?'

'Still unconscious. There's a police guard by the bed. Something's happened, but they won't tell me what.'

It was obviously connected to his sister, but I didn't feel she needed to be told why right now and either the police thought the same or were playing cautious. For all they knew Rob might be involved.

'I'll come down. Linda. I'll be there in a hour.'

Before I left I checked the answerphone and there were no messages.

A spasm of guilt hit me and I thought about ringing Jenny at her parents' house. I had told Alex I still cared for her, and I did, but what could I say that she didn't already know?

And it was too soon.

This was the final break and if it was to work there had to be a period of separation, so that a clear unbridgeable gap lay between us. Only then could we address what would happen in the future, discuss practicalities, finance.

The meeting, when it came, would have to be on neutral ground, Alex's house. He'd enjoy playing referee. A few more days, perhaps a week, then I would phone her.

The drive to Basildon Hospital wasn't a problem. The ankle held up well.

I found Linda in the waiting room outside a guarded side ward. She looked like she hadn't slept for a week.

'Any change?' I asked.

She shook her head. 'He's been unconscious since shortly after he was admitted.'

'What do the doctors say?'

'I can't get any sense out of them. All I know for certain is that he had a fractured skull and was bleeding internally when he was brought in.'

'What have the police said?'

Linda looked to her right at the police guard and led me a short way down the corridor, out of earshot.

'They seemed more concerned with his sister,' she whispered '– kept asking questions about her. I told them that I knew nothing. Rob wouldn't want me to tell them.'

'Tell them what, Linda?'

She hesitated. 'Maria, Rob's sister, has got herself into some trouble.'

'Drugs trouble?'

She looked in the direction of the police guard and walked me further down the corridor.

'Something else.'

'What?'

'Maria had got herself a job recently – she used to be quite good-looking, still would be if she cleaned herself up.

'Go on.'

Linda nodded. 'Maria used to be a dancer, a lap dancer. She always had a wild streak. She slept around and fell in with the wrong crowd.'

'Druggies?'

'No,' she corrected me, 'Pushers, big league stuff.'

'When was this?'

'Couple of years ago. She was glamorous then, a beautiful girl.'

'And?'

'She got into cocaine; inevitable in that company. At first she loved it, said it gave her a real buzz. Her boyfriend was controlling the drugs going through just about every other club around here.'

'Her boyfriend?'

'Karl Baker, and he is one nasty piece of work, Steve. He treated her well at first, but then abused her.'

'Abused her?'

'Got her onto crack. She lost a lot of weight and looked half-dead most of the time. It took over her life and she became very unreliable. Before long they sacked her as a dancer. Baker made her work for her crack after that – you know, with his mates, two or three of them at a time. Rob was beside himself.'

'That's hard.'

She sighed heavily. 'Maria got pregnant. God knows whose it was. She was in a dreadful state. Baker abandoned her and Rob felt that that was his one chance to get her away from her past life.'

'He started helping her?'

'In every way he could, but by then she was in a bad way and she used Rob, told him she was off the crack, but it was all lies.'

'It usually is. A crack-head can't tell the difference, Linda.'

The tears started to flow and as I put my hand on her shoulder she hugged me, turning her face into my chest.

'Rob didn't believe her, Steve, but wouldn't turn his back. She bled him for money. She got so much out of him we got into trouble ourselves. We argued about it – terribly. I hated her then. She'd ruined her own life and was ruining ours.'

'When are we talking about now, Linda?'

'The last few months. I put pressure on Rob not give her any more money till she promised to come off the crack and stay off it.

'And?'

'He did it. He said he'd help Maria only if she helped herself.' Linda took a handkerchief out and blew her nose. 'Then she turned up one night in a terrible state, demanding money. Rob was on night work and I told her to go to hell. Which she did.'

'I'm not with you?'

'She went back to Baker and begged him for crack. He laughed at her. Told her she was a whore and should earn her money on the street. She said that she'd do anything, so he promised to get her a job. But it was a sick joke. It was washing glasses in the same disco where she'd been a dancer.'

'She was working . . . she still works there now does she?'

Linda shook her head. 'No. The disco burned down two weeks ago. Three people were killed, over twenty injured. You must have read about it.'

25

I drove to the 1916 Club, Paddy's gym, straight from the hospital.

On the journey back I tried to get my head around all that Linda had said. Rob had been dealing with a nightmare, on his own, because he didn't want people to know what his sister had become.

I kept thinking about his sister and the old expression that if you lived with dogs you get fleas, but whatever my view on the stupidity of using coke, let alone crack, no one deserved to die like that.

Or the baby.

Did Linda say how many months pregnant Maria was? I couldn't remember. It was a complete nightmare, and for Linda and Rob it was still going on.

When I arrived at the gym only a handful of people were training. It generally didn't get busy until the evening.

Paddy was standing at the far end in deep conversation with Tug Hardy. Aaron, the son, was sporting a black eye and leaning against the wall with his hands in his pockets looking thoroughly pissed off.

As Paddy saw me he held a hand up and Tug Hardy gave a nod.

'Paddy, Tug,' I nodded. 'Something wrong?'

Paddy looked at Tug.

'He's gone back on the gear,' said Tug venomously, 'All that work blown because of . . .' he shook his head, anger cutting off his words. 'I'm sorry, Paddy. It's been an absolute waste of your time.'

'How did he get the eye?' I asked.

Paddy rolled his eyes as if to say shut up.

Tug Hardy looked at me evenly. 'I gave it to him. And if he goes back on the gear after this I'll punch him fuckin' sense-less.'

'I'm still willing to work with him, Tug, but not till it's out of his system,' said Paddy gently.

'D'you hear that?' Hardy shouted at his son. 'You don't deserve fuckin' help! There's a man here trying to help you and there's you pissing it up the wall.'

Aaron Hardy looked at Paddy and then at the floor.

'Sorry, Paddy,' he muttered.

'Sorry, Paddy! Paddy! Mister Fuckin' Ryan to you,' snarled Tug.

'Sorry, Mr Ryan.'

'You listen to your dad now, Aaron. Get yourself cleaned up and I'll see you soon,' replied Paddy.

Tug Hardy shook hands with Paddy and nodded to me. Then grabbed his son by the arm and frog-marched him from the gym.

'It's a shame, the lad's got potential, real potential,' said Paddy, shaking his head. 'Now, how's that ankle?'

'Getting better. It could use some treatment, I think.'

'Right. Let's get you up on the bench and take a look.'

We went through to the treatment room at the rear of the gym and Paddy examined the ankle, running his hands over the swollen joint, feeling for heat. Then he cupped my heel in one hand and gently manipulated the ankle with the other until I winced.

He puffed out his cheeks. 'Well it's not gone down as much as I hoped it might.'

'I'm afraid it got damaged again.'

'Eh?'

I told him about the cinema fire, but kept it simple.

'I swear you were born when lightning struck a goat. No wonder it's taking its time. Have you been icing it?'

'Religiously, Paddy.'

'Good. Now, are you working?'

'No, I'm off sick.'

'Well then, you've no excuse now, have you? Rest and ice it for fifteen minutes, twice a day.'

'Is there anything you can do?'

'Not much. I'll massage some of that fluid away, but rest, ice, compression and elevation will do the bulk of it.'

He felt the ankle again and got me to rotate the ankle. It hurt on the outside of the joint.

'You could have some ligament damage there, maybe tendons, not sure. If we can get the swelling down I'll start on ultrasound.'

For the next forty minutes Paddy massaged the ankle. Afterwards he gave me some heavy fabric tape and instructions on how to apply the tape in line with the tendons to take some of the strain off the joint.

'Now, take it easy. No charging about.'

I grinned. 'It feels better already.'

'Come back tomorrow, around five.'

We went back into the gym and found Tug Hardy training. He was hitting the bag ferociously and the shock of the heavy blows was making the bag jerk around.

Paddy nodded in approval. 'Now, that is the right way to hit a bag. The bag should jump when you hit it, not swing away. He was a good fighter, Tug Hardy.' Paddy cranked his head to one side. 'You know he blew it through drink?'

'No, I didn't.'

'Well he did. Beat the British champion in a non-title fight and then let it go to his head. That's why he's so hard on young Aaron. He's scared the lad will go the same way with drugs.'

'Explains a lot.'

'Can't live your life fighting shadows though, Steve. Face up to all things and be as kind to yourself as you can,' he held up a finger, 'and torture your body regularly in the gym.'

'Of course, Paddy.'

'You came back then, Tug,' said Paddy as we approached the sweating Hardy.

He stopped and breathed out audibly. 'I dropped him off and came back to beat the hell out of something. If I don't I swear I'll belt him again.'

'Is he back with that crowd again, Tug?' asked Paddy.

Hardy took his bag gloves off and threw them on the ground.

'Said he was going to visit his mother.' He shook his head in bewilderment. 'I can't tell him not to, can I? So when he's down there he looks up his so-called fuckin' mates.'

My ears pricked up. 'Back to Burnham Villas, Tug?'

Hardy's face was wary. 'Yeah. Why?'

I moved forward and dropped my voice. 'Has Aaron ever mentioned any names in connection with the drugs?'

There was a stillness about Hardy and had Paddy not been there I think he'd have torn into me.

'He's a firefighter, not a copper, Tug,' put in Paddy quickly.

'I still want to know why you're asking,' Hardy said, not taking his eyes off me.

'A friend of mine has a sister, she's got in with the wrong crowd, dealers, and she hasn't come out of it too well.'

'What does this have to do with Aaron?'

'She lives in Burnham Villas.'

Hardy's head came forward, inches from mine. 'And your interest is what exactly?'

'I've become involved.'

A malicious grin crossed his face. 'You mean you're looking to sort the people who got your mate's sister on to gear?'

'Thinking about it.'

'You must have some names yourself then?'

'One.'

'I'm listening.'

'Baker,' I said, 'Karl Baker.'

Hardy nodded. 'Well you're ambitious, I'll give you that.'

'You know him then?'

'Oh yeah, I know him. He's big league and if you don't mind me saying, you're not.'

'Well I might have to cheat then,' I said levelly.

'He's game, I'll give you that, Paddy, he's game.' Hardy picked up the bag gloves and put them back on. 'So if you catch up with Baker, and it's a big if, what d'you intend doing.'

'I think he topped my mate's sister. I want to see him go down for it.'

Hardy looked left and right furiously, then put his head against mine again. Paddy moved in and put an arm between us.

'You are a nutter,' hissed Hardy. 'Baker will have you chopped up. Now I'm telling you this cos you're a friend of Paddy's – don't go near Baker. He's evil – I mean raving-fuckin' mad evil.'

'You seem to know a lot about him,' I said, 'and it seems personal.'

Something came over Hardy's face then, a certainty, a measured ferocity. 'You're a clever man, but I'd watch that cleverness if I were you.'

'Is that why you're so angry with young Aaron then? Because Baker frightens you?'

Hardy grabbed me by the throat. 'D'you want to fight me?'

'Not unless you make me,' I said.

'Then fuck off. Fuck off now.'

I hesitated and Paddy pushed between us.

'Enough, Steve. Now you've had your say and then some. Let Tug train in peace.'

He pulled me away and led me to the door of the gym. When we got outside he shook his head from side to side and his face split into a fierce grin.

'Alex warned me about you. Jesus, but I've never seen Tug so wound up. I'd say you hit some very tender spots there.'

'But it does explain why he hit Aaron. He's scared of Baker, isn't he?'

'I'd say so, yes,' he laughed. 'But he gave you a lot of respect.'

'How do you make that out?'

'He didn't kill you.'

'I need him to talk to me, Paddy.'

He tilted his head to one side. 'Sit in your car. I'll see what I can do.'

Ten minutes went by and then fifteen. I'd just got to the point where I was about to drive off, when Hardy emerged and walked over to the passenger side of the car.

He tapped on the window and I lent over and wound it down.

'I'll give you five minutes. If you make a smart remark you'll not enjoy what follows. Understood?'

I nodded and opened the door. Hardy climbed in.

'Karl Baker?'

'What about him?' said Hardy.

'Where can I find him?'

'You don't want to find him. Believe me.'

'Humour me.'

'Basildon. Lives in a council flat. Rumour has it he has a place somewhere in Spain; something a bit tasty. He keeps his money abroad as well. There's never anything in the council flat so that if they nick him he's clean.'

'Where is this flat?'

'Off Broadmayne, Derry Close. I don't know the number.'

'How does he do his business?'

'Like the rest of the world I imagine – lock-ups. Rents them through lowlifes. If the lock-ups are discovered it's them that go down.'

'How do you know that?'

Hardy gave me an evil stare. 'If you ever repeat what I'm about to tell you to anybody, Paddy, McGregor – anybody, I *will* do you.'

'I'm suitably frightened, tell me.'

'He used Aaron to fetch and carry from a lock-up. Baker only uses one errand boy per lock-up. That way if the errand boy's nicked he can't go blabbing about anything else.'

'Go on.'

'Aaron was allowed to take his payment in gear. He abused it and nearly died in the process. I found him unconscious in a lobby of a block of flats on Burnham Villas. Since then I tried to get him away from all that. But Baker got word to him through his mother.'

'She's on the gear?'

'It's why I left the bitch.'

I nodded. 'Thank you.'

'If you meet with Baker you may regret those words.' And with that he climbed from the car and walked back into the gym.

26

Tug Hardy's warning was still ringing in my ears by the time I'd got back to the flat.

He was right, it was madness to go after Baker but, with Rob beaten to a pulp, I felt an obligation to redress the balance. Question was, which way do I go with it?

Common sense said hand everything over to Jo and stand back, but Hardy wouldn't speak to her and anyway it was Essex police area and Jo would have to pass everything on. A lot could get lost in the translation. The local drugs squad might go in half-cocked and Tug and Aaron Hardy could get some massive grief, one way or another.

No. I was outside the box. I was answerable to no one. I had freedom to roam and I could feed bits at a time to whoever, in order to get the result. Baker was as heavy as it gets, I'd seen the results, but he didn't know about me and what you can't see you can't hit.

I rang Jo and arranged to meet her around eight at the hotel. She said to wear a jacket; we were going to a smart restaurant.

That gave me plenty of time to ice the ankle and once again I found myself watching the news.

It was mainly a rehash of the previous days and the riots had slipped to second place in priority, being nudged aside by the reports of fraud amongst bureaucrats in Brussels.

The street disturbances still continued, but the news of the cocaine in Shenaz Rahman's body and the interviewing of Mohammed Ali Rahman by the police investigating her murder had spread uncertainty, resulting in sporadic protests rather than wholesale riots.

The politicians, local and national, now felt it safe enough to peep over the parapet and, whereas no one actually attacked Mohammed Ali Rahman, there were one or two barbed comments about the evil of drugs in the community.

It would have taken a blind man not to see that it had more to do with political assassination than outrage.

There must have been many who sighed with relief that, whatever the outcome, Rahman would not now get elected and all the major parties, that only two weeks before were falling over themselves to nurture him, were now backing off faster than a male praying mantis after securing its bloodline.

I left for the hotel just after seven, wearing a white cashmere jacket and black trousers with a collarless shirt.

The jacket was my one link with an earlier existence when money and promotion seemed to go hand in hand. If Jo and I were going to continue I had to find some way of improving my wardrobe.

The guy on the reception of the hotel recognised me, smiled and said, 'Good evening, sir?' and offered to phone up to Jo's room.

I shook my head and said, 'It's a surprise.'

I walked up the stairs to her room and tapped on the door.

'One minute,' called out Jo.

The door opened and I bit my lip. She looked stunning. The dress was black, low cut and made of gossamer.

'It that legal?'

She smiled. 'Like it?'

'They say you should never tell a good-looking woman she's good-looking, she hears it all the time. Apparently you should tell her she's intelligent, she'll appreciate it more.'

'Go on then.'

'Intelligent doesn't come close.'

She leant forward and kissed me and I took her waist.

'We might get arrested tonight,' I breathed.

'Indecency?'

I shook my head. 'Arson.'

We passed people on the stairs and heads turned. I didn't think it was my cashmere jacket.

'Where are we going?' I asked.

'Here. Members' dinner party. It's usually very good. I haven't been for a time.'

Jo led me down the stairs and out on to the patio.

Tables had been set out on the lawn in front of the patio with silver candelabra and vivid floral arrangements at each centre. Silver lanterns completed the setting by ringing the outside of the tables, making the lake glitter in the fading light. We walked to the edge of the patio and were immediately approached by a waiter and offered champagne.

I took two glasses and handed one to Jo.

Groups of people were stood around drinking and talking; the women in cocktail dresses and the men in tuxedos – mostly white jacketed as a concession to the late summer.

Without a tie I stood out and said so to Jo.

She blinked. 'I love that jacket. The tie doesn't matter, not to me.'

A couple in their fifties came over. He was heavy set and looked affluent business; she looked ex-model – tall, slim and still very attractive.

She also had soft brown eyes that were full of mischief.

'Steve, I'd like you to meet Richard and Emma. They're old friends of mine.'

We shook hands and Emma looked from me to Jo and gave a tiny smile, then linked her arm through Jo's and led her off.

'Jo looks very happy, how long have you known her?' asked Richard.

'Not long.'

'How did you meet?'

'Through work.'

He ran a glance over me. 'You're not a policeman, are you?'

'No.'

'Didn't think so. So what is it that you do?'

'Fire Brigade.'

'Ah.'

'And what about you?'

'Banking, I'm afraid. Very boring.'

He finished his champagne, turned and beckoned a waiter.

'Do you like champagne, Steve?' he said handing me another glass.

'Providing it's not too dry.'

'Ah, well, that tells me that you're an occasional drinker of champagne.'

'Does it?'

. He nodded, 'The drier the better, for a champagne connoisseur. You and Jo should come out to our house in France. Get's full up in the summer weekends with the same old faces. It'd be nice to have some younger blood.'

We were a million light years apart in lifestyle and attitude, but he seemed a genuinely nice guy and we talked easily enough for five minutes or so. He threw in the odd shrewd comment and it was enough for me to realise that he was probably worth whatever he was paid.

Then Jo and Emma appeared alongside us.

'I was just saying to Steve that he and Jo should come out to the house in Languedoc – be nice to change the mix.'

'What a good idea, Richard, we don't see enough of you as it is, Jo. Do think about it.'

'We might take you up on that,' said Jo.

'Good. Ring me, soon,' said Emma and she squeezed Jo's arm.

As they moved away Jo let out a delicious laugh. 'She likes you.'

'Likes me?'

'Yes, likes you. Wanted to know all about you. She's a bit of a girl is Emma. Still has an eye for the talent.'

'Does she?'

'Yes, she does. So behave yourself. I saw you looking.'

'She is lovely.'

'Not intelligent then?'

'Not so much as some.'

Throughout the meal a small orchestra played light classics and when they performed *Eine Kleine Nacht musik*, I chuckled.

'Yes?' frowned Jo

'Well I was just thinking that this would be the obvious choice and then they go and play it.'

'You like Mozart?'

'Depends. Timing has a lot to do with music.' I looked around at the other diners. 'Thank you for this.'

Jo took a sip of wine. 'I wasn't sure how you'd like it.'

'I wish you'd have told me about wearing a bow tie though.'

'You've got one?'

I smiled. 'No.'

'I'll buy you one,' she said suddenly serious. 'Would you like that?'

'Yes, yes, I'd like that very much.'

Her eyes held mine. 'Good.'

After the meal the orchestra changed tempo and played a mixture of Cole Porter, Irving Berlin and Gershwin.

And we danced.

I couldn't remember the last time I danced, but it was a night when everything came together – mood, atmosphere and the woman. And dancing seemed right, mainly the slow numbers. I was wine-mellow and Jo felt like electricity in my hands.

'Take me to bed now, please,' she whispered.

We made love slowly and rhythmically; rocking gently and

feeling each other build. Neither of us wanted it to end and when we could control it no longer Jo shuddered and gasped and I gripped her fiercely and released, feeling my whole body shake; the quivering continuing long after I'd stopped.

Bathed in sweat, we kissed long and slow and eventually I rested my head on her breasts, falling asleep as she wrapped her arms around my head and clutched me to her.

I woke later and could tell immediately that Jo was awake by her breathing. She must have sensed me stir.

'Hi.'

'Hi.'

'Are you awake now?' she asked.

'Yes.'

Her hand found me and we began again.

We made love in the same pattern throughout the night. Each time seemed more intense, more alive. Finally, just before dawn, I fell asleep exhausted and when I woke Jo was propped up on one arm, watching me.

'Morning.'

I kissed her. 'Morning.'

'You were sleeping like a baby,' she said.

'What time is it?'

'Nearly eight o'clock. Shall I run a bath for us?'

I nodded.

'Then we'll have breakfast here or on the patio?' she asked.

'Here'

Over breakfast I asked Jo if she had spoken to Bill Proctor about Basildon.

'I did. Why?'

'Just wondered if anything's happened.'

Jo lifted her coffee cup and peered at me over the rim. 'Vanzie hasn't reported for bail. A warrant has been issued for his arrest.'

'That means that they can drag him back in and have another go at him.'

She agreed. 'If they can find him.'

'Did Proctor say he was going to come back to you, about Basildon?' I asked.

'Not as such. I'll have to file a report because of my involvement. Something may come out of that. Why?'

I put down my knife and fork. 'Does the name Karl Baker mean anything to you?'

'Not straight away. Should I know him?'

'Could you ask Bill Proctor?'

'This is to do with Rob Brody?'

'I don't know. It may do.'

Her eyes became wary. 'Steve, when I was moved off the Rahman case we were free to get together. As a witness though I can't discuss the case with you. The only reason I told you about Vanzie is that it'll be released to the press later today. Likewise with this Basildon business, we're both witnesses and as such shouldn't discuss the matter.'

'I understand.'

She refilled her coffee cup. 'Karl Baker?'

'That's right.'

'And the reason you want me to find out?'

'Curiosity, Josefina.'

She smiled. 'My father always called me Josefina. He hated it when people shortened my name.'

'So you'll ask?'

'Maybe.'

27

11.20 Tuesday
29 September

When I got back to the flat there was a message from Alex to contact him straight away. There was also one from Linda Brody to tell me that there was no change in Rob's condition and that the doctors had said that there could be brain damage, but they weren't certain.

There was nothing from Jenny, for which I was grateful. A few more days to let any remaining heat dissipate and then I would ring her.

I went through the post and discovered a letter from the bank telling me that my account was overdrawn and asking me to ring them or pay some money into my account to meet my scheduled standing orders.

There had to be a mistake, I had enough to meet all monthly bills with a surplus of around six hundred for extras. In any case my salary would have been paid in on Monday.

I rang the bank. It wasn't a mistake.

Jenny had cashed a cheque for two thousand five hundred pounds on Friday morning; the cheque she'd got me to sign just before she'd left for pre-natal class.

Guilt balanced my anger, but what I felt wasn't the issue. The issue was that my salary for the month had disappeared and standing orders and direct debits would start ricocheting off all the walls over the next few weeks and each one that bounced would cost me around thirty quid extra.

Clever girl, Jenny. Nothing like desperation to bring me to the negotiating table.

I sat down and ran through options.

The bank wouldn't give me an overdraft because of past money troubles. I could ring Jenny, but she would stall, just to up the ante and her price would be more than the return of the cheque.

I could approach one of the phone-a-loan companies, but from past experience I knew I'd pay through the nose and in any case it would take three to four days to get the money into my account and by then the tremors would be rocking the account.

Today preferably, tomorrow at the latest, I needed to pay liquid cash into the bank.

Alex.

I sighed. It would mean taking the Khan job, but would Alex yield two and a half grand up front? Even if he did, it wasn't that simple because if the fire brigade found me out there'd be no second chances. I'd be sacked. Undeclared secondary employment was a discipline offence – working whilst on sick leave was an instant dismissal.

I rang him at his office.

'Stevie, what can I do for you?'

'I'm hoping we can come to a deal over the Khan job.'

There was a pause. 'Good man!'

'But I have a price.'

'I'm listening.'

'Jenny's cleared my bank account.'

'Ouch.'

'So I'll do the Khan job, but I need you to sub me two and a half grand.'

'Just like that?'

'Yes. And it needs to be today.'

I could hear him breathing on the other end of the line.

'I can't do that with the firm's money, Stevie, but I'll give you a personal loan till you're sorted out.'

'Conditions?'

He chuckled. 'On condition you take the job.'

'What do you want me to do?'

There was a pause. 'This could work well.'

'Why?'

He ignored the question. 'Be here at say . . . one o'clock. We're having lunch.'

'Talk to me, Alex. What's happened?'

He hung up.

I arrived at one sharp and Alex handed me two and half grand in fifty pounds notes. Then we went to lunch, stopping off for me to deposit the money on the way.

'Thank you,' I said as I climbed back into his car.

'You're going to have to sort this business out with Jenny soon, Stevie. Real soon.'

'I know.'

'She rang me last night.'

'Oh?'

'She hinted about the money.'

I turned to face him. 'So you knew I'd phone this morning?'

'I had an idea.'

'Am I that predictable?'

'No, Stevie. Usually you're very unpredictable, but interspersed with intervals of utter habit.'

'Thank you.'

'Not at all.'

'Where are we going for lunch?'

'Il Gallo Nero. Brentwood.'

'Why there?'

'Because I've got a meeting with Zahra Asif there.'

The drive took twenty minutes and try as I might I could get nothing more out of him.

The restaurant itself was just off the High Street; a typical small Italian eatery with nothing about the décor to suggest it was anything special. The one thing Alex did confide was that the veal was genuine, not tenderised pork, and the spaghetti vongole should be tried.

Armed with this essential knowledge, we entered and were sat at an alcove table towards the back, which had been reserved.

Five minutes later Zahra Asif entered and Alex got up and beckoned her over.

She wore a dark green suit with matching scarf held in place by an emerald brooch. She looked what she was; sharp, in every sense of the word.

'I believe you know Steve, Miss Asif?'

She shook my hand. 'Yes, how are you?'

'Fine, and yourself?'

'You've read the papers?'

'Yes.'

'Then you'll know,' she said coolly.

We ordered drinks. I had a scotch, Alex the same and Zahra Asif chose Perrier.

The atmosphere was a degree below comfort, which I put down to my last run in with her. Alex didn't miss it, but chose to ignore it and when the menu came he was the charming host, all suggestions and smiles.

After we'd ordered, Alex got down to business.

'Stevie, Miss Asif rang me yesterday and asked for this meeting.'

I looked at her. 'Can I ask why?'

She ran a glance past us both. 'I believe you are investigating Daud Khan?'

'Who told you that?' asked Alex.

'My brother, Iqbal. It came up in a family discussion. Naturally he didn't breech any confidence, but he mentioned that your loss adjusters had been asked to look into the background of cinema fire in Green Street.'

'And your interest is what exactly?' I asked.

The waiter brought over the drinks and we waited for him to go. I studied her and she seemed very calm, very in control.

'My interest, Mr Jay, is to protect Mohammed.'

'How so?' asked Alex.

'I believe he has been the victim of a dirty tricks campaign.'

'Meaning?' I asked.

'Meaning just that. I believe someone has made a malicious political attack on him.'

I looked at Alex and shook my head in disbelief. 'What, someone murdered his wife to stop him becoming elected?'

'Are you always sarcastic, Mr Jay?'

'Not always, there has to be a reason.' I took a sip of the scotch, still shaking my head. 'Okay, for the sake of argument, how does this involve Khan?'

'I believe Daud Khan has cash flow problems.'

'So?'

'He approached Mohammed for money and Mohammed refused.'

'Why? Didn't Khan help with the fund-raising for his political bid?'

'I don't know why and Mohammed wouldn't say.'

'But?'

'But I think it had something to do with the expansion of Daud Khan's business into non-Asian leisure.'

I didn't believe a word she said, but she looked like she did. 'Be specific?'

'Steady, Stevie,' put in Alex. 'Miss Asif will think you've got something against her.'

'Have you, Mr Jay?'

'No.' I took some of the edge off my voice. 'I repeat, why wouldn't Mohammed Ali Rahman help a friend?'

She placed her fingers together as though in prayer, and brought them up to her mouth, tapping them against her lips.

'I think that the venture involved licensed premises. Mohammed is a strict Muslim and would have nothing to do with it.'

Alex raised his eyebrows as if to say 'fair point'.

'I see. This is a feeling is it?'

'Sorry?'

I placed my drink down on the table and looked sideways at Alex to see if he was genuinely buying what he heard.

'How sure are you of this, Miss Asif?' I asked.

'As I said, it's a guess.'

'I'm still not following this. Are you saying that Khan tried to get back at Mohammed Ali Rahman? Because I simply don't believe it.'

'Someone is targeting Mohammed.'

'That might well be, but I don't buy killing someone's wife because you've got the ache over a loan refusal.'

'Pardon?'

Alex put in. 'Don't be obtuse, Stevie.'

'It seems a slight motive, Alex. Anyway, Miss Asif, if you believe that then why not go to the police?'

'Because Mohammed is under suspicion and they would just think he was trying to divert the blame.' She crossed her arms. 'You've seen the news reports.'

'Yes, I have and, if you'll forgive me, the police wouldn't bring him in for formal questioning in the present climate unless they had good reason.'

There was a definite quiver of her bottom lip. 'He loved Shenaz. It's unthinkable that he would hurt her.'

'A strict Muslim in love with a drug addict?'

The quiver disappeared and she fixed my eye. 'Shenaz would never take drugs. Never.'

'Apparently her body was full of cocaine . . .'

'I don't care! Shenaz was a good Muslim. Yes she was westernised, modern, but many Pakistani women are. I am.'

'That tells me nothing. How do you know? People can live secret lives.'

The quiver returned and her voice broke. 'Because she was my sister . . . and my closest friend.'

Alex held a hand up to stop me asking another question.

'Go on, Miss Asif, please,' he said gently.

'We grew up together in Lahore. I came to England with my elder brother Iqbal and worked for Mohammed. It was through Iqbal that Mohammed met my family and a marriage was arranged with Shenaz.' There were tears in her eyes.

Alex took out his handkerchief and offered it to her. She shook her head.

'I see. I'm very sorry for your loss, Miss Asif. Neither Mr Jay nor I knew'

Zahra Asif took a sip of the water and Alex gave her a couple of minutes to compose herself. He also shot me a look and I eased back in my chair.

He now took up the questioning.

'So let's go back to Khan, if we may,' he said. 'Have you anything specific you can give us on the cinema?'

'I know he was thinking of selling it.'

'Why?'

'It was losing money. It's part of the reason he needed to borrow.'

'How do you know he was thinking of selling it?'

'He told Mohammed. He said that he would pay Mohammed back when he sold the cinema.'

'You were there when he said this?'

'It was a private conversation, but I overheard.'

Alex paused. 'Would you swear an affidavit to that effect?'

'Yes.'

Throughout the meal I watched her and, despite my earlier scepticism, I started to buy her story. Once Alex had got the agreement on the affidavit he stopped the questioning. Instead he made an arrangement with her to come to his office and swear the affidavit to the firm's solicitor.

She left shortly after, barely touching her meal and Alex waited till she was out of the restaurant before he turned to me.

'So, what do you think, Stevie?'

'It directly contradicts what Khan said in your office.'

'Aye, it does and she's willing to swear it – what do you make of that?'

'I think she's one angry woman. But is she being straight with the reason why?'

'If it were your sister you'd want to see the right man get it in the neck too, Stevie.'

'You realise, Alex, that I can't now investigate Khan. If this involves Rahman in any way, particularly as it might be linked to his wife's murder, I can't be involved.'

'Yes. I do see that. I'll have to let the police know, of course, once the affidavit is signed.'

'No. No, let me do it. If this is genuine, then I know someone who would love to inform the murder team directly.'

28

Alex and I talked on the way back to the office and he was generous in offering two days' pay for my services, but I was now in a financial hole that was getting bigger by the minute.

Back at his office I refused coffee and said that I needed to go away and think things through.

He read my face. 'There's no immediate panic, Stevie. I'm not short of a bob or two and you can sort me out when the Sheldon case comes to court.'

'I know, but I owe you a fair bit as it is. At this rate when the Sheldon case comes in there'll be no money left over.'

He sat down on the edge of his desk. 'Talk to Jenny, Stevie. Get her to move back in – lead separate lives if you have to – till you've the money sorted out. It makes good sense.'

'Financial sense maybe.'

'She's carrying your child, Stevie. At the very least she deserves to know what the future holds – you both do. Sort it.'

By the time I'd got back to the flat I'd decided he was right and planned to meet Jenny to resolve all the issues. I wouldn't lie. My situation with Jo wasn't part of the equation and I wouldn't allow it to become one. The meeting had to be about the practicalities, but she also had to know there was now no going back.

Alex's one flat – separate lives idea wouldn't work. I intended to keep hold of Jo and Jenny wouldn't, couldn't stand by and watch that happen.

Reality and acceptance, that was all there was on offer. I didn't like myself for it, but that's how it was going to be.

I looked at the clock. It was coming up to half three and I had an appointment with Paddy at five; enough time for a coffee and the news.

As the half three bulletin came on there seemed to be some confusion between the newscaster and the studio crew. Papers were passed to the newscaster and she stopped to receive instructions through her earpiece.

With a glance to her left and a shuffle of the papers in front of her she began the bulletin.

'Good afternoon. In the past few minutes there has been a dramatic breakthrough in the hunt for the murderer of Shenaz Rahman. According to a police spokesman, the husband of the dead woman, Mohammed Ali Rahman, was arrested at his home shortly before eleven o'clock this morning. The police will give no further details, but they are believed to be digging in the back garden of the family home in South Woodford in North-East London. Reports that they have recovered something from the garden are not as yet confirmed. We will give you more later as we get it.'

I rang Jo.

'Hi. I take it that you've heard the news about Rahman's arrest?'

'I heard shortly after it happened this morning, Steve. Bill Proctor rang me.'

'What do you think?'

'I think they've found something in the back garden.'

'Something . . .' I stopped, incredulous. 'The head?'

'Looks that way.'

'Why would . . . no I can't buy that.'

'Bang-to-rights is the expression that comes to mind, Steve.'

'Well, if that's true, I may have something that really muddies the water.'

'Oh?'

I told her everything Zahra Asif had said about Khan.

'She may be right, but it doesn't make Khan the murderer – and *if* they have found the head in the back garden that looks pretty watertight.'

'A strict Muslim gets white racists to cut his wife's head off? You don't believe that.'

'Rahman's a rich man, he could afford to have it done. Probably didn't even know the people who actually did it. What better way to deflect suspicion?'

'And then bury the head in his own back garden? Why, for Christ's sake?'

'You'd be surprised how many wives have been dug out of gardens, Steve. In murder inquiries the simple answer is usually the right one.'

It got more unreal by the minute, but I wasn't on the inside and who knows what else the police had discovered?

'What happens now?'

'Now they'll interview him to a purpose and he has lots of tough questions to answer. It really is stacking up against him, Steve.'

'Look, I've one or two things to do, can we meet later tonight? I need to talk to you.'

'Okay. Where?'

'Not sure, let me ring you later.'

As soon as I put the phone down I rang Alex and he agreed with me.

'I smells like an old sea-boot, Stevie, but Jo's the detective.'

'Why don't you try to speak to Khan on his own?'

'He'll not move without Asif in tow.'

'That's iffy in itself,' I suggested.

'Not for a serious businessman like Khan. No, his financial dealings need to be examined in detail. An accountant might be of use, if I can get access to the books, which is unlikely.'

'Keep me posted.'

'Aye, I will.'

I left the flat in good time to make Paddy's by five and throughout the journey I kicked the facts, as I knew them, around my head. From where I was none of it made sense. Somehow Khan needed to be spoken to on his own.

On arrival at the gym I found just three of the usual faces training. I couldn't see Paddy anywhere and took a few minutes to watch the sparring.

One of the guys in the ring, Thomas B. Grant, was a one-time pro who'd fought for most of his professional career in the States – and it showed.

His fighting days were past, but he exhibited skills as smooth as the day he'd taken apart Reuben Barnard, a world title contender, and prematurely retired him from the ring.

Thomas never mentioned it, but I'd heard from Paddy and Alex that the only reason Thomas never got a title shot after that was the corrupt politics that infested the American fight game. Reuben Barnard had a lot of money backing him and Thomas had upset more than just Barnard's dreams.

The man Thomas was sparring with was Danny Carpenter, another ex-pro who always kept himself in shape. Carpenter was a man of few words who always had a serious air about him. I didn't know what he did for a living nowadays and was frankly scared to ask.

Come to think of it there were one or two like that in the 1916 gym.

When the buzzer sounded Thomas came over to speak and Danny Carpenter nodded to me.

'If you're looking for Paddy, Steve, he's in the treatment room with Tug Hardy's son. Don't know what's up, but things seem kinda tense.'

'Thanks, Thomas.'

I knocked on the treatment room door and opened it. The

atmosphere was heavy and, as Paddy looked up, his face was stone.

'Steve. Come in,' he said softly.

'You sure? I only wanted to let you know I was here, Paddy,' I said.

He shook his head and beckoned me in. Aaron Hardy made a move to go, but Paddy put his arm out to stop him. There was an awkward silence; Aaron Hardy obviously didn't want me there.

'Tell Steve what you told me, Aaron. Go on lad, you can trust him.'

Hardy said nothing, but didn't go. Paddy nodded and patted the youth's back.

'Tug's been hurt, Steve,' said Paddy.

'How?'

'He went to Burnham Villas last night to speak to his wife. He wanted her to leave Aaron alone, to tell her he was going to look after Aaron solely from now on.'

'What happened?'

'He ran into some of Baker's thugs. They beat him half to death, but not before Tug did some damage himself – busted a couple of them up.'

Aaron Hardy was looking at the floor as Paddy told me; his body language a mix of fear and guilt.

'How do you know this, Paddy?' I asked.

'Tell him, Aaron.'

The youth looked at me, but then looked away again. When he spoke it was barely a mumble.

'My mum. She says I've got to go back and live with her or else.'

'How did your father bump into Baker's thugs?'

He looked at the floor again and Paddy took up the story.

'Aaron's mother lives with one of Baker's muscle men, a vicious bastard called Lee Vanzie.'

I stood very still and tried not to show any reaction, but Paddy saw something.

'You know this man, Steve?'

'Maybe,' I admitted. 'Aaron, your father said that you used to work for Baker?'

His head lifted slightly.

'I'll take that as a yes, shall I?'

He looked at Paddy who pointed to me. 'He's asking the questions lad.'

The youth didn't want to meet my eye.

I sat down on the treatment bench and turned my body slightly away from him.

'Aaron, these people who hurt your father have to be stopped. It could be you next or your mother.'

For the first time he looked at me directly.

'I'm not a grass,' he said quietly.

'And I'm not a copper. These people hurt a friend of mine, Aaron – and I want to take them out of business.'

'If my dad couldn't beat them, you've got no chance,' he said quickly.

'I'll fight them a different way. I need your help, Aaron. I want these people to go down for a long time. Now will you help me?'

Instinctively he looked at Paddy.

'I don't know what Steve's got in mind, lad, but it's either this or the police.'

He glanced at the door and Paddy moved aside.

'No one's keeping you here, lad. If you go out that door though you'll have to deal with it on your own – and hope they don't come looking for you.'

His shoulders sank. 'What is it you want?'

'Did you ever come across a woman called Maria Brody?' I asked.

He frowned. 'Why?'

'Did you?'

'I knew her, everyone knew her. She used to be Karl Baker's bird – lost it, big time – became a rockhead.'

'I think Baker had her topped,' I said slowly.

The youth's eyes darted from me to Paddy and back again and for a moment I thought he was going to run.

'Aaron, why would Baker kill Maria?'

He was shaking. 'I don't know.'

'What was Baker into that . . .' I stopped myself. *The Disco!* 'Baker got Maria a job in the disco that burnt down, didn't he?'

His eyes couldn't settle to anything now and I tapped his shoulder.

'Aaron, what was so special about the disco that burnt down? Was Baker anything to do with the fire?'

'I don't know.'

I shook my head. 'But you know something about the disco, don't you?'

He fell silent again; his gaze fixed at the floor.

'Well, lad?' prompted Paddy.

He crossed his arms, trying to keep his trembling hands from view.

'I only know a little.'

'Tell us,' I said.

'The disco was important for the drugs.'

'Well there's only so much drugs can pass through a disco, no matter how big it is,' I said.

He shook his head. 'No. No, it wasn't like that. Baker owned part of the disco. He bought into it with his profits and used it to launder his cash.'

Paddy raised his eyebrows. 'Clever.'

'How do you know this?' I asked

'Lee Vanzie. He was always bragging to my mother about Baker and what they'd been up to. He's a nutter.'

'So Baker wasn't too pleased when it burnt down?'

'I thought he was going to kill me.'

'You? Why?'

'I wasn't supposed to know, it was a mistake.'

'What was?'

'I went to the disco to tell him I'd moved a lot of gear and needed some more.'

'And?'

'I overheard him talking about being stitched up by someone.'

'Stitched up? By who?'

'I don't know. All I know is that I heard him arguing in the upstairs office with his partner.'

'His partner?'

'His front man – the Paki.'

'Name?' I said slowly.

'It was weird. I don't think it was his real name. Baker always called him Dave.'

I closed my eyes. 'Thank you, Aaron.'

'Do you know this character, Steve?' asked Paddy.

'I'm beginning to think I know nothing, Paddy.'

The youth was watching me now, because he could feel the bite coming.

'Aaron, I need something on Baker,' I said. 'Something clean and uncomplicated that'll make him go down for a very long time. Think, Aaron. Think creatively.'

He looked physically uncomfortable and for a moment I thought he'd refuse. Paddy nodded slowly to prompt him.

'Do you know Burnham Villas?' he asked.

'Yes.'

'There's a way on to the estate, an alleyway that continues from the end of Harpers Road. Meet me there at eleven tonight and I'll show you under the Zigzag.'

'The what?'

'Baker's main stash.'

29

After Paddy treated my ankle I went back to the flat and found a message on the answerphone from Linda Brody. Rob had briefly regained consciousness that afternoon and had asked to speak to me. She left the ward phone number and I immediately rang it.

'How is he, Linda?'

'He's awake some of the time, Steve. When he first woke he asked for you. Since then he's alternating between sleep and being half-awake.'

I looked at my watch.

'I'll be there at eight.'

Between the hospital and meeting Aaron Hardy I realised that I wouldn't be able to meet with Jo so I rang her mobile and explained that Rob had asked to see me. I didn't mention Aaron Hardy.

'I understand. Don't go getting yourself into any more trouble, Steve,' she said half-serious. 'Ring me tomorrow.'

'Will do.'

Next I rang Alex at his home.

'Stevie, I'm glad you rung. I've been thinking about what I said to you earlier – I was wrong. I shouldn't be sticking my nose into yours and Jenny's problems. I broke my own rules.'

'That's because you're an interfering old bastard.'

He paused. 'That's me forgiven then is it?'

'Don't go sentimental on me, Alex. There's nothing worse than your best mate thinking he's your mum.'

'Aye. So what can I do for you?'

'I think I'm on to something with Khan.'

'Good man, Stevie. What have you found out?'

'It's complex. Hopefully, I'll know more tonight. I'll come and see you tomorrow and brief you. Oh and I shall want paying. If I can deliver Khan to you then I'll want a percentage, not a few hundred quid.'

'If you can deliver, Stevie, then you're in line for serious money.'

'How much?'

'Five per cent of what you save the insurance company.'

'Ten.'

'Andrew and I will only make fifteen – your five comes out of that.'

'Alex, fifteen per cent of nothing is nothing. I'm putting my arse on the line here, taking big chances and I want ten per cent.'

'Seven and a half.'

'Done.'

'Aye, I think I have been.'

'There's a lot going on around Khan, Alex. Now at the moment I've got him on the periphery of some pretty heavy shit and I'm trying to find out whether he's the hub or a spoke.'

'You're developing a colourful turn of phrase, Stevie.'

'It's the company I keep.'

'Take care – and don't put yourself at risk.'

I put the phone down.

It was going to be a long night and I decided to get some food inside me before it started. There were eggs and bacon in the fridge so I made an omelette, grilled the bacon and washed it down with three cups of coffee.

I left the flat just after seven with my ankle feeling better than it had for days. Before leaving I had packed a pair of thin leather driving gloves, pin-light torch and a steel biro.

I was ready.

The journey to the hospital took forty-five minutes and when I made my way up to the side ward where Rob was I found the corridor outside swarming with police.

News of Rob regaining consciousness had spread.

Linda Brody came out and told the doctors that Rob had asked to see me. There was a discussion between two doctors and Linda, with the police edging into the conversation.

A tall, thin-faced detective was unhappy with me going in, but his manner pissed the doctors off and I was allowed to go with Linda. The detective said he wanted a word with me the minute I came out.

As she took me into the ward she warned me that Rob was still drifting in and out of consciousness, but that when he came around now he knew who he was and was able to talk a little.

I knew he'd been in a bad way, but I wasn't prepared for just how bad.

His head was swathed in bandages and his face was black and swollen with one eye completely closed by a blood-filled swelling. He was hooked up to several machines and tubes ran everywhere.

Linda went up to the bed and leaned over. Then shook her head.

'Sleeping,' she whispered.

She retreated from the bed and we spoke in low voices in the corner of the room.

'How are you holding up, Linda?'

'Coping. The hospital has been kind enough to let me sleep here. I've been eating in their canteen. They bring me a cup of tea every so often.'

'How's your daughter?'

'Cassie's with friends. She misses her dad . . .' her voice broke, but she fought it and wiped at her eyes with a crumpled handkerchief.

'What *did* happen the day he was beaten up, Linda?'

She looked away. 'I told you.'

'Yes, but it wasn't quite true was it?' I said gently.

She looked at the opaque vision panel in the door. 'I don't want to say anything that might get Rob into trouble.'

'It won't go further than me, Linda.'

She peered over at Rob again and tucked the sheets under his arms. For a moment she stood and watched him. She looked terrible; her eyes were red with dark rings under them and she was pale, on the point of exhaustion.

'What good would it do to know the truth?' she sighed.

'What good would it do to let these people get away with what they've done to Rob?'

'People like that don't get stopped, Steve. The police get one or two of them, but there's always someone to take their place. Rob's alive, that's the main thing. I'd rather concentrate on us moving somewhere else; leave all this behind us.'

I nodded. 'I can see that, but I've got a feeling these people won't let it go at that. They have got to be put away, Linda. Then maybe you'll get the peace you're looking for.'

She fussed around Rob again and held his hand. When she looked back at me I could see she was at breaking point.

'You won't get them all.'

'I'll try, Linda – and I think I'll get enough to take them out of circulation, but I need your help. Please.'

'What will you do with the information?' she asked.

'I can make sure it reaches the right people.'

'Who?'

'A friend. A Detective Inspector who'll know how to handle it.'

She frowned. 'The woman you brought to the house?'

'Yes.'

'You and Jenny split up again then?'

'For good this time.'

'That's a shame. I always liked Jenny. I thought you two were matched.'

'So did I, Linda. Too much history.'

Rob groaned and Linda bent over him. 'He's been like that most of the day. Funny, it's horrible to hear him groan like that, but reassuring at the same time.'

'He'll make it, Linda. Next time he might not be so lucky.'

She held his hand and squeezed it gently. 'What do you want to know?'

'Tell me it all. Everything you left out last time.'

'Rob always said you were shrewd, shrewd and bloody-minded.'

'I still need your help.'

She closed her eyes. 'Maria got herself in big trouble with the crack. She was in such a state sometimes, screaming and shouting about what Baker and his thugs had done to her, having panic attacks, the lot. She was an embarrassment to them.'

'Go on.'

She let go of Rob's hand and came over to where I was standing.

'There were times when they wouldn't give her the drugs. Partly because she was causing a fuss and attracting attention, and partly to punish her. When she was really desperate they made her screw for it. Two, three, four or more of them at a time; they were animals.'

'You've told me this already.'

She nodded. 'Rob was going berserk. Eventually he said he'd get the drugs for her, that she was to stay away from Baker and all his crew.'

'Rob bought drugs for her?'

'Yes. He was trying to protect her!'

'It's all right, Linda. I'm not judging him and it stays with me.'

She still hesitated. 'Don't tell your friend what I'm about to tell you. Wait. Wait until you've spoken to Rob.'

'Okay.'

She took a deep breath and exhaled slowly.

'Saturday, before you came down, before you took him to the hospital, Rob had a phone call from Maria. She was upset, screaming. Rob tried to calm her down, but she was hysterical.'

'About what?'

'He wouldn't tell me. It frightened him, frightened him to the point where he said he was going to go to Burnham Villas and get her straight away. He told me to lock the door and open it to no one except him.'

'Then what happened?'

'You turned up at the house. I didn't know what to say.'

'And later?'

'When Rob came back on his own he was in a terrible state. I'd never seen him so frightened. I asked him where Maria was and he just shook his head. He told me we had to go, to get out and leave everything. I was only to pack one suitcase . . .' Her voice fell away as tears filled her eyes.

'Please – I need to know,' I prompted.

The words tumbled from her, but she was crying and I had to make her repeat herself.

'I'd nearly finished . . . packing when I heard this bang downstairs . . . it was the front door being kicked in. I was so scared I froze . . . Cassie hid under the bed and . . . and I told her to stay there. I could hear Rob's screams . . . it went on and on . . . I could . . . hear the noise as they beat him and beat him. It was horrible – like a heavy piece of wood hitting and hitting . . . 'Then Cassie started crying and I think they heard her. One of them came up the stairs, but I locked the door and shouted that I'd called the police. I think they went then, but I was too scared to move.'

'How long after that did I show up, Linda?'

'I don't know, an hour maybe more. When . . . when I came down Rob was still conscious. He said not to call the police . . . that he'd be all right. I should have called an ambulance . . . I should have . . .' She broke down in tears again.

I put my arms around her shoulders.

'It's hard, but you did the right thing. Had you come down sooner and they were still there they would have got you . . . and Cassie.'

It took me ten minutes to calm her.

She kept repeating that she should have gone downstairs and called an ambulance the minute they'd gone. She'd placed her and their daughter's safety before Rob's and she couldn't forgive herself for it.

We talked for an hour or so. A nurse came in periodically to check Rob and asked us if we wanted a cup of tea. We said yes and the detective who had spoken to me earlier brought it in.

He took a good look at Rob and ran what I imagine he thought was a serious stare over Linda and me. I would have wound him up, but Linda didn't need any more aggravation.

A few minutes after he went, Rob stirred.

Linda got up and went over to him. I heard him speak and she beckoned me over. Rob's one good eye opened and he said something I couldn't catch.

'He wants you to go near, Steve,' said Linda.

I bent over the bed and put my ear to his mouth. His voice was a rasp.

'I saw . . . him,' he whispered.

'Saw who, Rob?'

'Vanzie . . . I saw him at . . . railway . . . murder. He saw me . . .'s why I went . . . off sick . . . knew he recognised me.'

30

I stayed with Linda until gone ten. Rob had lapsed back into sleep and didn't wake again before I left. I told her that I had to meet someone and would look in afterwards, though I had no idea how long I'd be.

As I left, the detective who'd pulled me on the way in asked if Rob had said anything. I shook my head and brushed past him.

I reached Harpers Road at twenty to eleven and parked fifty yards away from the alleyway that led on to Burnham Villas. By looking in the rear-view and side mirrors I could see what I needed without being conspicuous.

Harpers Road was a total contrast to the estate. The neat semi-detached houses had small front gardens and each one had something of its own character.

The only indication of the proximity of the estate were snapped off saplings the length of the road – a gift no doubt from the estate's children.

As I settled down to wait it started to rain.

Aaron Hardy's choice of Harpers Road was a good one in that the road was very quiet with limited people or vehicle movements. The minutes crept by and eleven came and went and by a quarter past I was starting to wonder if he'd show.

The rain stopped.

At half past the waiting was getting to me and I thought of going back the hospital in the hope that Rob would again wake and give me something extra I could work with.

Suddenly Aaron Hardy emerged from the alleyway.

I switched my hazard lights on briefly and he started walking towards the car. As he reached me I opened the passenger side door.

'Get in.'

His face was flushed and he was jittery. He seemed to pick up on my own edginess which, despite my best efforts, I couldn't hide.

'Problems?' I asked as he closed the door.

'Not sure.' He snatched a glance at the passenger side mirror. 'There were some faces about the estate.'

I checked the rear-view – nothing. 'So?'

'I had to check the place out. I don't think they saw me.'

'What does that mean? Were you seen or not?'

Again he looked in the side mirror and then back to me. 'No.'

He held my eye, but I wasn't convinced. I was on the verge of calling it off, but told myself I was reacting to shadows.

'Before we go anywhere, Aaron, I need to know some more about the Zigzag.'

'I'll show you where it is,' he said.

'No good, Aaron. I've got to get in there. What if the cupboard's bare when the police raid it?'

His eyes wouldn't keep still. 'There's always gear in there, sometimes it's loaded to the roof.'

'And the Zigzag is what exactly?'

'The old community centre. It's boarded up because it kept getting wrecked. The council closed it down and put iron grilles on the doors and windows.'

'And where is it?'

'On the other side of the estate.'

'You're telling me that Baker keeps his main stash in an old community centre that's probably vandalised on a regular basis?'

'It's not in the community centre – it's under it.'

'Under it?'

He nodded. 'When the estate was built they ran a cable tunnel through the middle to supply all the electric. There's a side tunnel off the main one – they used it to store equipment there when it was built. When the work was finished they bricked it up and put a steel door in connecting it to the main tunnel. There's also a concealed manhole by an electrical sub station at the back of the community centre that leads down to the side tunnel – you'd never know it was there unless you were shown.'

'And the manhole leads to the side tunnel.'

'Yeah. Baker put the biggest fucking securi-lock you've ever seen on the manhole – you need oxy-acetylene to cut through it.'

'So how do we get in?'

'I'll show you how, but I'm not going down there,' he said firmly.

'We're both going. Now how do we get in?' I said.

He hesitated and I thought he was going to refuse, but then he nodded.

'We go in by the tunnel entrance. That's how they come and go without people seeing – there's another manhole that comes out behind one of the blocks of flats.'

'You still haven't told me how we get in?'

'Vanzie had a key for the steel door to the main tunnel. He was always getting stoned or pissed up so I got a copy made.'

'You were selling on the side?'

'Yeah, but it was insurance too. In case they ever came after me.'

'How old are you, Aaron?'

'Seventeen. Why?'

'Nothing. Go on.'

'We have to go through the entrance to the block of flats and straight out the back to where the rubbish bins are kept in a brick store. At the back of the bins is the other manhole. Unless there's someone standing next to you when you open it up no one would ever know. It's the perfect stash. Vanzie would visit it two or three times a week to get enough gear to supply all the small dealers.'

'Like you?'

'Yeah. We'd each have our own stash somewhere on the estate – a lock-up or bike shed.'

'Don't the kids ever explore the manhole by the bins? They must have discovered it.'

'Even if they did, it only leads down to the main tunnel. The entrance to the side tunnel is two hundred feet or more along it. Its cramped and there's no lighting.'

'Okay, Aaron, here's how we do it. You go ahead and I'll keep a short way behind you. If you see anyone that's a problem just bend down and tie your laces. I'll know that's something wrong and we'll go our separate ways and meet back at the car later.

He stayed where he was.

'What now?'

'Once we're there you're on your own. I show you the way and even unlock the side tunnel door, but then I go. That's the deal – take it or leave it.'

I studied him. I couldn't tell if it was rain or sweat on his face. He was shit scared and way out of his depth, and I knew he thought I was as well.

'Okay,' I said. 'Now tell me exactly where we're heading.'

'A block of flats marked Nos 100 to 120. Go down the alley that leads on to the estate and turn right. Keeping walking till you come to the square at the middle of the estate . . .'

'I know it,' I said.

He looked at me for a moment then made the connection. 'Maria?'

'Yes. Go on.'

'Go through the lobby of the flats and out the back. The bins are in the yard on the right. It's well dark.'

'I've got a torch.'

'So have I, but don't use the torch till you're in the bin store with the doors shut! I'll be inside the store waiting for you.'

And with that he got out the car and started walking back towards the alley.

I gave him a fifty-yard start and followed him down the alley.

The last time I was here I felt that outsiders were smelt the instant they crossed the pack boundaries, but there were few working streetlights on the estate and, given the late hour and the earlier rain, I felt confident that I could move about without attracting too much attention.

In the event the only people who saw me were the youth with the Vauxhall Astra and a few of his mates. He was still revving the guts out of the car, oblivious to the hour or the fact that he was slowly driving the residents out of their minds

I found Maria's block of flats and went thorough the pitch-black lobby out to the yard at the back. Then I stopped and half opened my mouth, listening. All I could hear was the rain and the sounds of distant traffic.

Keeping to the right I walked down the yard and found the bin sheds, prised open the heavy timber doors and slipped inside. A hand grabbed me.

'The manhole is right behind me,' he whispered.

I switched on the pin-light torch and shone it at the floor.

The pencil beam illuminated the metal cover and Aaron bent down and lifted the iron ring. The manhole cover was counter-weighted and opened without effort or noise. A Jacob's ladder led down to the bottom of the cable tunnel, ten feet below.

'Pull it closed after you,' he hissed.

He descended the ladder and when he reached the base I followed him.

At the bottom I shone the torch along the tunnel. It was about six foot high with heavy electrical cabling bracketed to the walls. The tunnel curved to the left and Aaron told me to switch the torch off and then led the way through the ink-black tunnel.

After about fifty feet Aaron turned his torch on again and I could see that the tunnel dropped in height to about four feet and narrowed until my shoulders were touching the cables either side of the tunnel. As a cache for drugs it was perfect; the smaller tunnel was intimidating with 'Danger: High Voltage' signs everywhere.

He turned the torch off again and we bent over and shuffled forward. A hundred or so feet further on Aaron stopped.

'Wait here!' he whispered and was instantly swallowed up by the darkness.

For a few minutes I could hear the shuffling of his soft-soled trainers on the damp concrete and then the shuffling stopped.

My senses strained for information.

That was the first time I caught the smell, a sickly aroma that hung in the still, damp air.

The minutes ticked by and I thought I heard a small metallic sound, but I couldn't be sure. The shuffling started again, coming nearer.

I switched on my torch and the beam speared into the dark, picking out Aaron Hardy's hunched-over form as he ran towards me. As he reached me he grabbed my arm and pushed me.

'Go!' he hissed.

'What?'

Without waiting for me to respond he tried to push passed me, but there wasn't room. I shone my torch in his face and saw he was shaking uncontrollably.

'Let me go!'

He dropped to his knees and crawled by me, then got to his feet and disappeared back down the tunnel to the entrance.

I shone my torch forward and listened.

Nothing.

I fought the urge to follow him, but instead edged forward, seeking out the way with the torch beam. The tunnel was smallest at this point, barely three feet high and only just wide enough for me to squeeze down it. And all the time the sickly smell grew stronger.

Thirty yards on the tunnel opened out again. Here it was six feet high and three feet wide.

The stench was overpowering.

The thin beam of my torch picked out an opening on the right. I edged forward trying to control the shaking of my limbs, knowing now what the smell was and steeling myself for what I would see.

The side tunnel opened out in the tunnel wall. I turned right into the opening and six feet inside was a brick wall with a half-open steel door at its centre. I could almost taste it. The thick pungent odour clung to the back of my throat and made me gag. I aimed the beam at the doorway, hesitating.

Come on, Stevie – do it!

I pushed open the door and shone the torch into the tunnel store.

It was empty save for one plastic refuse sack at the end. I held my breath, pulled open the plastic sack and found myself staring into the bloated, decayed face of Lee Vanzie.

31

Where was Maria?

Then it hit me. It was Vanzie that had been cut up in Maria's flat. They had killed him and then butchered his body.

Why?

And why had they not got rid of it?

Me.

I'd called the police and fire brigade minutes after they'd dumped the body in the tunnel. That wasn't in their plan. They'd wanted the flat to burn out – all traces of the blood vanishing in the flames. No body, no evidence of there ever having been a body; so no search. Dump the body – let things quieten down and then move it. But I happened along and instead the estate had been swarming with police for days.

They'd had to leave the body where it was – sweating that the police wouldn't explore the length of the tunnel. Knowing that they'd be all over the estate, knocking on doors, asking questions, digging around, making it impossible to move Vanzie's hacked-up corpse.

I adjusted the torch beam to maximum angle and it illuminated the side tunnel store. A Jacob's ladder in one corner ran up to a manhole, but that was it. Aaron Hardy said the place was usually full of gear, but apart from the plastic sack and its reduced occupant, it was bare.

A noise above made me look up. Someone was unlocking the manhole.

I switched off the torch, put it in my pocket and backed

slowly to the tunnel door, but as I started to go through I heard the scrape of feet in the tunnel and froze.

I was trapped.

The manhole flew open and I saw a bulky shape against the night sky. Then heard the splashing and caught the sweet metallic smell of petrol.

Get out.

I pulled open the tunnel door and ran back to where the side and main tunnels met and was immediately bathed in light from a powerful torch.

Decide.

I ran at them as fast as my ankle would allow and grabbed the head of the lead one as he emerged from the narrow tunnel, driving my knee into his face repeatedly.

He dropped the torch and in the dark I slammed his head against the side of the tunnel. He went down hard, but grabbed my bad leg and I stamped down on his forearm, hearing it crack beneath my foot.

The men behind him pushed forward and I couldn't stop them forcing me back from the narrow tunnel neck.

Inside the bigger tunnel with more room to manoeuvre they had the advantage and tried to surround me, but I stepped back, keeping them in view. There were three still standing.

One of them moved in and grabbed me and we struggled in the semi-darkness, the only light coming from the dropped torch.

I bit his hand to the bone and he screamed and pulled away, but I followed up by stepping forward, driving my thumbs into his eyes and butting his face. I went to throw a kick as a finisher, but a tremendous blow smashed into my right shoulder from what felt like a baseball bat.

I flew sideways and cannoned off the tunnel wall screaming, but now I was in shadow and they couldn't see me. Someone picked up the torch and swept the tunnel interior. I lurched towards it and threw a left hook, guessing where his head was. I hit something and there was a yell, but it was an unfocussed blow and I knew it would hurt, but not stop him.

I went crazy now, ignoring the pain shooting through my shoulder and lashing out at anything that came near me. I got hit from all sides, but did some major damage in return when one of them got too close; I kicked his legs out from under him and stamped on his face.

Suddenly there was a soft whooshing sound from behind and a wave of heat hit me, bathing the tunnel in yellow rippling light. I turned to see flames pouring out of the side tunnel, enveloping the wall cables and generating thick black smoke.

For the one and only time I saw the startled faces of my attackers and they saw me – silhouetted against the flame.

The one with the baseball bat saw the opportunity and carved vicious arcs in the air, driving me backwards towards the fire.

I had an instant to decide.

The flames were rolling out of the side store, along the roof of the main tunnel and hitting the top of the far wall.

As the bat went back to swing again I spun round and rolled under the flames, keeping my hands over my face until I was well clear of the heat. As I came to my feet on the other side my ankle gave way and I crashed back to the concrete floor with pain knifing through my injured shoulder.

As I lay there fighting the pain a hollow roaring sound came from the side tunnel and the flames grew fiercer – they were still pouring petrol down the manhole, the whole tunnel was filling with fire.

There was one option only; go deeper into the tunnel.

I dragged myself to my feet and limped away from the flames.

A few yards on the tunnel narrowed and dropped to three feet in height. I turned and looked back; behind me the flame and thick acrid smoke were spreading. If the manhole was still open the fire had plenty of air to breathe and the length of the tunnel to expand.

Unless I could outdistance it I was going to die.

Before me lay a narrow tunnel that might lead anywhere. Service tunnels sometimes came to a halt in a dead end, the cables disappearing up into the earth or split finer and finer until they took just one or two cables off in different directions.

All I could do was move and hope.

The smoke was pushing ahead of the fire, chasing me, so that I could feel it in my eyes and throat. I tried to ignore the pain in my ankle and shoulder, but it slowed me and breathing came hard from the exertion of having to move hunched over.

I used my torch to probe the darkness, but the beam petered out in the distance.

Then it hit something.

A wall.

Panic sent adrenaline screaming through my system.

The beam blossomed outward as I got nearer the wall. Twenty yards on I reached it and the cables split left and right down two opposite side tunnels each barely two foot square.

The smoke was becoming thicker.

Part of me wanted to scream, to refuse to die trapped in a narrow culvert choking and then burning to bone. I forced myself to focus, to deal only with what there was; to try.

I got down on my belly and shone the torch down each of the culverts. The left-hand culvert went in for maybe ten feet and then went off to the left.

Could I get through the angle? Maybe, maybe not.

The right-hand culvert stretched away into the distance, probably to finish in a blind wall with the cables disappearing through the brickwork.

Choose.

I flattened out and crawled into the right-hand tunnel.

The only way I could move forward was to stretch my hands out in front of me and push with my toes. My ankle rebelling the instant I put pressure on it.

Just do it!

There was no room for manoeuvre and I had to keep dead straight and steal inches at a time, the rough concrete floor tearing at my T-shirt and rasping the skin from my chest. With each movement my elbows lost skin and I banged my head on the brickwork.

I was drenched in sweat and caked in filth.

Thin wisps of smoke were now visible in the torch-beam and racking coughs convulsed me, slowing my progress, allowing the fire to gain on me.

Ignore it. Ignore it all and try!

I pushed on, knowing that my movements were becoming more feverish, more desperate. At one point a heavy cable had become detached from its wall bracket and blocked my path.

I tried to push it away, but it didn't move.

It invaded my path by maybe six inches, twenty-five per cent of the space I had to crawl through.

I flattened out as much as I could and wedged my head under it and wriggled, pushing it aside by sheer brute force and bloody-mindedness, but it cost me a strip of skin on my already damaged shoulder and the effort left me exhausted.

I sucked in the smoke-charged air and my chest constricted at the invasion of the toxins. I tried to breathe more shallowly, but there was an unsolvable equation between effort and the need for air and my body started to thrash around, robbing me of the will to think rationally, to co-ordinate.

I was slipping to the edge of defeat; dying.

The torch went out and took me to the down slope, to the point of submission. A small, but insistent inner voice said, 'You've done enough – lie still and surrender to it. The smoke will make you lose consciousness and you won't feel the fire that consumes you. No one will know, Stevie, no one will care. Sleep.'

It was almost euphoric; before, each second counted; now it didn't matter. I was going to die, alone, but at least with peace, with dignity – not scraping the last of life, not clinging to false hope.

All I had to do was lie there.

A sound carried.

In the distance something mechanical came and went; rose and fell.

It was on the very edge of my hearing and in my distracted state it didn't seem at first important, but as it continued it tugged at a memory. The sound meant something – I recognised it.

I cried out, a half-sob, half-laugh then stretched out my arms and clawed forward again. Breathing as shallowly as I dared, moving slowly and fighting the pain once again.

Try!

The anger was returning. I'd been given a straw of hope, a chance, a slim bone-bare chance.

I could see nothing. The darkness was total, but I turned my head and fixed on the sound and with each foot gained it grew.

I wanted to scramble towards it, to get out of the culvert, this would-be tomb, but a last vestige of training surfaced and counselled control.

Small bites, Stevie, small bites.

Pain and fear reached for me again and from somewhere I found the strength to put them aside.

I wanted to live.

Inch by inch, foot by foot I gained ground. There was no point in keeping my eyes open to the smoke, so I shut them and squirmed like a blindworm through the brick and concrete tunnel, knowing that the skin was being chaffed from my body, that tomorrow, if there was a tomorrow, I would have the luxury of pain and infection.

The mechanical sound was louder.

My fingers hit something and I opened my eyes.

A solid brick wall was in front of me, but with subdued light filtering into the culvert.

I turned my head and saw the light was coming from above – the culvert had changed direction. It was going up.

Twisting over on to my back I found myself looking up six feet of brick tunnelling at the night sky. I knew exactly where I was then. I knew that the noise was the youth mindlessly revving his car and breaking the balls of everyone in earshot; except me.

I was a fan.

32

Getting through the angle of the culvert was incredibly hard, almost impossible.

I laid on my back and reached up to the first cable bracket in the vertical part of the culvert, then dragged myself up until I was in a sitting position scraping my chest on the edge of the brickwork angle.

My shoulder protested and the throbbing snaked down my back. Getting my legs to follow wasn't going to be easy.

I sat, looking up, my back against the brickwork and my legs still laying along the horizontal culvert; sitting, seeing the escape, but unable to stand.

I knew the next bit was really going to hurt – my shoulder, my ankle, everywhere.

Reaching up I heaved myself upright and at the same time twisted at the waist to bend first one leg sideways and half bend the other leg.

Pulling hard and twisting left and right, I managed to get one knee beyond the angle into the vertical section. Then I heaved again and through a combination of brute strength and bloody-mindedness succeeded in taking skin off both shins.

But I got both knees through the angle.

Now I was twisted to the right at the bottom of the vertical section, but without the room to push upright.

I twisted my upper body so that I was facing the same direction as my knees, then pushed back and up.

I swore, heaved and sobbed from effort, but gradually straightened my legs.

Stood up I was below the parapet. I took hold of the parapet edge and hauled myself up, scrambling until all my upper body was out of the culvert, and I was looking into the startled face of the youth sitting in his car.

I leaned over, fell the two foot to the ground and lay looking up to the sky.

A couple more youths started to approach me, their bewildered anxious faces an indication of my appearance.

'Call the fire brigade – call them!' I rasped.

It was like I'd spoken a foreign language. They looked from me to each other and back again.

'Now!' I screamed.

They had another noiseless exchange of looks and then one of them pulled out a mobile and started dialling.

I rolled on to my front and got to all fours, fighting the urge to vomit. Then I climbed to my feet and lurched over to the youth in the Astra.

'Thank you,' I said hoarsely.

He looked at me like I was a Martian. 'Do what, mate?'

'Thank you,' I repeated, 'for being a total pain-in-the-arse. I really do appreciate it.'

His face was wary. 'You having a laugh or what?'

I reached into the open side window and pressed his road horn, the noise echoing off the blocks of flats.

'Have that on me,' I said, and limped off in the direction of Harpers Road.

When I reached my car I got in and turned on the internal light. It was twenty to one. In the visor mirror I saw my smoke-blackened and bloody face and examined my arms, legs and body as best I could.

I was a mess.

My T-shirt was shredded, my chinos were rags and every

expanse of visible skin was cut, chafed, bruised or covered in smoke-black and filth. A shudder went through me and despite myself I became emotional as I realised how close I'd been to dying – to being asphyxiated, to charring to the bone.

My shoulders shook, my lip quivered and tears filled my eyes, but I was alive. I'd beaten it – me and my moronic friend with the Astra. I closed my eyes and smiled as the tears ran down my face.

The moment passed and that inner voice said that priorities needed to be sorted now. Sleep, shower, coffee – any order, but above all I needed help to clean, wash and dress my wounds. I drove to the end of Harpers Road and stopped outside a telephone box.

Against the odds it wasn't vandalised; I phoned Jo.

The mobile rang and rang, then a sleepy voice said, 'Hello?'

'Jo? I need your help.'

'Steve?' she yawned. 'Where are you? What's wrong?'

'I'm in Basildon and it hasn't been the best of evenings – can you meet me at my place in forty minutes?'

'Why? What's wrong? Are you okay?'

'No. No, I'm not and I need your help.'

I heard her moving around. 'Do you know what the time is?'

'Yes – and I still need your help.'

'Okay, might be longer than forty minutes though.'

'Fine, but as soon as you can.'

I put the phone down.

Twice on the journey to Romford I stopped, once to throw up and once to manipulate my shoulder, which was starting to give me serious gip. In fact with the adrenaline flushed from my system, my whole body was aching or stinging and shock was converting into mind-numbing fatigue with each minute a battle to keep my eyes open.

The car must have swerved at some point, because a lorry

screamed past me with its horn blaring, jarring me back to concentration.

I reached Prentice Road and slumped forward, unable to climb from the car.

It was twenty minutes before Jo arrived and the only thing I'd managed to do in the interim was turn the engine off. Her face when she saw me said it all.

'My God, Steve, what on earth has happened?'

'Just get me upstairs, please.'

She pulled me from the car, put my arm around her neck and helped up to the flat.

Taking my keys she opened the door and half dragged me to the living room, easing me down on to the sofa. Then she stood shaking her head.

'Steve, you need hospital treatment.'

'No. Help me shower and . . .'

I stopped. Behind Jo, in the living room doorway, stood Jenny.

Jo caught my look and turned.

Wearing a black lace nightgown Jenny's pregnancy didn't show. She was sizing up Jo and nodding, as though it confirmed something in her mind. Then she gave her attention to me.

She did well to control herself, given the mixed emotions that must have been hitting her. What she did next was either humane or the smartest bit of thinking I'd seen in many a year. She came over, took my arm and said to Jo, 'Please help me get him to the bathroom.'

Between them they lifted me and took me down the hallway.

Only once did Jenny let her emotions show. When we reached the bathroom she said to Jo, 'I take it you've seen him with his clothes off? Good, then you won't mind helping me undress him?'

I wasn't able to stay with the minutiae of the interplay, but you'd have had to be dead not to feel the electricity. When Jo took off my briefs Jenny took a step back – whether that was recognition of the new proprieties or just to gauge Jo's comfort with the idea, I wasn't in any shape to say. But it did feel strange.

They showered me, Jo taking my weight and Jenny negotiating the areas of broken skin with a sponge. It stung like hell and I twitched and cursed as the raw patches took the force of the water or were grazed by the sponge.

Both Jo and Jenny got soaked.

The water turned black, then grey and finally ran clean. They patted me dry with two bath towels and then turned their attention to dressing my wounds.

Jenny used an antiseptic to dab at the raw and broken skin and Jo fashioned a support for my shoulder from a triangular bandage. She also retrieved two paracetamol from the bathroom cabinet and made me take them.

Then they carried me through to the main bedroom and put me in bed.

'Well, do you get in with him or do I?' said Jenny neutrally.

Jo took the remark in her stride. 'Do you mind?'

'Be my guest,' said Jenny and went into the spare bedroom.

With the door closed Jo slipped out of her sodden dress and threw it on the floor. Her bra followed and she climbed into bed with me, propping a pillow against my shoulder.

I watched her through half-closed eyes as she fussed around me.

'You'll have to sleep on your back,' she murmured, 'that chest is going to be pretty sore.'

She said something else, something soft that was followed by a kiss. Then sleep enveloped me.

33

When I woke it was just after eight and Jo was lying on her front watching me. She smiled, leant across and kissed me.

'Is it always going to be like this?' she said quietly.

'Did I dream it or was Jenny here last night?'

'Oh she's here all right, in the next bedroom.'

'Sorry. It must have been awkward for you,' I said.

'Well it felt strange sharing you in the bathroom. If I didn't know better I'd think that you planned it,' she smiled.

I laughed and every part of my body screamed keep still!

'I'm sorry, Jo. Jesus! Jenny in the next room.'

'You were probably too out of it to notice last night, but she loves you, Steve. And going into the other bedroom was the clear proof of it.'

I closed my eyes. 'Tricky then.'

'I'd say so, yes.'

'What happens now – between you and me?'

'I'd say that depends on you.'

I was about to ask her in what way when there was a knock on the door. I looked at Jo and there was another knock.

The door opened slowly and there stood Jenny, dressed in jeans and a blouse.

'Would you like coffee?'

Jo looked at me then at Jenny. 'Can I help?'

Jenny shook her head. 'You're a guest.'

'Coffee would be good,' I said.

Jenny nodded and went out, closing the door behind her.

Jo mouthed, 'Guest?'

I nodded and spoke quietly. 'Your status – destined ulti-mately to go.'

'She's very clever . . . and very attractive.'

'And over.'

Jo glanced at the door. 'How well do you know her, Steve? I mean really know her?'

'We were very close at one time; we both know each other inside out.'

'And her reaction last night? This morning?'

I nodded. 'Took me totally by surprise.'

Jo bit her lip. 'You two need to talk, and I'm in the way.'

I opened my mouth, but she put her finger to my lips.

'I'll go. Don't worry, I'm coming back, but right now you two need to discuss things. And you need to open your eyes and your mind.'

'Sorry? I . . .'

She kissed me again and then climbed from the bed and got dressed. I closed my eyes and was woken almost immediately by the sound of the front door opening and closing. Two minutes later Jenny brought in the coffee.

She sat on the bed and held the cup for me.

'So, that's her.'

'Jen, I know what you're thinking, but nothing happened between us until you went.'

She raised her eyebrows. 'But it would have, either way, wouldn't it?'

I breathed out slowly. 'Probably.'

'Is she married?'

'No.'

She swallowed. 'I have to move back in, Steve. I can't live with my parents and I have a child on the way. I need a home.'

'I'll move out,' I said.

'Do you have to?'

I studied her face. 'I'm not with you.'

'No, you're not, are you? I've spoken to Alex again. He suggested that we share the flat – one flat and two lives.'

'That's what you want?'

Her face set. 'No, Steve that not what I want, but it might be something I'd settle for until the birth, because I don't have a lot of choices.'

'I never meant to hurt you, Jen.'

'It's no more than I deserve.'

'It's not punishment. I've changed.'

She turned and looked over her shoulder at the bedroom door. 'Not that much.'

'I wouldn't have asked Jo here if I'd known. That must have hurt – I'm sorry.'

'Don't be. In a way I'm glad I met her. Not so pleased that she's so attractive, but at least now I have a face and a name.'

'*Could* you really live here? Separate lives I mean?'

'What, you want both of us?'

'No I didn't mean . . . sorry, yes I see, very funny.'

'It's not funny, Steve. It's anything but funny.'

'No. No I've been where you are and it wasn't funny, but I can't change how I feel.'

She brushed a lank of hair from my forehead. 'No, nor me.'

'I need to sleep, Jen. I want to talk, to deal with this, but I'm very tired.'

'I know.'

And then she did something that caught me totally off-guard; she lent over and kissed me.

I dozed off and on till mid-afternoon. A number of times I was aware of Jenny looking in to check on me, but she didn't speak, just stood there for a moment, watching, before closing the door noiselessly behind her.

I woke properly just after three and lay trying to pull together all the bits and pieces of the puzzle.

Khan was as guilty as sin, but of what?

Logic said to tell the police everything I knew and back off, but what did I have? Vanzie was dead, but why? And in whose interest was it to kill him? Something to do with Baker for sure, but what? An argument partially overheard by Aaron Hardy where Khan's nickname was mentioned was proof of nothing.

The one tantalising bit of evidence that could be checked out was Aaron Hardy's assertion that Khan was the front man at the Basildon disco that burnt down – there had to be paperwork on that – business records.

And that meant going back to Alex.

Baker had to have a different kind of record. I just didn't believe that anyone operating on the edge as he'd been lately hadn't made mistakes in the past. At the very least he must have attracted the attention of the local drugs squad. That meant going through Bill Proctor which in turn meant going through Jo.

I needed to make phone calls.

As I rolled over to get out of bed the pain from my shoulder convulsed me. Sweat broke out on my forehead and I stayed still until the worse of it past, then took a deep breath and tried again.

Shit!

The pain was so intense I cried out. There was the hurried scampering of feet down the hallway and the bedroom door flew open. Jenny's face loomed over me.

'Oh, Steve! What are you doing?'

'Trying to get out of bed.'

'Why, for God's sake? Just stay there.'

'Can't . . . need to speak to Alex.'

She eased me back to the centre of the bed and arranged the pillows to support me.

'Now stay still. I'll ring Alex.'

I nodded. 'Tell him I must speak with him this afternoon.'

'All right, but don't move,' she insisted. 'I'll get you some paracetamol.'

A few minutes later she came back in with the tablets. 'He's coming from the office. He'll be here in about half an hour.'

'Thanks.'

'Would you like something to eat?'

I shook my head. 'Coffee.'

Jenny disappeared and I went back to playing tennis with what I knew. Or more correctly, what I didn't know. Vanzie killed Shenaz Rahman. Vanzie worked for Baker. Baker was laundering money through a disco fronted by David Khan. Khan was an associate of Mohammed Ali Rahman.

And I didn't believe in coincidences.

Mohammed Ali Rahman not only had the reputation, he had the charisma, but so do the best conmen. Yet there was a peace about him; spiritual peace and that cut through the suspicion. But was that naïve?

Khan. There was the linkage. Then there was Maria and Rob Brody – was that connected? How? Why? There had to be something that pulled it together. Baker. Baker and Khan.

That was the hot spot.

34

Alex arrived, took one look at me and crossed his arms.

'Why do you always make me feel like a school teacher about to deliver a lecture?'

'Harsh as this sounds, Alex, I didn't do all this damage to myself just for you.'

'Merciful heaven, but you've excelled yourself, Stevie. Is it attention-seeking?'

'No. No, in fairness to myself I managed to do most of this alone and unobserved.'

'Tell me.'

I gave him everything. He listened without interruption, even through my discovery of Vanzie's body, though I could see a million questions were bubbling to the surface. Occasionally breathy noises emanated from him, like a set of bagpipes settling on a chair.

When I got to the part about arriving back here with Jo only to find Jenny had returned he shook his head in wonderment.

'Have you ever thought about going into entertainment?'

'Amusing then?'

'Aye, if you like your humour black.'

I moved my shoulder gingerly and shifted my weight, trying to keep the discomfort from my face. I could see Alex was linking it all together, so I said it for him.

'Khan then?'

'Yes, I agree, Khan. And this Baker character of course –

nasty piece of work him. But you've only brought me bigger questions, not answers, Stevie.'

'We need Khan on his own.'

He shook his head. 'It's way past that, Stevie. We need to hand all this over to the police. If not, we're withholding evidence in a murder investigation. At the very least.'

'What if I told Jo?'

'Sorry?'

'What if I gave it to her instead of the Rahman murder team?'

'You have got it bad, haven't you?' he said slowly.

'No, it's not that. Listen, everything I've found out is second-hand. It's not me withholding evidence. If anything, it's the people I've spoken to – though each has only part of the equation. Set up a meeting with Khan.'

'What have you got in mind?'

'Nudging him into talking'

'Why would he agree?'

'To save his own neck.'

'And your lady policewoman?'

'Will be an observer.'

'You're flying by the seat of your pants, Stevie.'

'Someone tried to kill Rob Brody. I'm not prepared to let that pass.'

'This meeting with Khan? When?'

'Tomorrow. Make it your offices. Ring him and say . . . say that something has come to your attention that he'll want to talk about, but not to bring a brief.'

'That'll make him dead suspicious, Stevie.'

'Probably. And tell him if he doesn't show, you'll go to the police.'

'Why would he come?'

'If he's guilty in any way he won't. If he's on the edge he'll see it for what it is, a chance to get from under. And if he's innocent he'll come, but insist on having his brief present.'

'You're a sneaky bastard, Stevie Jay.'

'It's the company I'm keeping.'

'I'm not totally convinced, but I'm willing give it a try. Will you be up to it tomorrow?'

'I'll be fine.'

He looked doubtful. 'Then stay where you are and rest.'

When Alex left I went back to the mental arithmetic. The more I examined the option I'd put to Alex the flimsier it looked. There were simply too many pieces of the puzzle missing. Tilting at Khan would only work if he saw an exit for himself.

What was his soft spot? Baker. And Vanzie? Did he know Vanzie? Probably. Did he know Vanzie was dead? Good question. What if Khan were led to believe that he was himself in danger?

I needed more. Otherwise it would be an exercise in blundering around blind trying to bump into the truth.

Frustrated, I closed my eyes again and slept till early evening. Jenny brought me in some pasta around seven and stayed to talk. She was unnervingly normal. No edge, no accusation.

She sat on the bed and watched me eat.

'I've not asked about what you've been doing, Steve, but I am concerned. Have you any idea how much of a shock it was seeing you in that condition last night?'

'Sorry.'

'What's going on?'

'I can't say, Jen. I will tell you, but for now it's best that I keep it to myself.'

'Yourself and Alex.'

'I suppose so.'

'Are you working for him again?'

'I'm not sure. It depends.'

'Is Jo involved?'

'Maybe.'

'She rang earlier, when you were asleep. She'll be over at eight to see you.'

I put down the plate and fork. 'This must be embarrassing for you. I'm sorry.'

'Yes, it is. But what can I do about it?'

'Tomorrow I'll ask Alex if I can move in with him. That will give you a home and stop you having to have all this under your nose. Financially I'll meet the bills, give you what you need.'

'What I need,' she repeated wistfully as she stood up. 'This really is it, isn't it?'

'Yes, Jen. It is.'

'I thought you'd always be part of my life.'

'Part wasn't enough for me.'

'No. I see that now. Do you love her? No, don't answer that. She's gorgeous, Steve, gorgeous and smart.'

'She said much the same about you.'

'There you are then, the perfect substitute.'

At eight o'clock Jo arrived and Jenny said that she was going over to her parents for a few hours. The look she gave as she left chilled me to the bone; Jo was right, she did still love me.

As the front door closed, Jo kissed me. 'How have you been?'

'Sleeping when I can. The shoulder is giving me hell when I move it.'

'I still don't know what happened last night?'

'I think I ran into the same people that beat up Rob Brody.'

'Has this been reported?'

'Not yet.'

'Tell me more.'

'I can't, yet, but I want a favour.'

'I'm listening.'

'Have you ever met Daud Khan?'

'Why do I know that name?'

'He owns the cinema that burnt down in Green Street – and a disco in Basildon that burnt down a couple of weeks ago.'

'Go on.'

'He's also an associate of Mohammed Ali Rahman.'

'What is it that you're saying, Steve?'

The phone rang.

Jo got up and went through to the living room to answer it. She came back and said that Linda Brody was on the phone.

'Help me up.'

She frowned. 'Can't I take a message?'

'No. Help me, please.'

Jo rolled her eyes and with a struggle, got me to my feet. My head swam and every part of my body begged to lie down again, but I concentrated on putting one foot in front of the other.

In the living room Jo sat me down and brought the phone over to the armchair.

'Linda? It's Steve.'

'He's awake, Steve, and asking for you. He says it's about what happened at the railway track.'

35

Jo refused to take me to Basildon.

She said I wasn't in any fit state to go and she was right. When I said that Rob would be able to throw light on what happened to his sister, she agreed, but said it was a matter for Essex police.

'If you don't take me I'll call a cab,' I said.

'You won't even get down the stairs, Steve.'

'That's why I want you to take me. Rob's one of my watch, Jo. He's asked for me and I have to do this.'

She looked down. 'It's not fair on those around you. Jenny's got more than enough to come to terms with, don't you think?'

'I won't die, Jo. It'll be very uncomfortable, but I'll get through it.'

'A cab?'

'If I must, yes.'

'It's madness.'

'But you'll take me?'

She sighed heavily. 'Let's get you dressed. If we can even get you into the car I'll be amazed.'

Getting my trousers on was hard. Getting my shirt on was pure agony. I elected for a button-up rather than a T-shirt. It was easier, but only relatively. When Jo had finished, I was biting back the pain and trying to act normally, which alone convinced her I was in serious pain.

Walking was a joke. Although the only part of my legs that

had been injured were my thighs when they had been scraped
on the culvert brickwork, my bad ankle had taken a lot of
abuse in the fight and had swollen up to ugly proportions
again.

'You are a bastard for making me do this, Steve. It's not
fair.'

'I know.'

It took ten minutes to get me down the stairs and by then I
was sweating and cursing. Any pretence of having been under
control had gone.

'Well we're going to Basildon Hospital one way or another,
Steve, because I don't think I can get you back up those stairs
on my own. If the A and E department set eyes on you, they'll
admit you.'

Jo drove steadily and we made it in three-quarters of an
hour. She parked as near to the main block as she could and
told me to wait. She disappeared and five minutes later came
back with a wheelchair.

'Where did that come from?'

'It seemed to be going spare, so I retrieved it.'

'That's theft, ma'am.'

She smiled. 'Borrowing.'

I gave her directions and she took me to the side ward where
Rob Brody was lying. I got a nurse to fetch Linda and when
she saw me her hand went to her mouth.

'I wouldn't have asked you had I known, Steve. You look
terrible. How did it . . . ?'

'The same people that did Rob, or at least the same mob.
How is he?'

'Awake and talking,' she looked over her shoulder at the
police, 'but they don't know that yet. They've spotted the
rushing around though because I had to call a nurse, when he
was sick.'

'Can I get in to see him?'

'Yes, but you'll have to be quick, his vision is very blurred and there's a doctor on his way down to examine him.'

'Jo, could I ask you to wait here?' I said.

'I'll go outside and smoke.'

'Thank you. I squeezed her hand and Linda raised an eyebrow. As she wheeled me along the corridor, she asked how Jenny was.

'We've split up. It's been coming for a long time.'

She didn't reply to that.

Inside the side ward Rob lay with his eyes closed. Linda left me by the door and went over to the bed. She spoke softly to him and then came back and wheeled me to the bed.

'Guv?'

'I'm here, Rob.'

He moved his head slightly towards me. 'Sorry . . . about . . . about all the grief, guv. Linda told me how you got me to the hospital . . . touch and go, eh?'

'Just checking up on you, making sure you weren't working part-time.'

He smiled. 'Least . . . least of my troubles. Listen, guv . . . won't have long. The murder of that woman on the railway track – I recognised one of the murderers.'

'Lee Vanzie.'

'How . . . how did you know?'

'I recognised him in a police line-up.'

He closed his eyes in acknowledgement. 'Vanzie . . . recognised me, 's why I went sick . . . Maria. Linda's told you about her problems?'

'Yes, Rob.'

'Knew that they'd try to stop me . . . testifying. They threatened her . . . no choice.'

'Things have moved on a bit from there, Rob. Vanzie's dead.'

'Dead?'

'Hacked up and put in a plastic sack.'

He closed his eyes again and breathed out slowly. 'Makes sense . . . a lot of sense.'

'Why?'

'Maria . . . talk to Maria.'

'Nobody's seen her, Rob.'

He opened his mouth to speak, but the effort was tiring him. He looked past me to Linda. 'Tell him.'

I turned toward Linda Brody and she put her hand on my shoulder. 'Maria's here, Steve.'

'Here?'

'In the car park. She's waiting to speak to you.'

I looked at Rob and he nodded. 'Talk . . . to her.'

'She won't talk directly to the police, Steve,' said Linda. 'She's terrified.'

'But she'll talk to me?'

'Yes.'

'Then let's do it.'

Linda wheeled me out from the ward and down the corridor towards the main exit where Jo was smoking. When she saw us she threw away the cigarette and came up to us.

'How is he, Steve?'

'Talking, but very tired. Linda wants to talk to me outside. We won't be long.'

Jo looked from me to Linda Brody. 'Okay.'

I could feel Jo's eyes on me as Linda wheeled me away. Anyone would have been suspicious and Jo wasn't just anyone. To her credit she hadn't pushed it and I knew she was giving me a lot of leeway.

But trust can only go so far and a copper's a copper, no matter what shape they come in.

At the edge of the main hospital building we turned left and went the length of the car park. In the far corner was Rob's Mondeo and sitting in the back you could just make out the head of someone lying back into the rear seat; if you weren't close and looking you'd have never seen her.

The previous night's rain had dissolved the heat wave and the late September air felt cool.

Linda helped me into the front passenger's seat and then left us alone.

It was gloomy in the car with the only illumination coming from a lamppost twenty yards away, but it was light enough to catch the fear in Maria Brody's eyes.

I turned in the seat and my shoulder warned me to move slowly.

'I'm Steve Jay, Rob's boss.'

She leaned forward slightly and when she spoke her voice caught me off-guard. It was light, husky and more educated than I expected.

'Rob tells me that you saw the murder of that woman – on the railway track?'

'Yes.'

'It was Vanzie who killed her.'

'I know. I picked him out in a police line-up.'

'Karl Baker was there as well.'

'Baker? Are you sure?'

'Vanzie told me.'

'When?'

'The day they beat up Rob.'

'Why would he tell you, Maria?'

'Rob told you I have . . . problems.'

'He told me,' I agreed.

'I was strung out. I needed some crack.'

'Go on.'

'I got one of the kids in the block to go over to Vanzie's pad ask him if I could . . . could have the usual.'

'The usual?'

She was nervous and even in the bad light I could see that she was trembling.

'I need . . . I needed to have some . . . and I didn't have any money. Vanzie used to give me some . . . to keep me going. He would trade me, sleep with me in return for what I needed.'

'Okay.'

'About a couple of hours after I sent the kid, Vanzie and that other bastard, Mickey Preston, turned up.'

'Don't know him,' I said.

'Another one of Karl's thugs. He helped Baker and Vanzie kill that woman.'

That made three of the four, if she was telling the truth.

'Four people killed that woman. Who was the fourth?'

'I don't know, Luke Todd maybe. They were Karl's enforcers.'

'So Baker, Vanzie and Mickey Preston for definite?'

'Yes.'

'Go on with what you were saying, Maria.'

'When Vanzie and Mickey Preston turned up they'd been drinking. Vanzie was the worst . . . he had a full bottle of scotch with him and he insisted I drink from it.' She paused and I could hear the anxiety in her voice. 'They said that they were going to give me a good seeing to . . .'

She stopped and I let her get back to it in her own time.

'Vanzie . . . Vanzie tied me up . . . tied me to the bed and they . . . took turns. They . . . abused me . . . they . . . Vanzie was getting drunker and he started talking about Rob.'

'What about Rob?'

'He said that he knew what Rob knew . . . that if Rob didn't keep his mouth shut he'd be dead meat . . . that they'd cut his head off, like that Asian bitch. I didn't know what he was talking about.'

'He said Asian bitch, you're sure?'

'Yes. Vanzie didn't see it, but I could see that Mickey Preston was furious. Vanzie . . . Vanzie had me again . . . and then he fell asleep on top of me. I pretended to be asleep as well. Mickey Preston tried to make a call on his mobile, but you can't get a signal in my place . . . it's a dead spot.'

'So he went outside to get a signal?'

'Yes. Mickey Preston was calling Karl, I was sure of it. I was scared of what they'd do to me. I managed to untie myself and hid in the kitchen. When Mickey Preston came back I slipped out behind him and ran for it. I rang Rob.'

'And Rob came and got you out of it, but they caught up with him?'

'Yes. But there's more.'

'What?'

'Vanzie said something else . . . about Baker and the Pakistani.'

36

When Daud Khan and his solicitor Iqbal Asif turned up at Alex's office they didn't know that the agenda had changed. As far as they were aware they were attending a meeting about the cinema fire. So they were polite, but businesslike and when Alex offered them tea they accepted.

'Well,' said Alex, 'you both know Steve Jay. He's been taking a look at the background to the cinema fire and he's come up with some interesting facts. Steve?'

I nodded at Khan. 'Did you part own a disco in Laindon, Basildon that burnt down two weeks ago?'

'What has this to do with . . .' began Khan.

Iqbal Asif interrupted him. 'Don't answer that.'

I nodded. 'Okay. Let me ask you a different question. You didn't own the cinema in Green Street outright did you?'

'I don't have to answer that,' said Khan.

'Oh yes, you do,' said Alex. 'It states on the insurance that you had a sleeping partner. If you make a claim on your insurance, and you did when it burnt down, that partner is a co-beneficiary. You have to name him to be paid out.'

Again Iqbal Asif stepped in. 'He doesn't have to answer that here.'

'No. No, he doesn't,' agreed Alex, 'not here, but in making a claim you have started a process. This interview is part of that process, failure to co-operate will mean that the company will not pay out.'

'And if I withdrawn the claim?' said Khan.

'Why would you?'

'My partner may wish to protect his identity. It may be worth more than the money to him.'

'Now, that would be interesting,' I said.

'Pardon?'

'Mr Khan I said that it would be interesting, because your partner is not a "he".'

Iqbal Asif frowned and looked at Khan. 'What does he mean?'

'I mean, Mr Asif, that your client went into business with a woman. He approached Mohammed Ali Rahman for a loan because of a cash flow problem. When Mohammed Ali Rahman turned him down he approached your sister.'

'Zahra?'

'No, Mr Asif. Shenaz.'

'Mr Khan?'

Khan looked at Asif. 'You're my solicitor. I don't have to answer these questions.'

'Tell Mr Asif about Karl Baker,' I said. 'Tell him about the disco you were a would-be partner in with Baker, a major drugs dealer, and how after Mohammed Ali Rahman turned you down for a loan you approached Shenaz Rahman, who had her own money.'

Iqbal Asif's face was stone. Did you? Did you approach Shenaz?'

'Tell him what you told Karl Baker, that Shenaz had promised you money to finance the disco at Basildon and how she'd let you down, leaving Baker no option but to burn the place down to recover some of his money.'

Khan got up to leave, but Alex crossed the room in a flash and pushed him back down again.

'He was going to lose big time because of you, wasn't he? Baker was earning a fortune through the disco, but he needed a front man – you. Because although he could launder the money through the disco he couldn't own it – that would raise questions about how he got the money. Only you had bluffed and had stalled for time to come up with your share. But you couldn't afford it because you'd over-extended yourself.'

'He's lying,' said Khan.

'And when Mohammed Ali Rahman turned you down because the place was licensed, you told Shenaz that you needed the money for the cinema. Your mistake was to tell Baker it was Shenaz who was loaning you the money, and you blamed Shenaz when she backed out, having found out it wasn't for the cinema, but the disco.'

'This is all lies!'

'So you were in a hole and Baker got heavy, because that's how Baker does his business. Pay up or shit out. He believed you when you told him Shenaz was to blame and he had her killed. And when he told you to find the money, you had the cinema burned down.'

'That was racists!'

'Racists? Gaining access to an all-Asian cinema? Someone wedged the doors of the theatre. Someone who could move around undetected, an Asian – you or someone paid by you.'

'You don't know this. It's guesswork, all of it.'

'Is it? You pleaded with Baker not to kill you. You begged him and he gave you one chance – burn down the cinema, claim the money and hand it over. Only the day you pleaded for your life you were overheard. One person, a small-time pusher for Baker who wasn't supposed to be there, heard some of it and someone who was so despised that she was treated like wallpaper overheard all the conversation.'

Khan tried to get to his feet again and I called out.

The door to Andrew's office opened and Maria came into the room with Jo.

'Maria, is that the man you saw and heard talking to Karl Baker?' asked Jo.

'Yes. Yes, it is.'

Jo took out her warrant card and showed it to Khan. 'Daud Khan, I'm arresting you for conspiracy to murder Shenaz Rahman and for murder and arson at the Asian cinema, Green Street. You are not obliged to say anything, but failure to speak now may harm your defence in court.'

37

It was on the following Tuesday that Zahra Asif contacted me on behalf of Mohammed Ali Rahman.

The press in the meantime had spun three hundred and sixty degrees – effortlessly, proclaiming Mohammed Ali Rahman as a victim and loudly decrying 'his faceless detractors who had been only too quick to attack the reputation of an innocent man'.

Rahman for his part criticised no one.

Not one word of recrimination passed his lips – not for the police, not for the press, not for 'fair weather political friends'.

Zahra Asif had got hold of me through Alex and had invited Jo and myself to his house, a huge Queen Anne building in North London that was decorated in a fusion of western and eastern styles.

When we arrived we were shown into a large room with eastern tapestries on the wall and thick Persian rugs on the floor.

Mohammed Ali Rahman appeared dressed in traditional long shirt and loose trousers. He looked very much what he was: intelligent, sensitive and spiritual.

'Please,' he said, 'please sit.'

Jo and I sat on a teak-armed sofa, Zahra Asif stood and Mohammed Ali Rahman sat in a leather armchair.

'I am told that I have you both to thank for my release from custody. Thank you. Thank you for your courage and your determination to get to the truth.'

I looked from him to Zahra Asif. 'I have to tell you that my motives were not quite that pure. I wanted revenge, you see. Revenge for the beating my firefighter took and for what I believed to be the murder of his sister.'

He didn't answer at first; instead he studied me and then smiled. 'Forgive me, Mr Jay. I feel you may be doing yourself a disservice. You obviously have a strong sense of right and wrong – don't look only at the dark side of that. Compassion is a Muslim belief. It is also a Christian one. Compassion for yourself as well as others.'

'Compassion?'

His eyes rested on me. It was almost uncomfortable to see someone so still, so sure. 'All morality is based on compassion. There can be no right and wrong without it. Do you remember the saying of Mevlana – the founder of the Sufis?'

'Either exist as you are or be as you look.' I quoted.

He smiled. 'I am right about you. Forgive me, but I also try to write and I have found that these lines have helped me focus my life.'

I took the proffered paper and read it.

> In loving men, love yourself
> In loving women, be yourself
> In loving yourself, be a child

'I don't know what to say.'

'Say nothing, but read and use them when you must.'

Jo was watching me and I knew she was as affected as I was.

'Did you know,' he continued, 'that the woman you saw

when you stopped your fire engine at the cemetery was my
mother?'

'No.'

'My wife was on her way back to Pakistan with my mother,
to visit relatives. Her car was intercepted – the rest you know. I
did not report Shenaz and my mother missing because I
presumed they had caught their flight.'

'I see. And what happened to your mother?'

'She is ill, because of what happened. Disturbed. She
wandered the streets for days. Because of the riots no one
thought it amiss that an old woman should be so distressed.
Thank you for your compassion in trying to help my
mother and my wife that day. I will always be grateful
to you.'

'What will you do now? Will you go back to politics?'

'No. There will be much to do in the community, but I'll
take a different route from politics.'

We left after an hour and on the way back Jo brought me up
to speed with the investigation aftermath.

'I'm allowed to show my face around the station again,' she
said simply.

'That's it? No apology, no praise for arresting David
Khan?'

She shook her head slowly. 'I got a pat on the back from
Howard; very informal, very out of the way. In effect I'm back
at work. People know what happened, but there's still that
shadow and some people are saying the right things, but
keeping their distance.'

'What about the head they were supposed to have found in
Mohammed Ali Rahman's house?'

'No head. It was bones they found – animal bones apparently. Red faces all round.'

'What happens now? Between you and me?' I asked.

'I've been thinking about that.'

'And?'

'Jenny needs you, Steve.'

'I need you.'

'Oh, I'm not going away – and I've told Jenny that.'